# Leaving Lonesome

A NOVEL

*Love and Blessings Paula*

# PAULA SCOTT

LEAVING LONESOME
by Paula Scott
www.paulascott.com

This book or parts thereof may not be reproduced in any form,
stored in a retrieval system, or transmitted in any form by
any means—electronic, mechanical, photocopy, recording, or
otherwise—without prior written permission of the publisher,
except as provided by United States of America copyright law.

This is a work of fiction. Names, characters, places, and incidents are
products of the author's imagination or are used fictitiously. Any similarity
to actual people, organizations, and/or events is purely coincidental.

Cover Designer: Jenny Quinlan
Editor: Jenny Quinlan, Historical Editor, historicaleditorial.com
Editor: Susanne Lakin, livewritethrive.com
Copy Editors: Abby DeBenedittis and Judy Gordon Morrow
Typesetter: Susan Murdock

ISBN-13: 978-0-578-69765-9

Blessed are the merciful, for they will be shown mercy.

MATTHEW 5:7

# Table of Contents

# Prologue

If a man committed suicide, could he still go to heaven?

He would soon know.

He believed in heaven and hell, and death scared him. But not enough to stay his hand. He held out hope that God would be merciful.

*Forgive me for what I'm about to do.*

It seemed fitting. A life for a life. Except he'd need to die more than once to make things right.

The New Mexico desert around him was cold and lonesome as the sun went down. The breeze traveled with the smell of sagebrush, biting and whispering, waiting to usher away his spirit. He was ready to go. He placed the gun in his mouth.

A raven squawked overhead and it startled him. He removed the barrel from his lips, trying not to lose his nerve. The bird's dark shadow slid across the ground, rolling right over him. He shivered. Ravens reminded him of death and the devil. And he was dancing with the devil, tasting the barrel on his tongue.

Three years ago, he'd made a deal with the supply sergeant to keep his army-issued pistol before heading back to the states. He had to take the .45 apart and mail it to himself in several pieces, then put it back together when he got home.

Now it would finally do the job. Just like the bullets that had rushed from this same barrel into those soldiers on Black Virgin Mountain. They'd died instantly, and he hoped he would too. No one out here would ease his suffering if the bullet didn't kill him. The sound of gunfire wouldn't alert anyone. The ravens, buzzards, and coyotes would feast for a day or two before someone spotted his car and notified the nearest town sheriff of his rotting body.

He left his keys in the ignition, hoping some lucky kid would find his Camaro and love it the way he had. He'd bought it that first Christmas after graduating from West Point before going to flight school. The vehicle had low mileage and still seemed new. It had sat in his parents' garage during his war years.

He thought about his mother, Maureen, and the Colonel without much regret. His parents were selfish and perhaps so was he. People said you had to be selfish to take your own life. But he didn't see this as a selfish act. He saw it as an atonement.

"God forgive me," he whispered, putting the gun back into his mouth. He clamped his teeth down on the barrel and pulled the trigger.

The gun didn't go off.

*Come on, Lucky John.*

He pulled the trigger again.

Nothing happened.

*One more time.*

He clicked the lever, producing silence. He must have put the gun back together the wrong way. He yanked the gun from his mouth. His Irish luck had run out.

Or maybe it hadn't.

He threw the .45 into the sagebrush and walked around to the trunk of his car as the wind hit his face. It was the sudden gust of wind that woke him up. He was still alive.

*Thank you, Lord.*

He looked around at the piñon pines, the red rock canyon. A dove cooed in a nearby pine and he closed his eyes.

*Thank you.*

The breeze felt warmer now. Almost like a caress on his face. Like God was in the wind.

He opened his trunk and reached for the letter still sealed in its worn envelope, lying there in a small cardboard box where he kept his whiskey bottle. Booze and the letter had kept him alive for the past three years. Under the envelope he found her picture. He picked it up and stared at the photograph as he had so many times before. She looked so pretty silhouetted by freshly fallen snow. There was no way around it now, he would have to deliver the letter to her.

# Chapter One

*Sutter County, California, 1972*

The crop-dusting company sat like an island surrounded by flooded rice fields. John wasn't fond of rice fields—he'd seen enough rice paddies in Vietnam—but the rice reminded him why he had come to this farming community in the middle of nowhere. He sighed, relieved that he had finally found the courage to come here. At least he was slipping toward sobriety now and ready to face what his demons dished out.

He stepped out of his black Camaro into the bright sunshine. To the east, beyond the endless farmland, the snow-covered Sierra Nevada dominated the horizon. A view of the west offered a handful of jagged hills strewn with rocks and oak trees and rolling green grass. The small mountains arose about two miles from where he stood in the parking lot of Callohan Dusters.

Don McLean's hit song "American Pie" drifted out of the dusting company's hangar doors. An old Studebaker was parked beside the rusting building. John knew the history of that black

Studebaker, with its faded red leather interior, almost as well as he knew his parents' aging Cadillac, the white sedan he'd totaled on his seventeenth birthday, drunk on the Colonel's finest whiskey. The music made him smile.

Like the Studebaker, everything about this place felt familiar. The crisp winter sunshine, the vivid mustard plants growing around the hangar, the surrounding farm fields, distant orchards, nearby mountains, and the faint smell of aircraft engine grease wafting up from the dirty gravel. He'd never been here until today, though he'd visited a million times in his mind. To finally arrive at Callohan Dusters felt like a miracle.

He reached into his pocket and felt the envelope, worn from the years he'd carried it. For a moment, he closed his eyes and steadied himself. It had taken him long enough to get here.

The sound of an incoming aircraft captured his attention. Opening his eyes, he spotted the biplane approaching. Shutting his car door, he stepped away from the vehicle. He watched the plane descend into its landing at the nearby airstrip. It sailed in shakily, as if blown around by a strong wind. The plane's wheels touched down and the Stearman rolled the length of the short dirt runway, bouncing along like an old Model-A Ford.

The plane came to a stop, and a slight figure stood up in the cockpit. A brown leather helmet covered the pilot's head. The pilot looked toward him, gave an acknowledging wave, and then climbed onto the lower wing before springing lightly down to the hard-packed dirt. The aviator removed flight goggles as he walked over. The helmet came off next. John was shocked to see a ravaged ponytail appear.

Adrenaline slammed through his veins when the late-afternoon sun hit her shining hair. Dressed in faded blue coveralls and worn cowboy boots, she stepped briskly across the lonely dirt runway. She had a smooth, no-nonsense stride that made the ponytail swing rather than bounce. From a stone's throw away, he stared at her face. She was smaller in real life than he figured she'd be, slender, and swift to close the distance between them. She brushed wayward strands of hair off her face as she looked up at him through the glare of the sun.

"I'm Swampy Callohan. What can I do for you?" A Southern accent edged her words. She spoke like she moved, quick and without nonsense. Hearing her say her name—a name like nobody else's—filled him with a mixture of joy and sorrow.

"John Reno." He stretched out a hand that trembled ever so slightly. As she shook his hand, she narrowed her eyes on him.

He held his breath, waiting for his name to click in her mind or for her to recognize his face. He released the air trapped in his lungs as her cordial expression didn't change. Lord, she was beautiful, her eyes deep with unspeakable things. Grief had stolen the youthful shine from her gaze. Loss ages you that way. You grow old in an instant when someone you love dies. The windows of your soul are never the same because death stays in your eyes.

He found it hard to breathe standing there with her. Now was the time. Her small hand still enfolded in his, he reached his other hand to his back pocket. He touched the letter, hesitated, then drew his hand back out. He just couldn't give it to her yet.

"So, what can I do for you, Mr. Reno?" She pulled her hand free and shifted on her feet. Perhaps he'd made her uncomfortable.

He tried to speak, but his throat tightened even more. His eyes burned as if a dry wind blew against them. He took a moment to calm his nerves, settling his gaze on the aging crop duster. The plane was an antique, a World War II trainer some twenty years older than the woman it now belonged to. It had a nice paint job, though, with *Callohan Dusters* in big red letters across a white fuselage. Dark red wings shimmered scarlet in the sunlight. He was glad he had the Stearman to stare at for a moment. Looking at the plane hid the tears that blurred his vision.

A door slammed, and he blinked hard before turning toward the hangar. A man exited the building, a nylon flight bag draped over his shoulder. He headed for a souped-up Chevy Nova in the parking lot, but when Swampy called, "Rex!" and waved him over, he swung their way.

"Why aren't you dusting?" she demanded when the clean-cut blond guy reached them.

"I'm hitting the road." He wore the same coveralls as Swampy and didn't look in John's direction.

"What?" She cocked her head as if she hadn't heard him correctly.

"I can't take any more of Lucy. I need to get out of here."

She gazed at the hangar, then back at the man. "The season's just getting started. I can't afford to lose you. There aren't any decent dusters left to hire around here."

"I'd stay if I could." He finally glanced at John, then gave Swampy a look of regret.

Normally, John would have extended his hand for a handshake, but the guy appeared sad, angry, and confused all at once. After sizing John up, he focused on Swampy.

"Lucy showed up at my apartment last night. I was drinking. I let her stay." He'd lowered his voice with the confession. John could hear the man's remorse. He knew the weight of guilt. The way it settled in your gut and stayed there like a millstone trying to drown you.

"I told you to stay away from her."

"I tried. A man can only resist for so long. She's been itching for a piece of me."

When Swampy lunged at Rex, swinging a fist into his aviator sunglasses, John instinctively stepped into the fray. He looped an arm around her slender waist, drawing her away from the man.

"Get your hands off me!" She strained against John's hold.

He quickly let her go, prepared to stop the guy from retaliating.

Rex ripped the shattered glasses from his face and threw them on the ground. His face reddened. "I tried to stay away from her!" He kicked the broken glasses across the gravel, tiny rocks flying in all directions.

"You're fired!" She cradled her fist against her coveralls, glaring at Rex with an intensity that reminded John of his first encounter with a drill sergeant.

Rex shook the bag thrown over his shoulder. "I'll drop by on Friday to pick up my check." He spun away, blood trickling from a cut on his nose.

"Don't bother. I'll mail it." Swampy straightened the flight goggles hanging around her neck.

Rex headed for his car. The Nova soon rumbled out of the parking lot and sped off down the lonely country road, its motor revving across the empty farmland.

Swampy watched him go, her hand tucked against her midsection, taking deep breaths as if trying to compose herself. When she turned to John, her eyes shone with grief or fury, he wasn't sure which. "So, what can I do for you?" she asked with a calmness that surprised him.

"I'd like to see your hand."

She kept it pressed against her coveralls. "My hand is fine."

He reached out and took her wrist gently but firmly, pulling her hand away from her belly. Blood was smeared across her coveralls. The gash on her knuckles bled freely. "You might need stitches." He studied the wound, looking for glass in the cut.

"I don't need stitches. I need a new duster." She jerked her hand away, pressing it back against her stomach. He could see she was used to being in charge. He found her spunk endearing.

"Put pressure on that wound." He went with the feeling rising in his gut like a phoenix, though he was afraid he'd regret it later on. "I'm looking for a flying job." He spoke loud and clear, like the military officer he'd once been, surprised that the old bravado was still in him. A surge of hope hit him too. He hadn't felt hopeful in a long while.

She didn't need to know why he was here. He reached into his pocket and fingered Jimmy's letter. Maybe he could just place it on the seat of her cockpit on the day he moved on. Because he'd have to move on. The thought of leaving left him cold, but right now he could help her.

Her gaze lingered on his long, unkempt hair and then his face. "How long have you been flying, Mr. Reno?"

"Long enough. Please call me John."

"How long, Mr. Reno?" The proud tilt of her pointed little chin couldn't hide the tiredness etched deeply on her delicate face. She was even prettier than her photographs, though she needed some more meat on her bones. In Jimmy's pictures, she hadn't been this thin.

"I could fly your plane through a five-foot spread of electrical wires, then land on your front porch without making your dog bark." His light talk didn't ease her level gaze. He said softly, "I'm the best pilot you'll ever come across."

Their gazes held. He was sure she had no idea who he was. His heart did a funny little flip-flop. "You should see a doctor for your hand."

"Can you really fly?" The excitement in her voice made him feel like a man again.

"I've been dusting full-time for several years. I'm a mighty fine duster."

"Rex was a mighty fine duster too."

"I'm not Rex."

*I'm far worse than Rex.*

He'd made her life bleed with sorrow, but she didn't know that. That old ache he knew so well rose up and washed over him. He waited for it to pass, like always.

"Since I'm now in need of another duster, I'll let you show me what you can do after I see your license. If I bring you on, you'll be careful with my Stearmans. They're tricky old characters that need a good pilot to keep 'em in the air. If you plan on flying fancy, you won't be flying for Callohan Dusters for long."

She continued looking at him in that hard, speculative way. He decided not to tell her that her old Stearmans were neither little nor tricky as far as airplanes went. Stearmans were forgiving old gals with a nice comfortable girth. They were easy to fly, sweethearts in the air. It was only on the ground that Stearmans got a little ornery due to their narrow landing gear and slightly top-heavy build.

"I'm sure I'll have no trouble flying your Stearmans nice and sensible. Crop dusting is a sensible job. Like driving a tractor in the sky." He smiled.

She adjusted her stance and squared her shoulders, making herself appear taller. "Crop dusters see themselves as a different breed. An elite group of flyers. We certainly don't see ourselves as cloud plowers."

There was the pluck—he'd heard about that plenty. Swampy Callohan had moxie to spare. But he also knew a thing or two about dusters. He'd flown across the United States, living from one dusting job to the next, learning the trade. He understood the mentality of dusters. Most were self-taught daredevils, aviators bred from a long line of flying folks. Some of the best pilots he'd ever come across were dusters. Still, they flew long, monotonous hours from dawn to dusk, planting, fertilizing, and spraying fields, just like tractor-driving farmers. Not much glory there, but he wasn't about to inform her of that.

The afternoon moved so quietly the hum of a tractor could be heard a mile away.

She impatiently eyeballed the sun once more. "Come back tomorrow morning bright and early. We'll talk about the job then." She turned to go.

"I'll be here at …" He left the statement for her to finish.

She swung back, giving him a little smile that made his heart flip over again. "Six a.m." She walked to the hangar, calling over her shoulder, "Don't be late. You won't even get a trial run if you are."

She left him standing at the edge of the deserted airstrip, which stretched from the tin hangar across the flat farmland to the south like a road to nowhere. He stared after her until she disappeared into the hangar. Would she find a doctor to sew up her hand?

A flock of snow geese sailed through the sky in a V-formation, the leader of the geese taking the brunt of the effort, the middle geese not as taxed, and the ones at the end just cruising along. Each bird flew slightly above the bird in front of it to reduce the wind resistance. When the lead goose tired, he would fall back and let another goose take over breaking the wind. The V-formation also made it easy to keep track of everyone in the flock. Pilots used this same formation in combat.

A battle played out in his mind. And in his heart. He'd come to give her the letter that was still in his pocket, but if he could just help her for a little while, maybe she wouldn't look so tired. He could break the wind for her until she found another duster. Because he had nowhere else to go, he slid behind the wheel of his Camaro and followed the geese into a westbound sun.

# Chapter Two

Swampy picked up a pencil and clamped it between her teeth as Billy stuck the needle into her hand. She did her best to hold still as he stitched up the cut between her knuckles without anything to dull the pain except the pencil she bit down on. Hard. She wiggled her toes, a trick her dentist had taught her, focusing on her feet to distract her from the sting shooting up her arm.

*Damned Lucy.*

Rex wasn't the first pilot they'd lost because of her.

She turned her eyes back to her brother, Billy. Beads of sweat clung to his pale brow. He was completely focused on closing her wound, and with his dark hair and handsome features, he looked so much like Daddy when he was young. Watching him stitch up her hand reminded her of when he'd tried to save a little sparrow that had flown into the window of their trailer when they were kids. After several days in Billy's care, it died and he freaked out and ran away. Alone at eight-years-old in the bayou.

He was gone for two days, and Mama lost her mind. She blamed Daddy. Their fight over Billy bloodied both of them, fueled by panic and whiskey and the bitterness of a marriage on the brink due to Mama's infidelity and Daddy's drinking. When Billy finally came home, Mama threw a party for him, making a big pan of macaroni and cheese, Billy's favorite—after Daddy beat the hell out of him with a belt. He had beat Mama too. She made Billy's dinner with one of her eyes swollen shut, then later that night, Mama left. The following morning, Daddy walked out into the bayou and blew his brains out.

Mama returned in time for Daddy's funeral with a new boyfriend she married two months later. The marriage didn't last, and it was just the beginning of a string of husbands Swampy despised.

Even before that sparrow, Billy had always been trying to save wounded things. Small creatures he'd rescued from the swamp. Birds and baby possums, squirrels, even little alligators. Maybe he'd married Lucy trying to save her too. She was a wounded creature, raised by a stepdaddy who did her wrong. Sick and wrong. And all she'd done was twist Billy up in her sick, wounded world.

Swampy was happy to see Lucy go.

Neither of them talked as Billy closed her cut with careful stitches. She flinched when he pulled the thread tight. Swallowing hard, she spit out the pencil. It clattered on the cement floor. "Lucy reminds me of Mama." There, she'd said it. She'd been wanting to say it for a long time.

Billy paused tying off the thread, then finished a little too roughly. "Don't compare my wife to Mama."

"We lost Rex because of Lucy."

"Maybe we lost Rex because of you. You work everyone too hard." Billy dropped the needle into a little Dixie cup beside his

medic bag. He pulled out some Merthiolate and poured a little on
her wound, staining it red.

She jumped up, cursing as fire tore up her hand. That antiseptic
medicine really worked, but it stung like crazy.

Billy leaned back on his stool, balancing on his only leg. "I'm
sorry. I know that Monkey Blood really stings, but you got problems, sister. You're too damned hard on people."

It bothered Swampy that he kept the bag he had carried in war
full of his favorite medicines. She knew he still took illegal drugs
too when he could get his hands on them. He'd learned to give
himself a little morphine in Vietnam to dull his feelings as he did
his best to save men's lives. After suffering his own traumatic inju-
ries over there, his drug use spiraled out of control. She forgave
Billy for saying she had problems, though forgiveness wasn't her
strong suit. Of course, she had problems. She was born with problems. "I wish you'd get a new medical bag. One that isn't army
issued and doesn't smell like 'Nam."

She sat back down on her stool, blowing on her stitches, trying
to cool the fire from Billy's Monkey Blood. That's what Mama had
always called the burning Merthiolate—Monkey Blood—and used
it whenever they got hurt. Both Swampy and her brothers, Billy
and Blue, began to hide their cuts and scrapes when they were kids
because Mama's Monkey Blood hurt worse than getting injured.

"If I could trade this bag for my leg back, I would." He held it
up for her inspection. "Not a scratch but look at me. This here's a
miracle bag. It survived a Bouncing Betty."

"You're the miracle, Billy." She leaned forward and squeezed
his remaining leg. It made her sick that Lucy was cheating on him
again. Billy didn't deserve it.

"Are you picking up the kids or is Mrs. Larson bringing them home?" Swampy blew on her stitches some more, the Monkey Blood still burning.

"Mrs. Larson's dropping them off."

"Are you okay?" Billy's state of mind bothered her. Mama had been a pretty runaround too, just like Lucy in her short skirts with those long strawberry-blond curls she was always swishing at men. Mama had driven Daddy to his dark end. She worried the same would happen to Billy.

He laughed but not a happy sound. "What's making you go all tender on me today?"

"Do you know what today is?" She leaned back on her stool.

"The day you fired Rex the Flex?"

Rex had gotten the nickname because he was always flexing his muscles. But Swampy had paid him no mind, even though he'd tried to get her attention. The last thing she wanted was a man in her life. Unless somehow Jimmy could come back to her.

"Today's my anniversary," she said.

"What anniversary?"

"My wedding anniversary. Jimmy and I have been married five years as of today."

Billy blinked. The sadness he often wore on his face settled back over him. "I don't think you should look at it that way."

"Why not?" She looked down at her hand. He'd done a fine job stitching her up.

"It just don't seem right to count it like that."

"I'll count it however I want. You and Lucy will have been married five years too next Friday. Want a drink to celebrate?" She slid off the stool and walked to the refrigerator and grabbed two ice-cold Millers from the shelf.

She came back and handed him one. "To the high life." She tapped her beer against his, then opened it and took a long drink.

Billy set his can on the workbench, unopened. "I'm not toasting to your dead husband and my dead wife."

She almost choked on her beer. "Don't talk like that, Bean." She looked hard into his eyes as she swallowed the icy beer. The refrigerator froze everything. They needed a new fridge but didn't have a dime to put toward it. The truth was they didn't have money to fix anything. The Stearmans were held together with baling wire and Billy's ingenuity.

"I won't kill her. She's the mother of my kids. But she's dead to me. I know why you busted Rex in the nose." Using his crutch, Billy stood up and put his medic bag in an overhead cabinet. Then he sat back down and opened his beer. "Blue ain't done a lick of work today." That was so Billy, unwilling to talk about his wayward wife but quick to pick on his older brother.

"Blue flagged for me all day." She knew this was Billy's way of deflecting the blame off of Lucy. He always protected Lucy. No matter what.

"Well, he didn't come by here to help me." Billy looked tired.

Swampy ignored his irritation with Blue. "You got dinner ready upstairs?

"No. I'm not hungry."

"You want me to make you something to eat before I head home? You gotta eat, little brother. I'm gonna weigh more than you do."

"You're skinny as a fence post too. Don't kid yourself, Silver."

"Don't call me that. It reminds me of Mama." She held up her beer. "This keeps weight on me. Drink up.

You want me to take the kids home to my house tonight and feed them?"

"I asked Mrs. Larson to feed them before she brought them home."

"Okay." She finished her beer and really wanted another one. Her hand throbbed and was swelling around the knuckles. Walking back to the fridge for another beer, she finally allowed herself to think about John Reno instead of worrying about her brothers.

Why did his name ring a bell? She just couldn't place him. He had strong, clean hands, even though he looked pretty down on his luck. She always checked a man's hands. If a man had long or dirty fingernails, she didn't trust him. If he couldn't take care of his own hands, he wasn't going to take care of other things either. She didn't want a man like that around.

But even with his shaggy beard and long hair, John Reno was far too attractive. She didn't like hair on a man's face, but those bright blue eyes had stopped her in her tracks. He was tall and well-built with wide shoulders and narrow hips. When he'd grabbed her around the waist and pulled her away from Rex, she'd felt his muscles, and his touch had excited her, even though she was embarrassed she'd lost her temper in front of him.

What were the chances he could really be a duster? She'd never finish the dusting jobs by herself and couldn't trust Blue to fly the Stearmans. He was crazy and would crash one of her planes. That would end everything for everyone. The point was to keep her brothers alive and save Callohan Dusters too. She doubted she could hold on to the business with the way things were going, but if nothing else, she was persistent. "You're as determined as a bulldog, Swampy," Daddy used to say.

She wouldn't give up. She wouldn't lose her brothers or the company. *God give me strength.*

She wasn't sure she believed in a benevolent God, but she prayed to him anyway. And she drank. Because a few beers at night took the edge off, and her edges were sharp.

She took another frosty beer from the refrigerator and held it against her swollen knuckles. The cold felt good on her throbbing hand. She grabbed another Miller for Billy as well. Had Jimmy been here, she'd be celebrating with him tonight, probably not drinking beer. Jimmy hadn't been much of a drinker. Maybe they would have danced in the kitchen to Jerry Lee Lewis until they were too tired to dance anymore. She could still hear Jimmy singing "Great Balls of Fire" the night before he'd headed to Oakland, then on to Japan and Vietnam.

She stuck a beer in Billy's hand. "I gotta get home. My horses are hungry. I'm sure they're waiting at the barn. Happy anniversary to us." She tapped Billy's beer with her own.

"It takes two people in love to make an anniversary. You're a widow, and I'm a fool. One of these days, I won't take her back."

"Famous last words?" Swampy toasted the air and then took a drink.

Billy popped his can open in response. "How's your hand feeling?"

"Better than my ego. I shouldn't have hit Rex. That was dumb. I need this hand to fly."

Billy grinned. When he smiled, his whole face lit up. "Thanks for punching him for me. And don't worry, I know you can fly one handed. You could probably dust with your teeth if you had to."

She laughed. "It felt good to bust him in the nose."

Billy laughed a little too. He stretched out his leg, blessedly all in one piece, and balanced his torso in the chair. His other leg was gone, his pant leg sewn up at the top of his right thigh. Most men lost more than a leg to a Bouncing Betty. She knew Billy was in pain when he stretched out this way.

"You've always had my back, Silver Susanna. Thank you." Closing his eyes, he took a deep, long drink, like a man kissing a woman with his eyes closed, longing all over him. Maybe he missed Lucy. Or maybe he just loved the taste of a cold beer.

"Please don't call me by that name. It reminds me that Mama was crazy."

Olivia Sullivan had named all her children after her favorite colors. Fortunately, Daddy had given them all nicknames. Mama always called Billy "Whitey" because she'd named him White William. To Daddy's credit, he'd called his youngest son "Billy Bean" from the day he was born, so everyone just said Billy and sometimes Bean. Blue Donovan, the name of Swampy's other brother, had stuck. Probably because Daddy's name was Donovan, and he liked having a son named after him. Blue didn't mind. He said he was blue like jazz, smooth as butter, and he often blew on a saxophone he couldn't play worth a hoot. Swampy and Billy made fun of Blue when he brought out his beat-up old sax. And her name, Silver Susanna Sullivan, was an awful name. Thankfully, Daddy had quickly renamed her Swampy, much to Mama's frustration.

Billy opened his eyes after that long, soulful drink of beer. "God rest Mama's wild Irish soul." His lips twisted wryly. He didn't really mean it. None of Olivia Sullivan's children really wanted her to rest in peace. She'd died in a car crash with husband number four, a no-good gambler and drunk. Mama had always picked the drunks. The last one had driven her off a cliff on the way to a Lake Tahoe casino.

Every time Swampy turned around, someone was dying. Nightly body counts on the evening news with Walter Cronkite made death inescapable in everyone's living room.

Oh, how she missed Jimmy.

When she got home, she pulled out the shoebox of Jimmy's letters and carried them to the porch swing. For a while, she sat there rocking the shoebox in her arms like a mother rocked a baby, feeling the enormity of death that had become such a part of her life. The grief was always there. Dark and inescapable. All-consuming and eating her alive when she let it loose. Finally, she opened the shoebox full of letters and pulled one out.

*September 12, 1969*
*Dear Swampy,*

*I miss you really bad, honey. You're always on my mind. Remember the day we met? I was thinking about that tonight. How pretty you were walking down the hall on that first day of school and how all the girls didn't like you when you showed up. You had a way about you that set everyone aback. They made fun of your name, where you came from, and the way you wouldn't smile. But I made you smile. Remember?*

*I know you hate being called a southern belle, but nobody was going to put you in your place in our little Podunk town. You were really something. I just had to meet you and make you smile. When I introduced myself to you saying, "Welcome to my Podunk high school," you informed me the word "Podunk" actually meant "swampy" and that was your name. Then you finally smiled. I thought you were smart as hell. Pretty and smart. I had to make you my girl. Now you're my wife. I still can't believe how lucky I am.*

*How are you and Dad getting on? Dad told me that you're doing the books for the company now. Mom used to do that. I sure am proud of you, honey. I told Dad you're good at math. You're good at everything. I can't wait to be with you again.*

*They've placed me on a search and rescue team with a guy everyone calls Cool Hand Luke. He's following in his famous father's footsteps. His pops is a Korean War hero, now a full-bird colonel making the calls over at the Pentagon. It gives me hope that Luke's daddy is part of the show. His son is fighting this war too, just like us poor boys. Maybe things will turn in our favor, and they'll let us really finish this war instead of pulling us back like they've been doing. Every time we take territory, they pull us back and give it away.*

*I don't understand this war. I don't know what we're doing over here. But Luke seems to know. He graduated number one in his class from West Point. Volunteered for war duty instead of being drafted like most of us. The guys are always*

*playing jokes on each other in the hooch, ribbing each other
without mercy but nobody messes with Luke. Not because
they're scared of him, but because the pilots all like and
respect Luke. I can't believe they assigned me to fly with him.
Luke is calling me Duster, not hard to figure out why.*

*First thing he said to me was, "So I hear that along with
being a crop duster, you're a high school football star," and
I laughed and showed him your picture. I told him you outskated me in the local roller derby in high school. He got a
kick out of that.*

*"That little gal outskated you?"*

*"She sure did," I told him.*

*"What did you do after that?"*

*"I married her," I said.*

*Our wedding seems like yesterday and yet forever ago.
It's hotter than blazes over here during the day and freezing
at night. I miss that little cabin in Tahoe where we honey-
mooned. The snow was so pretty. The moon reflected off the
snow when we bundled up and took that walk around the icy
lake. You were so beautiful in the moonlight. I'll never forget
that trip with you. When I get home, let's go to Lake Tahoe
again. Let's rent that same little cabin and walk in the snow
under a full moon together.*

*The moon brings out every kind of critter here. There's no
screen door on the hooch, and you can't believe what comes
in and makes itself at home with us. The beetles are big as
birds. They fly in and out like they own the place. One flew
right into my head last night. Felt like a baseball hit me. I
killed it with a can of Coke. The monkeys are into everything,*

*so you can't leave any food out. They eat everything. We have two cats and a stray dog we've befriended, and even the cats and dog let the monkeys run amok. Guess they're afraid of them. Every insect on the planet lives in Vietnam. Snakes too. You know how I hate snakes. I thought the rattlesnakes were bad in California. Forget about it. Those rattlesnakes are nothing. 'Nam's snakes can kill you in five minutes.*

*Did I say I missed you? Lord, how I miss you. I'm the only married guy in our hooch. The other guys talk about girlfriends or lack of girlfriends. I talk about you. I dream of the kids we will have when I get home. I wish we already had a baby, like Billy and Lucy.*

*I sure hope your little brothers make it out of here in one piece. I hear things are bad down in the rice paddies where Billy and Blue are. There's no place to hide if you get shot down in the paddies. At least we have the jungle here. Landing is a real problem, though. It's hard to find a hole in the canopy. But once you're on the ground, there's all kinds of places to hide. I know you're strong, so I can share my worries with you. I pray for Billy and Blue every day. I pray for the guys here with me. I never pray for myself. Don't know why, but I'm not afraid. I've made my peace with the good Lord. I go to prayer meetings now. It's not like church at home, sitting with you and Dad, but it feeds my soul. All is well with my soul, Swampy. I pray it is well with your soul too. I can't wait to get home to you, honey. I love you.*

*Always yours,*
*Jimmy*

# Chapter Three

John parked on a dirt road surrounded by rice fields. A lonely sign weathered by sun, rain, and years read The Sutter Buttes, and he finally remembered the name of this little mountain range just beyond the fields. Geese circled overhead, then descended and disappeared into a billowing blanket of a thousand other snow geese. While he sat in his car watching the geese, he noticed swans, to his surprise.

He stepped out of the Camaro and retrieved a pint of whiskey from his trunk before climbing up on the hood, kicking his legs out in front of him, and reclining back against the windshield to watch the swans.

As the sun descended into that little mountain range, he cracked open the last bottle of booze he ever planned to buy. He held the whiskey above his head as the sun sank behind the Sutter Buttes, and when the last rays colored the sky a real pretty red, he made his belated New Year's toast. "To promises to keep and only a few more miles to go before I sleep. I'm here, Jimmy." Then he took a sip.

He pulled an envelope out of his back pocket, remembering the day Jimmy had handed it to him. Jimmy had said, "I was going to mail this, but I can't bring myself to do it. I've rewritten it ten times."

John hadn't liked the look on Jimmy's face. "What is it?"

"A goodbye letter to my wife."

Jimmy stared hard at him. "I had a dream."

John laughed a little, but his laugh was hollow. "Dreams of dying don't mean anything. We all have them. Yesterday I dreamed a spider monkey stabbed me in the heart with my own knife while I was sleeping. I hate these wild monkeys. I wish we had a screen door on the hooch to keep them out."

"This dream was different. It still feels real." Jimmy pressed the envelope into John's hand. "Don't open it. I know this is asking a lot, but if I die, don't mail this to Swampy. I want you to hand-deliver it to her. Only she can open it. I don't want you reading it."

"Sure, okay. Anything you say." John shoved the envelope into his flight suit pocket. "I hope to God I never have to deliver it. We're lucky bastards, right? We'll get out of here in one piece."

"I don't believe in luck anymore. I'm going to the prayer meeting tonight. Want to come along?"

"Nah." John smiled, shifting on his feet, eager to leave with Jimmy pushing religion now. "I'd rather listen to Rudolph sing."

Rudolph wasn't CW2 Chester's real name, but because his nose was always red from allergies, the guys called him that. He was a pilot who liked to get drunk and sing. He had enough talent to be entertaining and sounded a little like that new singer Neil Diamond.

Jimmy stared at him for another long, hard moment. "I've given my life to the Lord."

John didn't know what to say. Jimmy wasn't making this easy for him. "Well, I guess it's true what they say: there are no atheists in foxholes." He patted Jimmy on the shoulder, then quickly walked away.

That night John had gotten drunk and sung "Solitary Man" with Rudolph while Jimmy was at his prayer meeting.

John pulled the envelope out of his pocket and ran his fingers over the yellowing paper as he had a hundred times before, wondering what the letter said as he sipped whiskey and watched the swans. They mated for life, swans. He couldn't think of a woman from his past he'd wanted to spend his life with, except maybe Mary Jane.

They'd met their freshman year of high school and gave each other their virginity at sixteen. They stayed together until graduating high school, but their relationship hadn't survived him going to West Point without marrying her. His parents hadn't approved of Mary Jane. His mother complained she was from a poor family and had bad teeth. Mary Jane's crooked teeth hadn't bothered him. He'd liked her uneven smile.

"No men in her family have ever served in the military. You can't marry that girl," the Colonel had said. "What kind of people don't serve their country?"

John had been on the fence about Mary Jane. Newly eighteen and just graduated from high school, he certainly wasn't ready to get married. And that broke Mary Jane's heart. In her family, everyone married right out of high school and some even married during high school, which appalled his mother. "They marry young because they're uneducated," she'd said. "That's why they're stuck in poverty. You need to take a good look at General Robison's daughter if you think you need a girl already."

John wasn't surprised when Mary Jane broke it off with him in a Dear John letter and married his high school buddy Leroy. That hurt. A lot. When he was in Vietnam, he sometimes thought maybe he should have married Mary Jane before he went to West Point, so he'd have a wife sending him pictures and care packages like Jimmy did. The truth was, he had envied Jimmy, and even now really wanted to read the letter he carried.

Of course, he wouldn't.

He should just give it to Swampy and get out of here.

How many times had he closed his eyes in Vietnam and imagined Swampy was his wife?

When had he fallen for her? Maybe it was before Jimmy died, when he had talked about her all the time. Maybe it was when he'd seen her pictures. Swampy making a snowman in Tahoe on their honeymoon and the one of her by the lake, tan and thin and so sexy in that pink polka-dot bikini. Or maybe it was when Jimmy shared her care packages with him. In the middle of eating the chocolate chip cookies she'd baked that were a little stale from the mail, had he realized he was falling in love with his best friend's wife? Meeting her in person had sealed it. It was true and unexplainable. He loved Swampy.

Had she punched Rex because of jealous rage? He didn't mind sharing her with Jimmy, but he sure didn't want to share her with anybody else.

Jimmy always said she was a blazing Cajun. Now he knew exactly what that meant. *She's still Jimmy's wife. Get her back on her feet till she finds another duster, give her the letter, and move on as fast as you can.* But he didn't want to move on. He wanted to stay with her forever.

He groaned and tried not to think about Swampy as he drank more whiskey. The memories of other women he'd known whirled through his mind. He'd never been short on girlfriends, though most of them hadn't meant anything more than a moment of pleasure. After Mary Jane, he hadn't wanted a serious relationship—until Swampy. He got to know her through Jimmy's adoring eyes and all those letters in 'Nam. Something about war made it easy to fall in love. Maybe it was the urgency to live after watching men die. To hell with being cautious with your heart. In an hour, your heart could take a bullet and stop beating, so it was easy to fall in love over there. He was in love with Jimmy's wife and now that he'd talked to her, touched her, looked into her eyes, he was a goner.

He put the bottle to his lips and tried to drown out her memory by drinking more. He thought about Jimmy. All the missions they'd flown together. The soldiers they'd rescued and sent home to their families alive. That had been their real mission in the war. They'd decided to hell with the government and fought for one another. Keeping each other alive was their cause. It was a good cause. Worth fighting for.

He took another gulp, finishing off the whiskey. He liked the burn in his throat, the warm buzz that softened the chill seeping into his bones, into his soul. It was cold out here in the rice paddies. Tired, freezing, and out of whiskey, he got down from the hood of his car and retrieved his sleeping bag out of the trunk. He'd been sleeping in his car for more than a year now and was used to the discomfort. The backseat wasn't so bad. It was better than trying to assimilate into life back home in McLean, Virginia, after the war. Country clubs, church pews, and potential wives lined up by his determined mother—what a nightmare that had been.

The Colonel had welcomed him home as if he was a war hero. The Silver Star, Distinguished Flying Crosses, and Purple Heart, along with a dozen other medals he'd been awarded in battle helped. Finally, after all of those years working his tail off trying to please the Colonel, he'd done it—his father was proud of him.

His mother, who rarely showed emotion, grew distraught when he'd returned with scars on his face. "You were so handsome before the war," she said, her eyes wide when she saw where the shrapnel had ripped up his right cheek. "You'll have to grow a beard to cover those awful scars."

"He can't have a beard," the Colonel said. "He's in the military."

"Look at him!" his mother cried, surprising both him and his father.

"He finally looks like a real man, not your little pretty boy, Maureen." The Colonel smiled. "I'm proud of you, Son. Don't mind your mother. The ladies will still want you. You're a Reno with the scars of war now. You're irresistible."

His mother, who never cried, left the room in tears. John tried to let go of the disappointment he'd always felt concerning his mother. He didn't understand her and probably never would. She was a cold woman. His father called her a tall glass of water. And she was. Classic ice water.

John smoked a cigar and drank brandy with the Colonel in his study after his mother went to her room. The Colonel showed him his own old wounds on his legs from Korea, talking about how he got the scars. It was the first time his father had opened up to him about anything.

"So, tell me how you won the Silver Star—the real story. Not that pretty memo I received from your commander. I know how war goes. Are you an accidental hero or did you really deserve it?"

"My gunner deserved the Star. He saved my life. I'm just the one they pinned it on." John wanted to impress his father with his war deeds, but when he'd won the Star, it felt like good fortune, not courage. Like he was surrounded by a supernatural shield he'd attributed to the men he flew with and his Irish luck.

The Colonel's mother was full-blooded Irish, her blue eyes always smiling like she had a delightful little secret. She was John's favorite person in the whole world. She'd called him "Lucky John" from the day he was born. Probably because his siblings, two brothers before him, had died shortly after birth, arriving too soon and unable to breathe on their own, much to his parents' secret heartache. His mother and father never mentioned the lost babies. His grandmother told him about the infants when he'd asked her when he was ten years old why she called him lucky. He'd never told his parents that he knew, and they never mentioned the babies either, but they didn't like his grandmother calling him Lucky John. She also took him to her Methodist Church, and his father and mother didn't approve of that, either.

The Colonel tolerated his wife's Catholicism, maybe because he'd admired President Kennedy and had been distraught when the president was assassinated, but for some reason his father deeply disliked the Methodists he'd grown up with.

"You really want to know what happened with the Star?" John ran a hand over his high and tight haircut. He'd just visited his father's barber that morning and felt kind of naked with his hair so closely shorn. He'd gotten used to longer hair in 'Nam. Thinking about the war was hard, but his father had never given him this much attention. He didn't know if he liked it or not.

"I really want to know." The Colonel puffed another cigar to life. "Not many men are awarded the Silver Star."

"All right," John picked up his crystal glass, shooting the top shelf brandy down in one long, delicious gulp, which he knew his father wouldn't appreciate. He asked for a refill before telling his story.

# Chapter Four

When a colonel gave an order, you didn't question it, you got it done. So, John kept his reservations to himself as he transported Colonel Christopher Kane to the higher support base on top of Nui Ba Den, the Black Virgin Mountain, despite drawing heavy enemy fire. The Ho Chi Minh Trail ended just a few miles west of the Cambodian border, and the Black Virgin was a battlefield both sides refused to give up on. The mountain, an extinct volcano, rose from the Mekong Delta jungle and flat farmlands, a single cinder cone with a saddle and bulge on the northwest side. The top belonged to the Americans, and they'd taken the bottom now as well, but in between these two strongholds, the North Vietnamese Army had dug in deep—caves, tunnels, and trails entrenched all over the middle of the Black Virgin.

John had flown the mountain before and knew this was a dangerous endeavor, but the colonel said he needed to get there pronto, so it was balls to the wall. They came in from the south at top speed and immediately drew fire. John turned the lightly armed Huey around, heading for the east side of Nui Ba Den as Cobra gunships, flying one thousand feet behind them, began strafing the enemy on the south. The whup-whup-whup of helicopters and explosions of firepower in the distance filled John's ears, along with comments from the colonel coming through the radio, though the colonel and his sergeant major sat directly behind John in the chopper.

His door gunner, nineteen-year-old Staff Sergeant Kelly, was harnessed in the open doorway with his M60 on a swivel mount, watching the dark green jungle below. He was a big, strong kid with an even stronger determination to do his job well. Kelly had enlisted in the army straight out of high school and was nearly done with his one-year tour. John would be sad to see him go next month, since he'd flown with the kid for nine months now and thought of him as a younger brother.

John's copilot was Lieutenant Lancing. Tall, slim, and soft-spoken, Lancing was cool-eyed and calculating as he too monitored the jungle and the instrument panel in the cockpit. They all wore ceramic body armor, "chicken plates" across their chests to protect them from ground fire. John was nearly through his first tour and unfazed by the tracers streaking from the mountain and the colonel shouting in his ear. Like his father, Colonel Kane was a Korean War hero and wasn't about to let a little NVA firepower stop him from reaching the command post that afternoon.

John turned the Huey around and approached from the west but drew fire there too. He tried coming in from the east next, and on short final, about a quarter of a mile from touching down, took massive fire, at least fifty rounds through the bottom of the helicopter. Tracers streaked past in drifting yellow and orange lines splitting the sky. The fireworks show would have been beautiful if it wasn't so deadly.

Bullets banged into the underside of the Huey. Warning lights flashed on the instrument panel as gunfire raked through the transmission and tail rotor. SSG Kelly answered the firepower with the M60, opening up the jungle as blue smoke began billowing from the aircraft.

Blue smoke was the last thing a pilot wanted to see. It meant the engine had taken a hit. The Huey tilted. John wrestled to keep control of the aircraft, working the pedals as the tail rotor went out. They were heading for the side of the mountain when the sound of whirring machinery disappeared altogether and only gunfire and explosions remained. The engine had failed.

John did what he could to put the Huey down skids first, as wind howled through the cargo door. Everyone braced themselves for the crash landing. The rotor blades contacted the ground first, and the helicopter rolled onto its side on top of a large bomb crater.

SSG Kelly was out of his harness first, yelling he'd spotted NVA soldiers coming down the trail about fifty yards to the right of the smoking aircraft. Thankfully the aircraft didn't catch fire. John hollered for everyone to grab their weapons and exit the left side of the helicopter as he pulled the release on his safety harness and got out of his seat, making sure Lieutenant Lancing exited the cockpit before he did.

They scrambled away from the wreckage and found another bomb crater about a hundred yards from the crash. SSG Kelly arrived with his M60 and the dazed sergeant major, joining John and Lieutenant Lancing in the hole on the side of the mountain.

Explosions thundered in the distance—Cobra helicopters blasting the enemy. They immediately began setting up a defensive perimeter with the enemy they'd spotted up the trail beyond the crashed Huey.

"Where's the colonel?" John pulled his .45 caliber pistol from his shoulder holster. He'd dumped his helmet while exiting the aircraft.

"He got out of the helicopter," said the graying sergeant major, wiping blood from his brow.

"He must have exited the right side," said SSG Kelly. "I don't have the M60 ammo case. I'm going back to get it and find the colonel."

"I'll get the colonel and the ammo case," John said. "You all stay here and defend the perimeter." He scurried up out of the crater and realized SSG Kelly was right behind him.

"I'll get the ammo case. My M60's useless without it," SSG Kelly explained, though he didn't have to. Everyone was functioning on high adrenaline and the need to stay alive. "That was a good landing," he told John as they jogged back to the helicopter.

When they arrived there, SSG Kelly scrambled into the helicopter in search of the ammo case. John found Colonel Kane in the crater under the aircraft being beaten by three NVA soldiers. Two of them were holding the colonel by the arms, and another was pistol-whipping him. His face was badly lacerated. He was bleeding profusely. Of course, they wouldn't kill him. He was too valuable as a prisoner.

John shot two of the soldiers before they realized he was upon them. They dropped dead, and the other one let go of the colonel's arm and looked at John like he was a ghost. The last soldier was no more than a teenager, his face feminine like a young woman's, his brown eyes widening with fear. He looked at the gun aimed at him and then back at John. Their gazes held for a timeless moment before the boy began fumbling to pull out a weapon. John just couldn't shoot the teenager while staring into his frightened eyes. The young soldier found his gun, but John still couldn't pull the trigger.

SSG Kelly, with the M60 ammo case under one arm, jumped into the hole and fired his .38 caliber Smith and Wesson at the boy's forehead. The teenager dropped as if his legs disappeared. He was dead before he hit the dirt.

SSG Kelly looked at John, obviously wondering why he hadn't shot the boy, but neither of them said a word. John stepped over and picked up the colonel. He wasn't a large man, and John outweighed him by a good thirty pounds of height and muscle and was thirty years younger too. After getting a good hold on the colonel, he hefted him up off the two dead NVA soldiers without looking at the boy who had fallen backward. The colonel was unconscious but came to as John lugged him over and lifted him up to SSG Kelly who'd crawled back up into the helicopter—the only way out of the hole was through the mangled aircraft. As John climbed into the chopper, he told SSG Kelly, "Grab the grenades." The kid could pick the grenades like grapes right off the cable running along the backside of his gunner's compartment. John helped the half-conscious colonel out of the crashed aircraft on the other side, calling over his shoulder, "We need first aid kits."

"I'll grab those too," SSG Kelly called back.

The colonel's right eye was hanging out. John hoped the kid grabbed all four of the first aid kits in the bird.

They made it back to the bomb crater where Lieutenant Lancing and the sergeant major were still reinforcing the perimeter. They heard the Cobras coming in, and soon the gunships began strafing their side of the mountain with rockets, blasting the trail beyond the helicopter. John and the sergeant major packed the colonel's face in compression pads and sterile gauze, then wrapped it in bandages, leaving his nose and mouth free to breathe. They heard the Huey coming in before they saw it. Every American soldier in Vietnam knew that sound. It was the sound of freedom.

The slick hovered down, and the pilot set one skid on the side of a rock on the outside of the crater, hovering since there was no place to safely land on the side of the mountain. John and the sergeant major lifted the colonel up to the men reaching down from the Huey and then hoisted Lieutenant Lancing up after him. "You're next," John told the sergeant major, and the man didn't argue. SSG Kelly grabbed the sergeant major in his muscular arms, and he and John shoved the man up into the hovering helicopter.

"You go," said SSG Kelly, but John knew the last man in the hole would have no way to get up into the helicopter. The Cobras had left the mountain, headed down to the bottom of the Black Virgin where a hot refueling point was set up. They'd be back, but maybe not soon enough to hold off the NVA.

"It's your turn." John slapped SSG Kelly on the back before getting a firm hold on him and lifting Kelly straight up toward the helicopter. "You did good. You saved the colonel's life. And my life." He had to speak loud over the pounding of the rotor blades.

"No, captain!" the kid yelled, but the men in the helicopter grabbed him and pulled him into the bird.

John waved them off, knowing they needed to get out of there. Without the gunships defending their location, the Huey was a sitting duck. He rushed over to the M60 and was relieved to see Kelly had it locked and loaded, ready to rock the NVA. The slick rose into the sky and headed off into the blue.

The afternoon was suddenly eerily quiet. The humidity wasn't as bad on the mountain as it was in the delta valley, but it still made him sweat profusely. Or maybe it was the enemy nearby that caused his body to let loose all the moisture it harbored. Perspiration ran down his back and chest and cheeks in steady streams. He was battered and bruised, his legs and arms aching, his chest burning with each breath he took. Maybe he'd cracked a rib or two.

But he was happy he got everyone out. He was the pilot in command and like a captain that goes down with his ship, he wasn't about to get in that rescue chopper and leave his door gunner behind. SSG Kelly had a young wife and baby at home. He stared at his crashed helicopter, and the realization hit him—that Huey was a command and control aircraft. A lot of sensitive equipment was on that thing.

He found the pile of his gunner's grenades right at his feet. He picked up the two thermal grenades, and after scanning the perimeter for any movement, scrambled out of the hole and ran to the helicopter. Pulling the pin on both grenades at the same time, he dropped them into the fuel cell area of the aircraft and ran back to the bomb crater. He hit the bottom of the muddy hole as the blasts went off. The grenades ignited the fuel tanks, and a wave of fire consumed the wreckage.

For a few minutes, he lay at the bottom of the hole and the world stopped. His senses became acute. He could see the crevices in the rock that had been blown in half when the crater was made by an American bomb. He finally got up and situated himself behind the M60, watching flames consume the Huey. At least the NVA wouldn't be able to get their hands on any of the radios or sensitive equipment. Plus, that burning aircraft blocked the trail to his location. He'd bought himself some time to wait for his own rescue as he listened for the Cobras, hoping to hear the gunships returning.

He thought of the strangest things while he waited. The bacon and eggs he'd had for breakfast. Every day he saved a piece of bacon for Rufus, the stray dog all the soldiers loved back at the base. Rufus was everybody's dog and nobody's dog. The medium-sized black mutt with a white star on his chest had once belonged to a pilot that left one morning and never returned— shot down and missing in action. Dead or a prisoner at the Hanoi Hilton or another location in the North where American airmen were tortured and starved to death. The guards of the prisoners were selected from families of those killed by American bombs. They were particularly sadistic, taking their revenge slowly and painfully making the airmen wish they were dead.

Rufus refused to leave the hooch where his pilot had lived. The dog would roam the base all day, wagging his tail, visiting everyone but growing attached to no one. Every soldier wanted Rufus to be their dog, but Rufus returned to his pilot's hooch every night, refusing to sleep inside with the airman who now lived there. Each night, Rufus waited for his master to come home, curled up outside the door of the hooch, no matter how cold it was outside. He just wanted his pilot. John loved that dog. And hoped to be loved like that by someone someday.

He wiped at the sweat running down his face but found tears instead. The only person who'd ever really loved him was his grandmother. That little woman with the smiling blue eyes the same color as his. She had died just last year, and he'd been unable to return to the states for her funeral. He hadn't cried when he got the news—he'd flown a mission that day and saved seven soldiers' lives—but he cried now.

Silent sobs overtook him as he stared down the barrel of the M60, manning his weapon while weeping. Thinking about his grandma and the two human beings he'd killed that day and the young soldier who died while staring into his eyes. His father had never allowed tears when he was a boy, but the tears wouldn't stop now. He'd never killed a man before, but that didn't bother him nearly as much as watching that bullet strike the boy's smooth, feminine forehead and seeing death overtake the teenager.

He cried in a way he never had before, a way that completely surprised him, that came upon him like a storm unleashing something profound in him. Something very deep. All the pain he'd ever masked. All the rejection from his mother and inability to please his father. He lost all track of time in the hole, holding onto the M60, staring down the iron sights dripping with his tears. Until he heard the sound of freedom, and stood up, looking around for the incoming rescue ship.

He probably hadn't waited long, but it felt like half his life. The Huey came in and lowered a winch that he hooked to his survival vest after gathering up the M60, its ammo case, and the remaining grenades. He wasn't about to leave any weapons behind the enemy could use on other American soldiers.

The helicopter lifted him to safety, and months later, he was awarded the Silver Star. SSG Kelly was given a battlefield commission by Colonel Kane, who was now missing an eye but recovering well and in good spirits. Colonel Kane told the kid to choose any college he wanted and Uncle Sam would pay for it. SSG Kelly chose Nebraska, home of Herbie Husker, the mascot farmer in bib overalls. John missed that big, muscular Virginia farm boy with a heart just as big as his chest. SSG Kelly returned to his family and a brand-new life on a college campus where he wrote John a letter, saying he'd made it onto his college football team and his wife was pregnant with their second child.

A tear slipped down his cheek as he finished telling his father how he'd won the Silver Star. The contempt on the Colonel's face over that single tear was too much. John stumbled to his feet and off to bed without saying goodnight. Reliving the story was harder than he'd thought it would be. Killing a man as you looked him in the eye was not an easy thing. The cost of war on a man's heart and soul was high.

His promotion ceremony the following week felt like a farce. His father pinned on his medals and shook his hand, telling him what a great military career was ahead of him now that he'd been the tip of the spear in Vietnam. But that night, roaring drunk at the O Club, he tossed his oak leaf into the Colonel's whiskey and 7.

He wanted to drown away that promotion. Most of all, wanted to drown away his pain.

"I'm not an officer anymore!" he yelled in his father's face. "I don't want to be a major in your army! Choke on your damned oak leaf!" His tirade had been laced with profanity as well. Before Vietnam, he'd thought of himself as an officer and a gentleman and didn't speak crudely like other soldiers. But that officer and gentleman was as dead as Jimmy. They'd both succumbed in the jungle, where he'd been determined to outdo his father in war. He'd wanted the Distinguished Flying Cross more than anything. His father didn't have that medal. But after he'd won two Flying Crosses and then the Silver Star, which his father respected even more, he'd grown too bold, too arrogant, too blind. He'd felt invincible after being awarded those medals. And that's exactly when he became vulnerable. And so had his men.

He strode out of the smoke-filled club and caught a taxi home to pack his bags as his mother slept in the three-story brick mansion his parents owned in McLean, Virginia. The mansion had been in his mother's family for generations. It was more of a museum than a home. All the priceless antique furniture remained the same as his mother grew up with. She'd been born into wealth, unlike his father, who came from a long line of distinguished war heroes, not wealthy men but impressive soldiers. Officers other men deeply admired. And nothing about his parents' marriage had changed. His father still preferred the Officers' Club, and his mother her own bedroom on the third floor.

Without any direction and still raging drunk, he got in his Camaro and headed west on Route 66, driving until he was too tired to drive anymore. He finally pulled over and passed out in the backseat of his car. There was a time he would have judged a man for sleeping in his vehicle, but not anymore. Sometimes it happened. A man lost his way.

He grew a beard to hide the scars on his cheek—mostly from himself—and disappeared into the American landscape of war protests and free love, sleeping on and off in the backseat of his car for several years as he made his way crop-dusting across the South. Some called him a hippie, and he looked the part, but he never stopped flying. The sky was his refuge by day, and he hid in a bottle at night. Now he'd finally reached California. And Swampy. He didn't know where things would go from here. But he was here.

# Chapter Five

Sometime in the night, John roused himself from a familiar nightmare. The helicopters of his dreams were always burning. Sometimes he was burning too. He sat up, bumping his head on the car's black leather ceiling. He cursed as he kicked off his green military sleeping bag. The cold slipped in upon his sweat, chilling him. He pulled the sleeping bag up over his body, lying there in the predawn darkness, listening to the field of swans and geese that, like him, waited impatiently for the safety of sunrise. The birds called back and forth to one another, their nervous chatter floating through the car's busted-out driver's side window along with the cold. He looked at his watch but couldn't make out the time in the dark. It felt like morning. He searched around until he found his flashlight, then climbed out to retrieve a fresh set of clothes from the duffel in his trunk. In his underwear, shivering, he dressed quickly, standing out in the open beside his car.

After throwing on jeans and a worn flannel shirt, he climbed into the front seat of the Camaro. He gave the car a few minutes to warm up and then headed east toward Live Oak, a single-stoplight town with big oak trees. He found an open gas station and cleaned up in the one-stall bathroom. Brushed his teeth. Washed his face and hair and underarms in water too cold. He took scissors to his scraggly beard and then finally finished it off by shaving, which felt discomforting but necessary. When the scars on his cheek appeared under his razor, he hurried through his task, wanting to escape that cracked mirror. The scars were white now—less noticeable but still there. Like a brand that would always remind him he'd been wounded in a way that could never be healed. But he knew by the way Swampy had looked at him yesterday that his appearance didn't jibe with her cardboard cutout of a crop-dusting pilot.

He thought about the clean-cut Rex. For some reason he felt compelled to clean himself up as best he could to ease some of the doubt he saw in Swampy's eyes.

With dawn haloing the distant Sierra Nevada, he drove to the dusting company. The heater roared warm air into the car's interior, but the broken side window sucked it out as quickly as the heater released it. He'd busted the window out after locking his keys in the car somewhere in the middle of the Nevada desert and didn't know when he'd fix it. A broken window was the least of his worries. Everything was broken in his life. Brokenness was in his bones now.

He couldn't wait to see Swampy. She was all he could think about since yesterday. He hoped she didn't ask about his scars. What would he tell her?

When he pulled up to the hangar, he noticed the building had once been painted a canary yellow, but most of the bright paint had chipped away. Largely iron-gray tin now, the hangar looked formidable and lonely illuminated in the Camaro's headlights. He parked alongside a '54 Chevy pickup. The paint job had worn down to the primer. Dents, abundant as a redhead's freckles, dusted the truck's sides. An American flag was draped across the rear window. The tires, frame, and large fenders were covered with mud. The driver's side door sported a black slogan, a striking snake wrapped around the name Blue Blazes. Soldiers painted slogans like that on their aircrafts in 'Nam.

He glanced around the empty parking lot, made small by the early morning duskiness of an encroaching fog. The mist oozed across the darkness like spilled milk. There would be no flying in this pea soup today. He squinted through the shadowy haze, looking for the owner of the Chevy, but didn't see anyone. He glanced one last time at the truck as he headed toward the hangar.

He pushed open the hangar door and walked into the dim building when a body hit him full bore. The impact knocked John off his feet. When he hit the concrete floor, he rolled instinctively. His attacker tumbled with him, fists slamming into every vulnerable spot on his body. The punches avoided the muscular plane of his torso. Targeting his ears, eyes, and groin. He was up against a dirty fighter.

He protected himself with well-honed fighting instincts; he'd been a champion wrestler in high school and a decent boxer in Vietnam. Still, the wiry attacker slipped in here and there as they thrashed around on the cold concrete floor. His eye took a nasty blow. He tasted blood from a split lip. A fist landed on one of his ears, and his ear wouldn't stop ringing.

A meager light bulb glowing in a distant corner of the hangar illuminated the building. John cursed the poor visibility. He was having a hard time getting a good punch in. His fist connected with a bony shoulder, then a skinny leg, and then the hard sole of his attacker's boot. Both men swore repeatedly as they landed blows. Their breathing was coming hard now. A fist caught him in the gut, knocking the wind from him. A bony elbow slammed into the side of his head. Knuckles followed the elbow. John dodged the punch by twisting his body sideways toward his attacker. He threw his arms around the man's chest, and his head snapped back as a fist smashed into his jaw. He ignored the jarring of his teeth, finally getting a solid hold of his attacker's scrawny neck. It took him five minutes to squeeze his opponent into submission.

"Blue Blazes, it's over," he said, somehow knowing the man he'd pinned to the concrete floor owned the mud-covered Chevy in the parking lot. The skinny man smelled of marijuana and engine grease. John released his hold on his throat and smacked the guy in the eye, then climbed off him. Rising to his feet, his eyes finally adjusted to the meager light inside the building.

Blue sat up, putting a hand to his injured eye. "What'd you do that for? I surrendered to you."

"I wanted us to match." John looked at the man's clothing—the same green jungle fatigues soldiers wore in Vietnam. "Where's your boss?"

Blue probed his swelling eye as he got to his feet. "Who?"

"The man who pays you to act like a jackass." John reached up to examine his own eye, which hurt more than any of the other sore places on his body. Touching his throbbing eyebrow made him wince.

*Where was Mr. Callohan?*

He both dreaded and deeply looked forward to meeting Jimmy's dad. He needed to look Mr. Callohan in the eye, shake his hand, and tell him what a fine son he'd raised. That old familiar ache hit him. His throat grew tight. He glanced around, hoping to see a tall, older gentleman with graying hair and an easy grin that matched Jimmy's.

"I don't work for a man. I work for my sister."

"Where's Mr. Callohan?"

"He's dead."

John caught his breath. He hadn't expected this but wasn't willing to lose the upper hand here by letting Blue see his shock. Anger rose in him, not really at this knucklehead but because Mr. Callohan was gone. Mr Callohan was the kind of father he'd always wanted. "What's the matter with you? I'm sure your sister doesn't want you to beat people up."

"I guard the hangar."

"From what?"

"The Viet Cong." Blue looked as lean as he'd felt when John had finally gotten a hold of him. His body was nothing more than muscle and bone and chestnut hair that favored red, clinging to his head in a long crew cut. He looked like a soldier straight out of the Vietnam bush, down to the single-shot shotgun strapped to his narrow hip and thigh. The stock and barrel had both been sawed off. Guys did the same crazy things to guns in 'Nam.

"Well, the Cong aren't going to get you in California, but I might if you jump me like that again."

Blue laughed as if he was having the time of his life. As if attacking John was the most productive thing he'd done all month.

His hearty laugh had a cackle to it. The sound reminded John of the geese he'd listened to in the rice field that morning.

"So you're the new pilot." Blue's gaze lingered on John's long hair and then his face. "You need a haircut. I could have pulled your hair, but I fought fair."

John laughed in unbelief. "That was fair?"

"I didn't use a knife or my gun." Blue patted the weapons strapped to his belt. "If I'd known you knew how to fight, I wouldn't have taken it easy on you."

"Blue!"

Both men turned toward the light from the opening door. The rising sun's rays stabbed through the fog, framing a woman in golden mist. She stepped through the door, hitting several switches that filled the building with light. She had a bandage on her hand. Her gaze swept John's face for a moment before she lasered in on Blue.

"Why weren't the lights on? Why aren't the doors open? Is Billy up yet? I guess it doesn't matter. It's too foggy to fly this morning." Swampy finally took a breath. "Hello, Mr. Reno."

"Good morning, Swampy." He tried to smile and winced because his lip was cut.

She turned back to Blue. "What have you been doing? I told you and Billy to have the planes ready by six this morning."

Even though Blue topped her by nearly a foot and wore a sawed-off shotgun strapped to his lanky hip, he looked abashed at having displeased her. John got the feeling only this woman could cause Blue to make the excuses he made now.

"Sorry. I heard on the news it was gonna be foggy, so I figured we wouldn't fly. I was just gettin' ready to open the doors when this cowboy stepped into the hangar. Thought he was out to sabotage our planes, so I boogered him up good."

Swampy turned to John. Her gaze lingered on his bruised eye. Embarrassed, he concentrated on tucking his torn flannel shirt back into his jeans.

She turned back to Blue. "It's a good thing you didn't hurt Mr. Reno. We need another pilot to get us through the season."

John ran a hand over his disarrayed hair. His lip throbbed, but his ear had finally stopped ringing.

Blue laughed. "If this cowboy hadn't said my name when he did, he'd be takin' a six-foot-deep dirt nap now. I was gonna bury him out back behind the old tractor."

Swampy waved an introducing hand between them. "John, this is my brother Blue. He acts like he's still in a war zone. We just accept it around here."

John held out his hand for a handshake.

Blue grabbed his palm in a firm, enthusiastic grip.

As they shook hands, Swampy continued, "I won't be able to start you dusting this morning on account of the fog. Which is good, looking at your eye."

The swelling was starting to interfere with his eyesight. He felt a little confounded standing there, looking at her out of a blackening eye. He'd met some crazy people in 'Nam, but these two siblings were something with their flying fists. Blazin' Cajuns, Jimmy had called them.

"Do you want to take a look at my licenses or something?" John reached into his back pocket for his wallet and felt the folded envelope. He quickly moved his hand away. He just couldn't give it to her yet.

"You got a license to fly in pea soup?"

"Not in a Stearman."

Blue chuckled. "Should we let this cowboy fly the jet we got stashed out back? I'll program the location of the orchard into the instruments, and he and his fancy licenses can dust today."

Swampy ignored her brother, finally smiling a little at John. "I don't need to see your license until I stick you in the cockpit. Besides, you can't fly worse than Blue. He flies like a warped-winged paper plane."

"I fly better than you, LG."

Swampy slapped Blue on the shoulder as she stepped past him. "Dream on." She gave John an apologetic look. "Take care of your face and come back tomorrow. Fog or no fog, I'll put you to work. If you can stand Blue, you should do just fine around here." She disappeared into the depths of the hangar.

John turned to Blue beside him. "She always this friendly?"

"Nope. I believe that mention of a fancy flying license sweetened her up. She's been wantin' to hire a real hotshot. Thinks a bang-up pilot can save the company."

John smiled. "Really?"

"She can't pay you much. We're barely gettin' by as it is." Blue appeared rubbed the wrong way by John's pleased grin.

"Pay's not a problem. I've come for the work."

"Baxter's Flying Service is looking for a pilot, and their pay's twice as good. They've got Ag Cats. Wouldn't you rather fly a new Cat? Our Stearmans are falling apart. We're lucky they're still in the air." Blue adjusted his mangled shotgun.

"I'm not interested in anything long-term. I'm just here for a gig or two."

"A gig or two? We need someone to work the whole season."

"How long's the season?"

"That depends." Blue narrowed his eyes and pursed his lips. John waited for him to explain California's crop-dusting season. When Blue remained silent, John prompted him. "Depends on what?"

"Frost in February. Rain in April. Hungry bugs and flying fungus. You name it, we spray it."

Shaking his head, John turned to leave. "When I come through this door in the morning, I'll be ready for you, Blue Blazes."

Blue laughed, that wild cackle, and then appeared deadly serious. "No one's ever ready for me, cowboy."

"Now that I believe. See you in the morning, Blue."

Blue's manic laughter followed him out the door.

# Chapter Six

John arrived at Callohan Dusters the next morning at five forty-five, but this time the fog beat him there. Walking from his car to the hangar was like trudging through a snow tunnel. The air smelled wet and cold. His lungs tingled as he sucked in the cloudy mist. All around, the world was white. In the distance, he heard the geese. He didn't need a watch around here—the birds announced morning, coyotes welcomed the night, and the afternoons were filled with the hum of distant tractors.

He paused before opening the hangar door. His left eye was swollen and sore. He glanced around, his senses on high alert as he stepped through the dark entrance, looking for Blue. The cackling laugh came from the depths of the hangar.

A light switched on.

"I see you've learned not to prance into a place like a circus pony. I taught you a good lesson yesterday."

"Morning, Blue."

"Mornin', cowboy."

"I sure could use a cup of coffee."

"How 'bout a shot of brandy?" Blue pulled a flask out of the thigh pocket of his fatigues and offered John a drink.

John stared at the flask for a moment before shaking his head. He'd made a New Year's promise to himself and to Jimmy. No more booze.

"It's hard to say no to the devil, ain't it?" Blue smiled, unscrewed the flask, and took a drink.

A car pulled up to the hangar, tires crunching on the gravel, and Blue hurriedly tucked his flask away.

Swampy soon walked through the door.

"Blue, go get Billy up. It's a good morning to fix *Old Dan*'s stress fracture. We can't fly till the fog clears." She dismissed Blue by turning to John.

"Mornin' to you too, LG," Blue called as he trotted away.

"I could use your help around the hangar this morning. Grunt work, ground pay. You interested?"

John opened his mouth to answer, but Swampy went on. "If you plan on working here, you'll need to be an all-around type of employee. We're no fancy flying business, but you'll rack up the flight hours once the weather clears."

He smiled to put her at ease. "Sounds good."

She ignored his smile. "Don't worry, I'll fly your tail off and then some when the sun comes out." She glanced at the watch on her wrist of her bandaged hand. "I've got a few things to take care of before we get to work. Look around, make yourself at home."

He took a deep breath, telling his heart to quiet down as she strode away. She wore blue jeans and an oversized man's sweater. Her hair was in a ponytail. She looked really good. He closed his eyes, reminding himself she would always be Jimmy's.

To give himself something to do other than think about her, he walked over to the Stearmans. The two planes sat side by side inside the big hollow building. A hand-carved wooden sign hung over each aircraft, dangling on rusted chains from the rafters of the ceiling.

*Molly* and *Old Dan*. The names were also painted in black letters on the nose of each Stearman. He smiled at the planes, and the urge to introduce himself welling up within him. *Molly, Old Dan—John Reno. Nice to meet you. I've heard a lot about you Stearmans.* He shook his head, pulling a stick of gum from his shirt pocket and popping it in his mouth. Savoring the fruity flavor, he stared at the planes a moment longer, reliving the instant Swampy Callohan had crawled out of one of these cockpits a couple days ago.

He hadn't been prepared for that. What he'd been prepared for, he didn't know. Thinking on it for a moment, he decided he wasn't ready to resolve much of anything right now, least of all his feelings about being here. He just wanted to look around at all the dragons he'd slain to get here and feel content for as long as he could.

Swampy paced the small confines of the hangar's cluttered office. She flipped on her clock radio and browsed from station to station before settling on a country program. After a second look at her new pilot, doubt plagued her. He now sported a black eye, thanks to Blue. She was afraid to let him drive the

Studebaker, let alone fly one of her Stearmans, but she had to admit his freshly shaven face proved as striking as she figured it would be, even with those scars on one cheek. What had happened to him? He was battered and worn, but still too good-looking. She'd described him to Billy as Hollywood handsome, if he ever cleaned himself up. All together, his tall, broad-shouldered frame, direct blue stare, and disarming smile created an enduring impression. He was older than she was—most people in the flying business were—but if he had busted out of his thirties, it was yesterday. She wondered for the umpteenth time if he was a real duster as she shuffled through the stack of mail on her desk. The sensation of being watched hit her.

She looked up and there he stood in her office door frame. It was as if his sharp blue eyes could see her uncertainty, her loneliness, her cracked central core she hid from the world. In the one sickeningly long second John Reno stared at her, Swampy was sure he perceived all this about her.

She imagined him seeing her after the sun went down when she was home alone, tired and drained and utterly depressed, sitting on the porch swing, sipping her fourth lukewarm Miller High Life, watching the moths attack the front porch light. How, after polishing off a six-pack on the really bad nights, she often got the hiccups and then would start to cry. Or was it she'd start to cry and then get the hiccups? They always started about the same time, halfway through that last beer, and she would hate herself, telling herself what a pathetic, weak, and forsaken human being she really was.

"Would you like some coffee?" she asked to cover her nerves. She pointed to a crowded corner where a dirty coffee machine sat under unrolled flight maps. She didn't drink coffee. The pot hadn't been used since Jimmy's dad passed away.

"I'd love some coffee." His quiet, raspy voice was pleasant. She liked the sound of it. There was a calm strength about him she appreciated. She remembered how it felt to be in his arms when he'd pulled her away from Rex. No wonder Blue had jumped him. Blue was threatened by this guy. She looked again for a ring on his finger, but he tucked his hands in his pockets, giving her a little smile.

Her face filled with heat. "The coffee is in the cabinet over by the bathroom. You can fill up the pot in the sink." She quickly returned her attention to the bills in front of her.

*Does he know I was looking for a ring? Please don't let him think that.*

She stared at the simple gold wedding band on her own finger and then shuffled some papers, her stomach flipping over.

*Look busy. You are busy. Why is he just standing there?*

When he remained in the doorframe, staring at her as if he, or she, had nothing better to do, she finally leaned back in her chair and gave him her full attention. She didn't like that he made her nervous. She couldn't remember the last time a man made her feel this way. She took a deep breath through her nose and let the air out of her mouth slowly. A grief counselor, the one and only time she'd gone at the insistence of Mr. Callohan, had taught her how to breathe deeply to calm herself after Jimmy died. A couple more deep breaths, slowly released, and she didn't care about John Reno. She didn't care that pilots never stayed. He would come and go too. Hopefully after she found another duster to take his place. An older pilot with a gut and gray hair. Yes, that's what she needed, a crop-dusting grandpa. Gathering herself together, she locked eyes with him.

"Is there something I can do for you, Mr. Reno?"

"You promised to call me John."

Nothing about this man was boyish—except his smile. He looked ten years younger when he smiled. He ran a hand through sun-streaked brown hair that suited his chiseled face. She didn't care for long hair on a man but had to admit he was far too sexy, even with long hair. The scars on his cheek didn't bother her. Without those scars, his face would have been too perfect. *Get a grip, Silver.*

She called herself Silver in self-loathing, hearing her mother's voice.

*"Silver Susanna, you're such a skinny thing. It's a shame you didn't get your mama's bodacious tatas. Thank God you got my brains. Your daddy was a jarhead Marine. But he got one thing straight: you look like something the swamp spit out. You're all eyes and lips, like a little hoot owl. I sure hope you grow into your looks when you're older.*

That did it. Thinking about her mother always filled her with a fighting spirit. "Why are you interrupting me, John?" There, she'd said his name like he'd asked. She was the boss. She could handle any man.

"I'm not sure," he confessed, and his smile grew.

She hadn't felt remotely attracted to a man since Jimmy. And she'd been a girl with Jimmy, young and hopeful. Now she was a widow and bitter, even though she tried not to be. She knew the cost of love, and the price was too high. She swung back to the desk, knocking over her habitual breakfast—a nearly full can of Pepsi.

A few quick strides brought him to the paper-littered desk, where she fought to rescue drenched envelopes. "Let me help," he said softly, leaning over her.

She stiffened. "I've got it." She tossed the offending soda into a trash can beside the desk. She stood up, tempted to push him away. He was way too close. Heat pooled in her belly, then raced down her thighs. Her breath quickened. He smelled so good, like soap and cedar. Like the trees in her front yard now covered with frost. She wanted to stay frozen like the trees. She didn't want to feel anything.

She closed her eyes.

"I'll get a towel." He turned toward the door.

She gritted her teeth at his helpful tone and opened her eyes, pointing him toward the bathroom. "Over there." She spun toward the other end of the desk to put some distance between them, but he stepped in the same direction at the same time, and to her horror, she slammed right into his chest.

His arms wrapped around her. After a moment of stunned silence, she whispered, "I'm sorry."

*What the hell was happening?*

He was a perfect stranger, wasn't he? She'd always been intuitive. Why was he holding her? Why was she melting against him? Why didn't either one of them step away?

*He's so appealing.*

*Dear Lord. . .*

*Walk away!*

But she couldn't move.

She felt paralyzed in his muscular arms. She'd been telling herself since Jimmy died that she didn't need a man's help or a man's touch or a man's love. Now here she was acting like Lucy. Like nothing else mattered in the world but a moment of stolen pleasure in a man's arms.

"Don't be sorry," he whispered back, and his voice sounded pained. "I went the wrong way. It's my fault." His hands slid over her back, almost apologetically down to the waistband of her jeans. Like he couldn't help himself. Like he needed to touch her.

His hands were silk and fire. Unexpected desire made it impossible to think straight. He was so strong. Not just his muscles, but his resolve to enter her life. To wake her up. To make her feel what she didn't want to feel ...

"Jimmy always said I was a spiller." She backed out of his arms.

"Jimmy," he softly repeated. He stepped back too, looking around as if lost.

She could see he was as shaken as she was. Blinking back tears, she pointed to a little yellow towel hanging on a nail near the light switch.

He retrieved the towel and returned to mop up the mess.

The room was so quiet she could hear the soda dripping onto the floor. "Did you know my husband, Jimmy? He died in Vietnam."

# Chapter Seven

She stood in front of him as he wiped the desk dry. She felt like a widow at a funeral waiting for condolences. John wouldn't look at her, but just kept wiping even once the spill was gone. After what seemed like an eternity, he said, "How long did your brother serve in 'Nam? He seems out of sorts now." He finally glanced up, but she didn't understand the look in his eyes. The light was gone from his gaze. It was almost as if he'd hit a switch and just turned himself off.

She wished she could do the same. Everything inside her felt alive. Wildly alive. Her heart pounded fiercely. Warmth flamed in her belly and spread through her limbs. She began to shake. He wasn't going to say he was sorry like everyone else did.

*Sorry.* It was the worst word in the world.

To the last person who offered her a "sorry," she'd actually said, "Why on earth are you sorry? Jimmy's death wasn't your fault. That damned war killed him."

She was so tired of hearing "sorry," but now, all of a sudden, she wanted to hear him say sorry more than anything.

Anger welled up, fierce and unexplainable, but not really. He'd awoken something in her that she didn't want awakened.

*Damn him.*

Why couldn't he say he was sorry? Why was he staring at her with that blank look on his face? Like she hadn't mentioned Jimmy at all. What was wrong with him?

"Blue did three tours in Vietnam because he loved it over there. He said Vietnam was like the swamps we grew up in. Wild and harsh and beautiful. Everyone hungry and poor and hardy as rats." She turned away, pressing her bandaged fist against her mouth as tears lodged in her throat. "I really need to mail these bills out today, Mr. Reno." She blinked the burning sensation from her eyes, regretting telling him she'd been raised in a swamp, that she'd once been hungry and poor, which was none of his business.

"I'm sorry I said Blue was out of sorts. War is hard on men." He clutched the sticky towel in both hands, his gaze upon her.

It was so awkward she wanted to punch him like she had Rex.

"I guess I'm still sore over Blue jumping me. Hell, I wanted black coffee, not a black eye." He motioned toward the old tin sign hanging on the wall behind her desk and read it out loud, "If I Rise on the Wings of Dawn."

"It's a verse from the Bible. Mr. Callohan loved the Bible. He died of a heart attack not long after Jimmy."

"I'm sorry about Mr. Callohan." He didn't say more.

Why couldn't he say he was sorry about Jimmy too? If she had a Bible, she would have thrown it at him. "Around here, the wings of dawn mean we start flying at daylight when it's not foggy." She couldn't get out of her office and away from him fast enough. She pushed past, bellowing, "Blue! Billy! We're burning daylight, let's get working!" She mashed Jimmy's sweater against her sides with frustrated fists. Her hand ached. Billy had done a fine job stitching her up, but her knuckles throbbed when she made a fist.

*This isn't going to work.*

*He's already under my skin.*

*Where the hell is Blue?*

Her brother finally trotted down the narrow wood staircase against the hangar wall. The maimed shotgun bounced against his skinny leg. Maybe Blue would scare John away, as he had so many other men. Rex hadn't paid much attention to Blue's erratic behavior. He came, he flew, and then he hit the honky-tonks after work most nights. Until Lucy had lasered in on him like a heat-seeking missile. Swampy had to give Rex credit. He'd resisted Lucy for a long time.

"Where's Billy?" she asked when Blue came over.

"He ain't feeling well. He looks hungover as a hound dog running all night in the bayous. The kids are still sleepin'."

"Has he heard anything from Lucy? Does he know where she is?" Swampy ran a hand across her forehead, battling a sudden headache. She did her best to ignore John standing nearby.

"No. But he said she called him half a man before leaving. Can you believe that? That little tramp will be the death of Bean. She wags her tail at more men than Lassie."

"Lower your voice. What if the kids hear you? What if Billy hears you saying that about Lucy?"

Blue didn't listen, he just kept talking in his normally loud voice. "It fries me to see Billy beat down. He looks like a dog pissed in his eyes, and it's more than the booze. He's been crying.

He says not to call Mrs. Larson to look after the kids today. He wants their company."

"Are the kids okay?" Worry washed over her.

"How would I know? I told you they're still sleepin'."

From the back of the hangar, Patrick called, "Uncle Blue, wait for me!"

Her nephew barreled around one of the Stearmans, racing toward them. He had on pajamas with fabric feet and a shirt with Mickey Mouse on the front. He was running as fast as his sturdy little legs could carry him. When he tried to stop in front of them, the slick feet of his pajamas slid him into a spin on the smooth concrete floor.

Before she could move, John swept past her and scooped up Patrick, holding him at arm's length like one would a wet cat.

"Patrick! Be careful." She grabbed her nephew out of John's awkward hold and cradled Patrick against her, smoothing a cowlick down and away from his startled little face.

He pointed at John. "Who's that? He smells like Juicy Fruit. I want a piece of gum."

Swampy was at a loss for words.

"I'm John Reno." John reached into the worn pocket of his Levi's jacket and handed Patrick a stick of gum wrapped in bright yellow foil. "Your aunt hired me to fly her planes."

Patrick grinned as he took the gum. "I bet you could fly a turd out of Mrs. Larson's old butthole."

"Patrick!" Swampy slapped his bottom." Where did you hear that kind of talk?"

"Uncle Blue says it all the time. Huh, Uncle Blue?"

She turned to her brother. Patrick clung to her more tightly. "Blue Donovan, I told you to watch that foul mouth of yours in front of the kids."

Blue let loose one of his goose laughs. "I didn't say butthole, I said asshole. Ain't that right, Packy?"

"I mean it. Patrick is starting to talk just like you. How can we send him to school next year with a Marine's foul mouth? They'll expel him from kindergarten, for Pete's sake."

"Oh hell, LG. They don't expel kids from kindergarten. Do they, Packy?" Blue narrowed his eyes on Patrick, giving him a little wink.

"Don't pay your Uncle Blue any mind. They kicked him out of school so many times they called him 'the visitor.' Your uncle's a smart man, but he just wastes his smarts running his mouth off. He could have been a doctor or even the president, but he's—"

"There's more to life than being a doctor or the president," Blue interrupted, his eyes beginning to shine. "Do you know what it feels like to be runnin' through the bush with an ass full of bullets? A knife in your teeth and a snake squishin' in your boot because you threw that boot on without checkin' it in the middle of a jungle with a boatload of Charlies comin' after you? You don't, LG, and that's livin'. That's feelin' the wind in your hair for the last time. That's the last sweat pourin' off your brow because you're about to die. How on earth can I be a doctor, sittin' around tellin' old people how to crap, or the president, sittin' in his fine White House tellin' us to call the Viet Cong indigenous personnel so we don't hurt their damn feelings before we shoot the little bastards? How can I live like that after livin' wild in 'Nam? How, LG?!"

Swampy knew when to let something go. Especially when Blue got all crazy like this, his eyes wide and shining.

She set Patrick's pajama-slippered feet on the floor and told him to go get dressed. "And don't run, Packy," she reminded him. Patrick hurried away—a swift walk that turned into a run as soon as he thought she no longer watched him. She turned her attention back to her brother. Blue was breathing hard, pumped full of fretful adrenaline. His eyes were wide and shining. He looked out of his mind.

"Blue, I mean it. Start watchin' your mouth in front of Patrick. He's just a little boy. He doesn't understand when you freak out. He idolizes you, and all you talk about is that godforsaken war."

"I miss 'Nam." Blue's sigh of surrender relieved Swampy. He was settling down. That was good.

She turned away from him, and her eyes connected with John's. At least the light was back in his gaze. He smiled at her, and her stomach did another little flip, which she hated.

"Blue, show John how to help you fix the stress fracture. We'll leave Billy alone." She spun away from both men and headed back to her office. If John followed her, she was going to fire him.

# Chapter Eight

The '54 Chevy roared down a long country road that wound through orchards and fields and still more orchards, twisting away into the whiteness of a misty California morning. John stared out the passenger window, trying to relax with Swampy pressed against him. Beside her sat Patrick. Blue was driving and belting out a military cadence. Patrick sang along. The pickup blazed out of the fog like a freight train. The fog billowed wide when the old Chevy blasted through, then wrapped back around the lonely country road in the wake of the truck.

One moment they were in the fog, the next the Chevy broke through an invisible wall into a brilliant morning. The sun shimmered on the Sutter Buttes, those ten square miles of mountains rising above the valley floor like a fortress in a land of flat dimensions. At the drugstore in Live Oak, T-shirts and coffee mugs bragged that these buttes were the smallest mountain range in the world, and perhaps they were. John studied the circle of peaks towering above the farm fields before turning his attention to an orchard along the road, anything to take his mind off of Swampy beside him.

Trees as far as he could see were planted in rows perfectly spaced so that a tractor could roll through without touching the limbs. He leaned forward, looking through the Chevy's cracked windshield. "What kind of orchard is that?"

The poorly paved road turned into a long dirt drive winding through the same orchard. Blue and Patrick now sang an airborne cadence about an old lady and jump boots. John's conversation with Swampy seemed private with the other two concentrating on their boisterous song.

"A'monds." She pronounced almonds without the *l*.

"Almonds?" He repeated, putting the *l* back in the word.

"Out here they call them a'monds. 'When you knock them from the trees, you knock the *l* out of them,' the farmers say."

John laughed. "Why do the branches look red?" The sun slipped into the cab of the truck, warming his face.

"That's new growth. The trees are preparing to bloom. We'll be spraying these a'monds soon. They'll be covered with blossoms. From the air, they look like fields of snow."

She sighed before continuing. "Jimmy loved the a'mond blossoms. He'd pick me branches of the blooms and put them in a jar on the kitchen table. Mr. Callohan always did that for Jimmy's mom."

John leaned back against the seat. The memory of Jimmy settled between them like a heavy wedge waiting to be hammered in. He looked out the passenger window at the trees and the blue sky, but his thoughts soon circled back around to Swampy. She was always on his mind.

The truck suddenly slowed as it came to a bend in the road, tires squealing around a corner, Blue's foot heavy on the gas pedal. With the momentum of the turn, Swampy slammed into John, knocking him abruptly out of his reverie. Patrick's sturdy little body slid into hers, packing her against John.

"Dang it, Blue, you drive like rabbits … run," she finished abruptly, her cheeks turning red as the orchard's ripening branches. She tried to scoot back over into her spot.

"I know impatience to pick up the welder and get back to the hangar is eatin' you alive, LG. And seein' the sun out this way, you're probably chompin' at the bit to dust today too."

"We won't get anything done if you wrap us around one of these a'mond trees." She pushed Patrick into Blue and then slipped back into her space.

Blue brought the truck to a sliding stop in front of a big wooden gate. They all braced their hands on the dashboard so they wouldn't fly through the windshield as a plume of gravel and mud erupted around the truck. Everyone took a collective breath.

"Mind opening the gate, cowboy?" Blue smiled.

"Sure. Please call me John. Or Reno. Only my grandma gets away with calling me cowboy." John stepped out of the truck onto the muddy road.

"All right. Reno, Nevada. Nevada it is."

As he shut the door, John resisted the urge to fly off on another painful memory. Men had called him Nevada in Vietnam. Everyone had nicknames over there. Nevada was just one of his handles. Many of the guys had two or three nicknames depending on the company they kept. By the time he got the old wooden gate open and the truck drove through, he had control of his emotions. He closed the gate, then returned to the Chevy and climbed in.

They pounded over another dirt road, this one climbing a hill. Deep potholes rattled John's teeth as Blue gassed the old Chevy over the ruts. A bone-jarring bump bounced Swampy nearly onto his lap. He steadied her for a moment before letting her go. He needed to stop touching her.

"This isn't a race, Blue!" She righted herself on the seat without looking at John.

"It is a race!" Blue rolled down his window to hang his head out, watching something on the ground before sliding to another mud-spraying stop in front of a large barn.

"Didn't you see that rat dog runnin' after us? I tried to run him over, but the little bugger knows me too well. When are you goin' to let me cook that ornery little dog, LG? Everyone in 'Nam eats dog. Hell, I ate dog. Every bite, I imagined I was eatin' one of Mama's nasty little poodles. I swear I never tasted anything so delicious as that dog I ate in 'Nam."

"You ate dog, Uncle Blue?" Patrick's voice was high and shrill in the cramped cab of the truck. "You really ate dog?"

"That's it!" Swampy cried. "Let me out of this tin can. I can't take anymore. I mean it, Blue. You're drivin' me mad. If I hear one more word about the war, I'll black your other eye."

Swampy shoved John in her eagerness to escape the truck. He jumped out of the vehicle to get out of her way. She pushed past him and stomped around the Chevy, yanking open Blue's door. She dragged him out into the mud by his green army field jacket.

"Hear me, Blue Donovan?" she demanded softly, fervently.

"Sure, LG. All you had to say was 'shut up about 'Nam.'"

She leaned against her brother for a moment, but it was so brief John would have missed the tender exchange between the siblings if his gaze hadn't been glued on her. Blue patted her shoulder before she turned away to reach for Patrick, perched on the edge of the truck seat.

"Come on, Packy, let's go find that welder," she said.

John felt for her. Blue would drive him crazy too. He walked several yards from the truck and looked around. The Callohan ranch was just as he'd imagined it. Moss-covered rocks and ancient oak trees dominated the sprawling green hills. An old John Deere tractor, rusted by too many winters left out in the open, sat in the field as if one day it had broken down there and no one ever bothered to fix it. A pond in the distance reflected the weeping willow trees that skirted its banks. From his vantage point on the hill, he could see orchards stretched across the valley. A few barns and a home or two nestled among the sea of branches, only their roofs peeking above the miles of almond trees. Where the valley ended, distant mountains rose in all directions. A snow-covered volcano crowned the northern horizon.

He nearly jumped out of his skin when Blue spoke softly against his ear. "The Maidu Indians called these Sutter Buttes 'Spirit Mountain.' They believed their spirits came here after they died."

John laughed, a nervous reaction. "Guess my spirit was visiting that volcano over there." He pointed north at a majestic snow-covered peak.

"That's Mount Lassen." Blue smacked him on the back. "Come on, Nevada, we've got work to do."

# Chapter Nine

The drive back to the hangar was more peaceful than the drive out had been with Blue not aiming for potholes. John rested his arm across the seat back, ruffling Patrick's hair when the little boy grinned at him across Swampy's lap. They talked about who would win the Super Bowl. John was certain it'd be the Dallas Cowboys. Blue and Swampy talked up the Miami Dolphins.

"The Dolphins? No way." John smoothed his hair back as his eyes locked with Swampy's.

She laughed and didn't look away this time. His belly warmed as her gaze held his, and he laughed because she did. He got the feeling neither of them had laughed in a long while. Even after their laughter ended, she kept looking at him. Heat flamed through him. He tore his gaze away from hers.

He stared out the window at the farm fields blurring by, marveling at this turn in his life. Just two weeks ago, he'd been in New Mexico with a gun in his mouth. Today he felt grateful to be alive. The day was clear and bright, the fog completely gone. They came upon a pretty little church sitting back off the road in a grove of valley oaks. The church looked small and hopeful surrounded by the massive old trees and sweeping farmlands. It seemed like the mercy of God that he was here with Swampy.

"Ever been to that church?" He didn't look at Swampy when he asked. He couldn't. Surely, she would see his heart in his eyes.

"Hell, no," Blue said as he blasted past the church turnoff like he couldn't drive by it fast enough.

"Our mama was Irish. Daddy was Cajun, so all of us were baptized Catholic. Slow down, Blue." Swampy poked her brother in the arm.

"Daddy never went to church a day in his life," said Blue. "But his dog tags read Catholic, so there you go. He beat the hell out of me and Billy for no good reason."

Swampy's smile disappeared. "You and Bean were always doing something you shouldn't have been doing. You set the neighbors' barn on fire."

"We set a bird on fire. It flew into the neighbor's barn. That wasn't our fault. You never got a beating." Blue sounded bitter.

"I hated it when Daddy got after you and Bean with the belt. Bean let me hide him from Daddy. You never hid. You always had to stand up to Daddy. That was dumb."

"I wasn't gonna hide from that mean old jarhead. And once I hit basic training, I thanked our old man for those beatings. He made a Marine out of me long before I went to boot camp. Basic was a joyride after the bayou with Daddy. Then there was 'Nam. Damn, I miss Vietnam."

Ignoring Blue, Swampy pointed back at the church they had just passed. "Wait until the daffodils bloom, all along both sides of the church driveway in February. I sometimes stop and pick a

few. Father Reggie doesn't mind." She leaned back against the
seat, closing her eyes.

He wondered if she picked the daffodils for Jimmy. He understood how she felt. You never escaped grief. You just figured out
ways to tame it. Beauty eased grief. Flowers, nature, a river rolling by. Beauty was a bandage that covered grief until it wasn't so
raw and painful. Until you could breathe again.

Blue turned on the radio, and he and Patrick sang along with
Johnny Horton's "Whispering Pines." John loved that old country
song, so he sang too. Swampy opened her eyes, a smile returning
to her face.

They pulled up in front of the hangar around mid-morning.
Once they were out of the pickup, Swampy plucked her little mutt
Gadget from the truck bed and placed him on the ground beside
her. John helped Blue unload the welder and lug it inside the hangar. Swampy was rattling off a to-do list. "Blue, drive the rig over
to the runway. We'll fill *Molly* with blossom spray as soon as we
pull her out of the hangar. I can get the orchard done today if I hit
it now."

Sun reflected off the hangar, its large doors standing ajar. The
Stearmans sat looking out, as if waiting to escape into the sky.

"I'm hungry," Blue complained as he and John plunked the
welder down inside the hangar where Swampy motioned them to
place it. "Just let me grab a bone before we start workin'." Blue
didn't look at his sister as he walked away from the welder in a
hurry.

"You can eat after you load *Molly*. We're running behind as
it is. The sooner we get the Sanger farm done, the sooner we get
paid," Swampy called after him.

Blue kept on walking, though he now appeared to be headed for the loading rig. "I know we need to work harder and faster than the companies with their fancy new Ag Cats, but I'm hungry."

She turned to John. "You'll flag for me today," she told him over the hangar radio blaring Creedence Clearwater Revival's "Fortunate Son." She strode farther into the hangar, motioning for John to follow her. "I want you to get a feel for the orchards before I start you flying. You know, how the trees lie, where the wires are located. How much experience do you have dusting orchards? They aren't like row crops."

John smiled at the back of her head with its swinging ponytail. He tried to estimate how long her hair was—past her shoulders, maybe to the center of her back? "I've got a gazillion hours."

"You don't look old enough for a gazillion hours." She walked over and turned down the radio, then headed for one of the biplanes.

"How you doing, Bean?" she said, stepping over something on the backside of the red-and-white duster.

John trailed after her, staring at that practical ponytail, imagining her hair loose. He all but tripped over the thing she had stepped over but glanced down just in time to avoid walking on a man's leg.

He stepped back, staring at one leg. He looked for too long and too far back into his memory, back to the streets of Saigon with its legless beggars. Crippled men, women, and children dragging themselves around on the dirty streets. Memorials of the bloody conflict their country had endured for centuries. All over, the reminders of war. A war the Japanese couldn't win. The French couldn't win. Now the United States was finding she couldn't win either. A war that was sending Americans home looking like the war-scarred people of Saigon.

The one-legged man pushed himself on his wheeled sled out from under the aircraft.

"Billy, this is John Reno. John, this is my brother Billy."

Swampy's introduction yanked him back to the present. He struggled to focus on the lean young man staring up at him. The guy's hair was messy, like he'd just rolled out of bed, and a stubble of whiskers shaded his cheeks and chin. In spite of his grime, he was a handsome guy.

"John Reno." John reached down to shake the young man's hand. He was so rattled at having been caught staring at the guy's missing leg that he didn't notice the oil coating his fingers after the handshake. He did what he always did when he was agitated— dragged a hand through his long hair.

Billy grinned. "These spray valves get real greasy," he said apologetically.

John removed his hand from his hair, wiping the remaining grease on a pant leg. "I used to slick up my hair when I was a kid. Wonder if this is the same stuff. Feels like what we used in the fifties." He ran his hand over his slimy hair again and then laughed at himself.

Billy and Swampy laughed with him.

A child cooed. John noticed a baby in the playpen. The little girl had mastered the art of sitting up, but it was obviously new to her. As soon as she got excited, she toppled over in the blankets and toys with a happy gurgle.

"Where did she get those big blue eyes?" John looked at the baby but kept his distance. It wasn't that he didn't like babies. He did, but small folks intimidated him. The littler, the scarier, he'd decided long ago.

"Her mother." Billy's good-natured smile vanished. "Nice meeting you, John. *Molly's* ready to go, LG. I'll get started on Old *Dan's* stress fracture."

"Thanks, Billy. You work too darn hard. I'd hire us another mechanic, but ..."

"Don't worry about it. I like to work. Unlike some people I know." Billy settled back down on his wooden creeper, rolling under the hanging spray valves as Blue sauntered up with Patrick on his shoulders. Patrick was the spitting image of the one-legged man under the plane. The new arrivals had sandwiches crammed into their mouths.

"I thought you were getting the rig ready." Impatience laced Swampy's voice.

Through a mouthful of his lunch, Blue said, "We gotta feed the kids once in a while. You and Bill would work a week through before you'd think about eatin'. Someone needs to nourish the next generation around here."

The baby in the playpen cooed, pulling herself back into a sitting position just in time to take the piece of pickle Blue held out for her.

"She can't eat that pickle! She'll choke." Swampy rushed over to the playpen but the baby had already locked it in a fat little fist, then stuffed it into her eager mouth.

"Dang it, Blue!" Swampy leaned into the playpen, wrestling the baby for the pickle.

"She loves 'em. Ain't that right, Packy? Gracie eats pickle sandwiches with us all the time. Don't you, sunshine?" Blue cooed to the baby.

Finally giving up trying to get the pickle, Swampy called to her brother under the plane, "Billy, you let this idiot feed Gracie pickles?"

"He might as well feed the kids. He don't do much else round here," Billy called back.

"If I worked like the two of you, these kids would starve to death."

Swampy glared at Blue. "I take good care of Patrick and Gracie, and you know it."

"Yeah, but they like me better, LG. I feed 'em pickles and play with 'em, and all you do is brush their teeth and make 'em eat grits. You may as well eat worm dirt, right, Packy? Grits is worm dirt."

"Grits are good for them. Kids need to live on something more substantial than the strange stuff you live on." She rested her hands on her hips. "We're wasting time. John and I will get the plane out of the hangar. Blue, have that rig ready to fill the hopper. Take Patrick with you, and make sure he stays in the truck until I head down the runway."

"What about the rat?" Blue eyeballed Swampy's dog dozing beside her leg.

"I'm leaving Gadget here. He's getting too old to fly anymore."

"How long you gonna be gone? Long enough for me to cook the little sonofa—"

"Blue!" she stopped him. "Take Patrick and get moving. The only time you move fast is when you're driving that dang truck or chasing women."

"Those are the only two things worth moving fast for. You and Bean just haven't figured out how to enjoy life yet."

"Get," she said through clenched teeth, then added more gently, "Patrick, give me a kiss. And stay in the truck until I'm in the sky, okay?"

The little boy on top of Blue's shoulders wiggled around with his half-eaten pickle sandwich until Blue sat him on the ground so he could go to Swampy.

The little boy planted a kiss on her lips, his mouth full of bread and pickles. After kissing the baby as well, Swampy turned to John in a brisk, businesslike fashion. He stared at her mouth, wondering what it would feel like if she kissed him too. To her, he was still a stranger, but to him, she was everything. When their eyes locked and held for a second, she spun away in a hurry.

# Chapter Ten

John watched her in the old red-and-white Stearman whine away toward the west. He floored the Camaro, keeping up with her pretty well as she headed for an almond orchard five miles away. Once there, he parked the Camaro along the road where he would be flagging and then pulled the big white flag out of the backseat window, which he'd rolled down to accommodate the long-poled banner.

She'd told him to count off thirty-three steps after each pass. The sun was high, the breeze up. He wondered if the wind would mess with her Stearman. So far, she looked pretty competent up there.

When she made her first pass over the orchard, she flew the swath low and slow, the old-fashioned way. She must have been trying to override the wind, not giving the spray much chance to blow away from the branches it was supposed to settle over. She pulled up steep when she finished her swath, steeper than necessary. Flying right over the top of him, she was flying too slow to be pulling up like that in a near vertical loop.

91

He watched with his heart in his throat, knowing she could stall the Stearman that way and she didn't have enough altitude to recover from a stall. She came out of the hairy turn beautifully, and he began to count off the first thirty-three steps between her passes, breathing easier. She'd been doing this without him for several years.

He stepped out the distance to his next position, the flag flapping noisily in the brisk breeze. Maybe she was flying low and slow because of the wind. Maybe she knew on the back swath she had a headwind to give her the extra lift to carry her out of that slow, steep turn. Maybe she had those bird instincts the great pilots had. Flying was second nature to her, just maybe.

He talked himself into relaxing. By the time he'd positioned himself in line with her next swath, holding the flag high, waving it back and forth so she could line herself up with it on the other end of the orchard, he felt better about her flying.

She came across the orchard low and slow again and did the same kind of turn that put his heart back in his throat. He took his thirty-three steps again, the flag held out in front of him, as he tromped along the old paved road with Swampy's plane heading back across the orchard, dropping spray as it went. The longer he watched her, the more upset he became. Headwind or no headwind, she was flying dangerously.

The wind beat Swampy's face as the wires of the bi-wings sang sweetly in her ears. She continued to fly her low, slow swaths. They weren't quite straight with the wind pushing her around, but each time she opened the hopper door, the spray settled over the branches just like it was supposed to. Flying made her happy. It was really the only thing that thrilled her anymore—except for the man flagging for her today. The way John looked at her made her warm all over. He fanned a fire in her she hadn't even known was burning. She wanted to know more about him. But asking questions would show her curiosity, and the last thing she wanted was for him to know she was interested.

Due to the wind, the sky today was clear as it could be, no fog or clouds, just blue for miles. She couldn't remember a day she'd enjoyed flying this much. Flying felt new all over again— the raw delight, the unbelievable power of speed in the sky, like the first time she'd soloed that autumn after Jimmy died—and it was new all over again because John watched her. She wanted to impress him. She flew the remaining swaths the same way as the first ones, using the headwind to make her steep turns. On her last swath, low-slung electrical wires lay in her path. A clearance between the tops of the almond trees and the wires left just enough room for the Stearman to slip through. She should fly over the top of them; high wires were safe to fly under, low wires were not.

*John's confident words came back to her: I could fly one of your planes through a five-foot spread of electrical wires ...*

Well, she had more than five feet here. She smiled momentarily, the wind roaring against her face and drying out her mouth. She didn't smile long for fear of getting a bug stuck between her teeth in the open cockpit. Compressing her lips, she flew under the cables, slipping the Stearman between the wires and treetops with deceiving ease. This was dangerous. But so was feeling the way she did about John Reno.

John watched her do it. He closed his eyes in a silent prayer and opened them again just in time to see her zoom under the wires like a swift little swallow. She pulled up several hundred feet, then thundered toward home the way planes in an air show roared away from the audience they'd just wowed to silence.

But he wasn't silent. His curses split the air as he threw the long poled flag onto the old paved road. He stared after her out there in the sky, humming away in the trusty old Stearman, and then scooped up the flag and jogged the length of the orchard back to his car.

*What the hell is wrong with her? Is she trying to kill herself flying that way?*

He gassed the Camaro all the way back to the hangar. Doing a hundred miles an hour on the narrow country road, the wind roared into his broken window like the wind that roared around Swampy up in the plane's cockpit. Tires squealed as he pulled into the parking lot. He killed the engine, then sat there behind the wheel, trying to calm down. He hadn't lived through Vietnam to watch her die in California.

She taxied the plane toward the hangar. Everything looked so serene now, the sun glinting off the red wings of her Stearman, the geese calling overhead. When the plane came to a stop, she stood up in the cockpit, pulling her leather helmet off. She removed her goggles and shook her messy ponytail into place. She was so beautiful, but he was fit to be tied.

He got out of his car. His brakes were smoking. They smelled fried. He walked slowly over to her.

"You did a great job flagging," she called from her raised platform in the second seat of the Stearman. The first seat was now the hopper, a stainless-steel vat where the seed, spray, and other chemicals were stored. She grinned, a big smile that said everything. She was proud of herself.

His heartbeat slowly returned to normal. His pulse no longer roared in his ears like the sound of the Stearman's 450-horsepower Pratt & Whitney engine. As she climbed down from the cockpit, he reached up and snatched her off the wing into his arms.

"Don't ever do that again," he said softly, cupping her cold cheek with his hand as he looked into her eyes. He wanted her to know he was serious. He couldn't lose her. It would kill him.

"Do what?" Her eyes widened in confusion and then astonishment. A blush colored her cheeks.

"Take those kinds of risks up there." He let go of her face. "That plane has limits, Swampy! You could be the best pilot in the world, but you push that old Stearman past its limits and that's it. You're done. You stall a Stearman that low in one of those loop-de-doop turns you were doing and it's over. That reliable old plane will fall out of the sky, and you'll fall with her."

"I had a headwind." She raised her chin stubbornly, glaring up at him.

"What if the wind changed on you? What if the plane stalled? And what was that crap at the end? Flying under those wires?

Damn it, Swampy! You're spraying an orchard. You're not flying a dogfight in some war. You're not saving anybody with your
daredevil flying skills. You're killing bugs and fungus and mold.
A farmer can just as easily hire some other duster to spray his
fields after you're dead." He squeezed her shoulders, trying to will
caution into her.

She shoved out of his arms. "That farmer hired *me* to kill his
bugs and fungus and mold! Bugs and fungus and mold that ruin
his crops. Crops that feed his family. I may not be a hotshot pilot
with a fistful of fancy flying licenses like you, but those farmers
depend on me. I do the best I can, the best way I know how. And
flying under those wires … that was for you!"

She looked so earnest. So determined. Wisps of hair had
escaped her ponytail and blew across her face. Her baggy blue
coveralls flapped against her legs in the crisp breeze. Her goggles
hung around her neck. Her cheeks and nose were crimson from
the wind, and she smelled like blossom spray.

She was also the prettiest thing he'd ever seen.

"You impressed me, hotshot. You really did. But no more
showboating." He captured wisps of her hair and tucked them
behind her ears. "Fly smart, Swampy. That's all I'm asking. Just
fly smart."

He looked over her head, finally noticing their audience standing there. Blue held Gracie. Patrick flanked him, holding toy
guns. Billy was propped on a crutch, the empty pant leg of his
coveralls tucked in a hip pocket. His other pockets were filled
with the tools he used to fix the airplanes: safety wires, pliers,
wrenches, calipers, files, nuts, and bolts. The coveralls probably
weighed a good twenty pounds with all the tools stuffed into

them, but the young man stood balancing on his one leg and a lone crutch, smiling at John and Swampy along with the rest of the family. Everyone looked thoroughly entertained by the scene John had just made.

Blue began clapping. Patrick joined in. Even Baby Gracie put her chubby little hands together in glee. Gadget darted out from behind Billy, racing under his missing leg. Billy swung the crutch out from under him, aiming at the quick little dog, but the bat-eared mutt seemed to know it was coming. He bolted under Billy, his jowls pulled back in what appeared a grin, his back legs comically scuttling up around his front legs as the wooden crutch smacked empty air.

"Damn it!" Billy whistled through his teeth, swinging the crutch back under himself as the dog raced over to Swampy. "One of these days that little sucker won't be so fast."

Blue quit clapping. He propped Gracie in one wiry arm, turning to his brother. "I'm tellin' ya, Bill, we need to get you one of them prosthesis. That way you'll have something to kick that little bugger with when he does that to you."

Gadget sat down beside Swampy. Billy laughed, so everyone else did. His laugh was infectious.

"He only torments you two because he knows you don't like him." Swampy said, as she stepped away from John in a hurry.

"Damned right we don't like that ornery ankle biter. There's nothin' worse than a little dog. Ain't that right, Bill?" Blue acted as if Swampy had betrayed them by defending the little dog.

"That's right." Another one of Billy's lively grins lit up his face. "The only thing rat dogs are good for is gator bait."

Gadget yawned as if bored by the whole thing.

Swampy flashed a pleased grin. "Well, we don't need the other plane filled after all. The sprayer worked beautifully today. I finished the whole orchard. I think the wind helped."

"So what did you think, Nevada? She flies by the seat of her pants, don't she?"

Before he could answer, Swampy said, "I've got more flying talent in my butt than you've got in your whole body, Blue Donovan."

Everybody laughed. Even Blue. It felt so incredibly good to laugh. John felt young again. He hadn't felt young in years.

"Let's go to dinner after we get the planes put away for the night," he suggested when they all stopped laughing. "It's on me. I'll treat. I saw a little Mexican restaurant in Live Oak yesterday that looked pretty lively."

Patrick jumped up and down. Swampy looked as if she was about to decline the invitation, but her nephew appeared to change her mind. Blue said he was all for it. Billy looked as guarded as Swampy.

"You all go on without me," Billy said. "I'm expecting Lucy home tonight. She's usually only gone a few days." Billy leaned heavily on his crutch after mentioning his wife.

Swampy took the baby from Blue. "Okay, Bean. Don't worry about the kids. We'll wear 'em out so they'll sleep good for you tonight." She grabbed Patrick's hand and headed for the hangar.

John assumed that meant she would go to dinner. He and Blue pulled the plane into the building. Billy went back to work on the other Stearman.

After helping Blue put the plane away, John went to his car to retrieve some clean clothes. He longed for a shower and said so to Blue when he came back into the building.

Blue pointed him to the back of the hangar where a primitive shower stood, concealed by an old tacked-up tarp. John quickly bathed the day's grime away with lukewarm water that sprayed out of a rusty spigot. He washed his hair, scrubbing out the grease from earlier when he'd met Billy, and put his hair in a ponytail. He stepped into clean jeans and a flannel shirt and slipped on his old cowboy boots. He hadn't cared how he looked in a long time, but now he did.

When he finished cleaning up, he found Blue, Swampy, and the children waiting for him at the front of the hangar. They all looked cleaner too. Swampy had removed the coveralls she'd sprayed in and changed into jeans and a green sweatshirt that made her eyes even bigger and brighter, if that were possible. He still hadn't decided if her eyes were blue or green. Her ponytail was neatly redone. She looked fresh and young and so pretty he ached inside. When he stepped close to her, she smelled faintly of orchard spray.

He was amazed she got ready to go so quickly. She even had the children in fresh clothes, their faces scrubbed. Patrick was asking if he could have his own bottle of soda when they got to the restaurant. Swampy, carrying the baby, herded the excited little boy out the door to the Studebaker. The child's anticipation filled John with joy accompanied by a wave of guilt. He should tell Swampy who he was and give her the letter, but how could he now?

# Chapter Eleven

In Betty's Mexican restaurant, with piñatas hanging from the ceiling, the locals stared at their corner booth, even though Blue and the children sat between Swampy and John. Never could John just eat a meal in peace after Vietnam. He was always tuned into his surroundings, watching for danger, the same way Blue still lived in a war zone inside his own head. John just hid the madness better.

A Mexican radio station blasted music from the front counter, filling the kitchen and dining area with the rhythm of Mexico. The smell of tamales and enchiladas permeated the place. Nobody was dressed up. A number of diners wore cowboy hats; others sported well-worn baseball caps with John Deere or Ducks Unlimited logos. Women wore jeans and boots just like the men. This was small-town America, and John liked it. He didn't miss his parents' DC world, where men wore slacks, jackets, and ties and women went to dinner in dresses. His mother was always perfectly put together no matter the time of day.

He could still hear her refined voice from when he was young. *"Don't touch me, honey. You'll wrinkle my gown."* He couldn't ever remember her picking him up or allowing him to sit on her lap, even at home. He looked over at Swampy with the baby in her arms. She looked like a sweet young thing with her hair in a ponytail as she ripped up tortilla pieces for Gracie.

They all sipped soda out of small glass bottles, chatting about President Nixon heading to China next month on a historic trip in an attempt to normalize relations between the two countries.

"I'd love to go to China," Blue said after quickly polishing off his meal. He ate like a soldier in the bush—shoveling food in fast, keeping an eye on his surroundings. John was relieved Blue had left his sawed-off shotgun in the car, but he knew Swampy's brother still had a survival knife hidden in his boot. No wonder people were leery of Blue.

Swampy gave Gracie her bottle. "Chinatown in San Francisco is close enough to China for me. I have no desire to travel out of the country."

"She's a homebody." Blue finished his third bottle of Pepsi, muffling a burp before going on. "I'd have stayed in 'Nam if they had let me. Or moved to the Philippines. The prettiest girls are from the Philippines, you know."

Blue obviously had enjoyed his meal. John had never seen a thin man put away that much food. He was happy he'd invited them all to dinner. "We should go to San Francisco sometime. Walk Chinatown. I've never seen the Golden Gate Bridge except in pictures." John hoped Blue was smart enough to know this invitation to San Francisco wasn't for him.

Blue said, "I'm gonna get a motorcycle and ride like Evel Knievel over the Golden Gate someday." When Swampy looked down at Gracie falling asleep in her lap with her bottle, Blue winked at John and said, "San Francisco is for lovers." Blue then leaned back against the booth with a smirk on his face.

Swampy ignored them, acting like she hadn't heard Blue talking about lovers.

Patrick had slowly migrated to John's side, finally managing to tuck himself under one of John's arms. The little boy tucked himself into John's heart that night too. In Vietnam, when he thought he was about to die, he'd regretted not having kids. Maybe all men felt that way in war. Wanting a son to carry on their name, and daughters to remember their hopes and dreams. For a moment, John imagined this was his own little family, Swampy and the kids. When Patrick looked up at him, John asked the boy, "Did you get enough to eat?"

"Yep." Patrick leaned back against John in contentment.

John felt content too. He could tell the little guy was sleepy. He waved the waitress down and requested the bill. As he paid, everyone headed to the Studebaker they'd rode in together.

On the way back to the hangar, both children fell asleep in John's and Swampy's arms as Blue drove home. Then the men carried the sleeping little ones to the upstairs apartment. Swampy led the way, a box of tamales in her hands for Billy. Her brother met them at the door. He was shirtless, his upper body whittled into hard muscles from all the work it did to make up for his missing leg. He leaned on his one crutch, smiling. John could tell he'd been drinking. A woman appeared behind him.

"Hi, Lucy." Swampy's tone was guarded as she stepped into the apartment. Blue and John followed her. "Would you like to tuck Gracie into bed?" Swampy put the tamales on the kitchen counter and then turned to her sister-in-law.

"No, you go ahead." Lucy had a Southern accent, soft and breathy like Marilyn Monroe. She wore a short silk robe. Her blond hair was tousled, her figure lush, and her big blue eyes were fastened on John.

He tried to look away. She wasn't properly dressed, but she came at him, smiling. "I'm Lucy. Who are you?"

He held the sleeping Patrick to his chest like a shield. She reeked of sex appeal and didn't seem to care her husband stood nearby. "John Reno. Swampy's new workhorse," he said softly, not wanting to wake the little boy in his arms as he looked to Blue for help.

"I see our little pigeon has come home to roost." Blue's smile didn't reach his eyes as he stepped between John and his sister-in-law.

"Hello, Blue," Lucy purred.

"Hello, pigeon."

Billy took the sleeping baby from Blue. He cradled the baby in one strong arm, using the other to balance with his crutch. "Thanks, Blue. Mind helping me put the kids to bed, John?"

"You bet." John was relieved to escape Lucy. He found the sight of the one-legged young man holding his baby and hobbling on his crutch deeply touching. Billy left the living room and John trailed him down the hall.

"Gracie needs a diaper change." Swampy entered the room behind them.

"I'll take care of it." Billy put the baby down in her crib.

Swampy smiled at John after he laid Patrick down on a twin mattress pushed against the wall. The room was just big enough for the bed, the crib, and the three adults. He smiled back at her, motioning for her to go in front of him out of the room as Billy saw to the children. They found Lucy sitting on the couch, a pout on her lips. Blue lounged impatiently beside the front door.

"I got things to do," Blue said with lazy indifference, his eyes narrowing on Lucy.

"It is about time for your patrol, isn't it?" Lucy sounded sugary sweet. "You never know, maybe you will scare up a Viet Cong around here, and then we'll all think *we're* the crazy ones."

"Lucy—" Billy limped toward her on his crutch.

"Never mind, Bill. I'm sure you'd rather have her runnin' off at the mouth instead of just runnin' off." Blue strolled out the door.

John quickly followed Blue after politely saying good night. He went downstairs to find Blue sitting in a thrashed lawn chair in the shadows, lighting a joint.

The tip glowed in the dark as Blue sucked in fiercely. He held his breath for several moments before blowing out the smoke. "Lucy's the dandelion in our lawn. She may be a pretty little flower, but she's screwing up this family's root system. She's a weed, Nevada. A nasty little weed. My brother's too dumb to see that. All he can see is her pretty little flower." Blue took another hit and held the fume in his lungs for a long time before blowing a smoke ring above his head and offering the joint to John.

John shook his head as Swampy stepped up beside him.

"Well, at least Billy's happy tonight," she said, and John could hear her sadness.

"So is a dog before you shoot it for chasin' sheep."

"We've all got our problems." Swampy glared at Blue's joint.

"You're right. Maybe Bill's the lucky one. I only get to smoke my problem. At least Bill can screw his. And you, LG …" Blue looked at John, then smiled ruefully at his sister. "Looks like your problems are about over."

"Blue, you're such a—" She whirled around and walked away. Both men watched her stomp off before resuming their conversation.

"She's always tellin' me to be truthful, but when I am, she rips my face off."

"What's LG stand for?" John asked.

"Little General. She's been bossin' Bill and me around since we walked out of the womb. She's older than us but not by much."

John laughed softly. He understood family dysfunction.

"She's had it rough since she lost Callohan. Me and Bill try to pretend we're here helpin' her, but it's really the other way around."

"Not too many families stay together these days. Swampy's lucky to have you here."

"I don't think Bill or I would have made it after the war if LG hadn't circled the wagons when she did. We both came home messed up."

John was tempted to tell Blue he had come home messed up too, but just couldn't do it. Not yet.

The old Studebaker revved up outside the hangar.

"I was hoping to talk to Swampy about my work schedule before she leaves."

"Better catch her. She's tough as nails but will give you a fair shot flying for us."

"I noticed she's tough. I like that about her." John smiled. "See you later, Blue."

When he trotted over to her car, Swampy rolled down the driver's side window for him.

He leaned his hands on her window frame, resting his forehead against the top of the cold metal as he looked at her sitting behind the wheel. "Do I get to fly tomorrow?"

She stared at him speculatively. "You'll be careful with my Stearmans."

He couldn't tell if that was a question or a command. He longed to tease her, but sensed her mood wasn't up for it. "I'll be careful with *Molly* and *Old Dan*. I promise."

"Be here at six. We'll see how you do in a loaded Stearman." She put the car in reverse and began to roll up her window, a smile slipping onto her lips.

Her smile made him happy. He stepped away from the sedan, watching her taillights fade into the darkness. Already he was willing to walk through fire for her. Her family had problems, but didn't everyone's? He hadn't spoken to his parents in a couple of years. Sometimes he dropped a letter in the mail for his mother, just to let her know he was still alive.

The Colonel had probably disowned him by now, and he was sure his mother was embarrassed he'd disappeared. He'd spent most of his life working hard to meet their expectations. He'd done his best to make them proud, aside from totaling the Colonel's sedan that one time and refusing to date the DC daughters, which had frustrated his mother and her highfalutin friends. Other than that, he'd done everything possible to please them.

On Christmas and Easter, especially, he'd really wanted to call them but didn't. They'd be at church and then on to a champagne

brunch at the Officers' Club. He didn't want to ruin their holidays
with his voice. And what would he even say?

*I've grown my hair long and didn't vote for Nixon a second time?*

He got in his car, started it, and flipped on the radio to turn off
his thoughts. The solitude of the night out here in these farm fields
suited him. A waning moon and a million stars pierced the darkness. He'd always thought of California as a far-out place with
neon lights, beaches, loud bands, and hippies sitting on the corner
of Haight and Ashbury, but it wasn't like that here in Sutter County.

Northern California was similar to the Southern states he'd crop
dusted in for the past several years, mostly agricultural land with
rivers running through fertile valleys and snow-covered mountains in the distance. He already felt at home in this little community with its four churches and two bars—he'd counted both—a
service station, some small friendly stores, a couple of mom-and-
pop restaurants, and pickup trucks whose drivers waved on the
back-country roads.

He parked in the same spot as he had the previous nights.
Retrieving his sleeping bag from the Camaro's trunk, he climbed
into the backseat, listening to the swans settle down as they grew
used to his presence parked beside their field. A half hour later, he
was asleep.

A rumbling truck pulling up beside his car woke him. Minutes later,
Blue craned his head through the Camaro's broken-out window.

"Nevada? What are you doin' bedded down out here?"

John twisted into a sitting position, his sleeping bag bunching around his waist which left his chest at the mercy of the cold. "Hey, Blue," he mumbled, running his fingers through his sleep-mussed hair. It always took him a while to get his bearings when he first awoke in his car. A bit dazed, he looked around, noting the impending dawn illuminating the sky behind Blue.

"I'm on my way to pick up Swampy." Blue made himself comfortable, leaning through the missing windowpane. "Studebaker's giving her problems again. Surprised the daylights out of me when I saw your Camaro parked out here in Swan Field."

"Is that the name of this place?" John looked out the window, searching the shadowy rice paddy for the birds, which he found silhouetted like decoys floating on the dark water.

"You need a place to live?"

John smiled. "Nope. I've never had such pleasant roommates." He motioned toward the swans.

"Swampy's barn has a loft in it. You should ask her about it if you don't mind roughin' it. The place has an old woodstove and a dusty bearskin rug. Kind of cozy, if you like the mountain feeling."

John sat up straighter in the backseat. "You think she'd rent me that room?"

"Maybe we could cut a deal with your salary. Take the rent for the loft out of your pay."

"Sounds good to me." John didn't try to hide his excitement.

"Just tread lightly. My sister hasn't given a man an ounce of sweetness since Callohan came back to her in a box. I'm surprised she even looks at you. And boy, does she look at you." Blue grinned, leaning farther through the window, gazing around the car's interior. His attention landed on John's army-issued sleeping bag.

"How long you been out of 'Nam?" Blue's voice became soft and reverent.

John opened the car door, motioning Blue into the backseat with him. He scooted over as Swampy's brother dug his flask out of his pocket and settled in beside him. Blue offered the flask first to John, but he declined with a shake of his head.

Blue took a long swig as John began to speak.

"I left Vietnam three years ago, but it feels like yesterday."

"I was a door gunner," Blue said. "What were you?"

"A Huey pilot. I flew more missions than I care to remember. A lot of men lived. A lot of men died."

Blue leaned his head back on the seat. "Why didn't you tell us you served in 'Nam?"

"I'm not staying long enough for it to matter. And Swampy wouldn't want me here." John looked out the window at the swans. With sunrise breaking, he could see the birds better now. He wasn't sure why, but those swans comforted him. They mated for life—maybe that was it. Loyalty was high on his list.

"I know how it is to walk around with all the memories chewin' at your insides until pretty soon you're so raw inside that nothing outside really matters," Blue said.

John closed his eyes. He should tell Blue about Jimmy. The letter. The promise to give it to Swampy. All of it, but then he'd have to leave. He didn't want to leave.

Blue drank from his flask and didn't seem to mind John's silence. "Bad things happened to the best of us in 'Nam. Hell, we all thought we were just gonna walk in the sun over there. That guerrilla army surprised us." Blue reached over and put his hand on John's shoulder. "We're all livin' with somethin', Nevada. We fought a hell of a war over there, but now we're home and nobody cares, and we just gotta make the best of it."

"Thanks, Blue."

Both of them understood their conversation was over.

Blue climbed out of the backseat. "I need to get going. Swampy's gonna be chomping at the bit when I get there. She's probably saddled up one of her horses and is already headed for the hangar."

"Blue," John said before Blue closed the car door, "I don't want Swampy to know I served in Vietnam."

"I'm not telling anyone." Blue smiled.

"Thanks." It may have been the first true smile John had seen out of Blue.

"You're welcome. Battlefield brothers?" Blue stuck out his hand.

"Battlefield brothers," John agreed, gripping Blue's hand and squeezing hard.

# Chapter Twelve

Swampy sprang out of Blue's pickup before he came to a complete stop at the hangar. John and Billy were on the airstrip with one of the Stearmans, filling it with spray. She strode across the parking lot, relieved to see them already working.

John looked ready to crop dust.

"You're all set to tackle an orchard?" She looked him over in his coveralls. Several inches of Levi's hung below the hems. The coveralls were only half-zipped up, his broad shoulders about to burst through the taut fabric. His long hair was in a ponytail, and his face freshly shaven. She'd already grown used to his scars. Had he gotten into a car wreck? Maybe even a plane crash? She liked the scars—they gave him a rugged look—but she wasn't about to ask him where they'd come from. That was too personal.

Billy smacked John on the back. "He looks good, don't he, LG?" Billy grinned, then spun on his crutch and hobbled away toward the hangar.

Blue walked over. "Them my coveralls?"

John looked down at the snug suit he wore. "Billy said you wouldn't mind, that you never wear them anyway."

"You look like a bale of hay with the center strand cut." Blue laughed, cackling like a goose.

"He looks just fine." Swampy tried not to smile. "The next time I go into town, I'll buy you your own coveralls."

John stared right into her eyes. He sounded so confident when he said, "I'm ready to dust. Just point me in the right direction, and I'll be on my way, boss."

She gave him directions to the field after telling him she'd be his flagger for the day. Then she and Blue watched him roll down the runway in *Molly*.

Blue grinned after John's perfect takeoff. Swampy grinned back, then raced toward the hangar feeling happier than she'd been in years. Obviously, the man could fly. And he looked so cute in Blue's coveralls. He sure was a fine figure of a man. She wished he'd cut his hair, though she appreciated that he'd shaved.

Blue was climbing into his pickup when she jogged back out the hangar door, carrying a big white flag and wearing her own blue coveralls.

"I'm taking your Chevy." She tossed the flag into the bed of his pickup.

"I was just headed to town." Blue got behind the wheel in a hurry.

Swampy grabbed his camouflage jacket and tugged him out of the truck. "Too bad. I need your rig. Go help Billy." She jumped behind the wheel.

"Can't you take Nevada's car?"

She slammed his truck door in answer. He trailed her out of the parking lot, calling, "Come on, LG, how 'bout I drop you off at the orchard and pick you up this afternoon when you're done?"

She ignored him and gunned his Chevy out of the parking lot, trying to catch up with John out there in the sky.

When she reached the orchard, he was looping around overhead. She quickly lined up with her flag, and he began spraying. Within an hour, she had tears in her eyes. He was better up there than Mr. Callohan. Better than Rex. Better than Jimmy. He was the best duster she'd ever seen. Tears streaked her face as she held the flag high and waved it for him. He was the answer to her prayers. Callohan Dusters' saving grace. She could see that already. They could dust together, doing twice the workload now. Blue would have to return to flagging, but that was the worst of it. With John flying too, she could turn the company around. She wept in relief. The tide had finally turned in her direction.

"Where's the hotshot?" Swampy asked Billy when she arrived back at the hangar late that afternoon after John had dusted all day. *Molly* was already parked in the hangar when she got there.

Billy pointed to the rear of the building.

"Where are you, John?" She had a big smile on her face, walking swiftly in search of him. She couldn't wait to tell him how pleased she was with his flying.

A moment later, he stepped out from behind the tarped shower area with only his Levi's on, and they weren't even buttoned yet.

His long hair was wet, hanging over his broad, bare shoulders, dripping water down his muscled torso. His half-dressed dishevelment stopped her cold.

"I thought I'd take a quick shower. Wash the spray off before you got back." His face reddened.

She could hardly breathe. "You're welcome to wash whenever …" Her face grew red as his as they stared at each other. "I'll be in my office." She spun away and took off in a hurry.

"Thanks for letting me make a fool of myself, Bean." She strode past Billy sitting in front of his workbench. He was tinkering with a plane part and drinking a beer.

"You're welcome, LG. He looks good after a shower, don't he? All twisted steel and sex appeal." Billy laughed as she slammed her office door with a bang.

When John finally knocked on her door and then poked his head into the office a while later, she still had not recovered from seeing him half-naked. He was far too attractive. And too good a pilot to get rid of just because he made her all weak in the knees.

"Can I come in?" he asked uncertainly. He wore a clean flannel shirt. His damp hair was combed back smoothly behind his ears. She couldn't tell if he had on the same jeans he'd worn under the coveralls or if he had donned a new pair just as faded. The old denim molded to his body in a way she decided should be illegal in the presence of a lonely widow.

"Of course, come in." She waved him over to one of her chairs, averting her eyes from his jeans as he sat down.

"I'm sorry," he began. "I'm kind of funny about chemicals sinking into my skin."

She shook her head, holding her hand up. "You don't have to apologize. That's why we have a shower in the hangar." Not that she or her brothers ever used it.

She felt as uncomfortable as he appeared to be. But then she remembered his flying and brightened. "That was some fine dusting today. I hope I can afford you."

"Whatever your pay … I'm happy for the work." He glanced around at the wood-paneled office. Her gaze followed his. Framed black-and-white pictures of men standing beside ancient crop-dusting planes adorned the walls.

"You can fly with the best of these guys. I'm so happy to have you join Callohan Dusters. If we fly together, we can take on more jobs. Would you mind flying with me? I never felt comfortable dusting with Rex and he didn't like flying with me. He said two planes in the sky was too risky, but Jimmy and his dad always dusted together."

John turned from the pictures, and the look in his eyes robbed her of breath again as he said, "I'd love to dust with you."

They both startled when Blue spoke from the door entry. "John needs a place to live. I told him about your barn loft."

She glanced from Blue to John and then back to her brother. Her smile disappeared. "The loft hasn't been lived in for twenty-five years."

"John's used to roughin' it." Blue stepped into the office and sat down in the chair beside John like they were best friends. Her brother usually didn't take to people this way.

"I like the mountain feeling." John nodded to Blue before turning back to her.

"You two already discussed it?" She pushed strands of hair off her forehead, her stomach twisting into knots.

"John says you can take the rent out of his flight pay. I hear he's a real hotshot. Hotshot pilots don't come cheap."

"I'm not worried about my salary," John said. "I'll pay whatever you want for the room, Swampy."

"What do you want for the room? If you're paying John the same salary you paid Rex, you better give him that room for free, LG."

She leaned back in her chair, staring at the two men who rose to their feet at the same time and stood shoulder to shoulder in her office. Blue was making this impossible for her. His sudden devotion to John astounded her. He never liked the pilots who came and went like the wind at Callohan Dusters.

"All right," she finally agreed. "John, you can have a look at the loft this evening. I'm heading home in about an hour. You can give me a ride since I'm out of a vehicle right now."

Blue slapped John on the back. "I'll break the news to the swans." Blue was grinning as he left the office.

"Swans?" Swampy's eyes widened in question.

"I'll wait for you in the hangar." John was quick to leave, quietly closing the office door as he departed.

# Chapter Thirteen

John parked the Camaro under a tall oak tree. They got out at the same time and walked slowly to the barn together. The grass was short and green, new growth rising with the winter rains. A hawk soared overhead, cutting through the twilight. In the distance, a horse whinnied, and another horse answered.

"My horses are hungry," Swampy said without looking at him. "I feed them this time of year. Just for another month, then I won't have to feed them again until fall because the grass is coming on. It will be spring in no time."

She was talking fast and wouldn't meet his gaze. Her nervousness brought a smile to his face. She'd fidgeted the whole trip here and talked about crop dusting like nothing else existed in the world. He wanted to tell her to relax but knew it would only intensify her uneasiness.

He made small talk, hoping to help her unwind. "Do you ride horses?"

"I used to, but I'm too busy flying now."

She sped up her walk to the barn and he fell in behind her, admiring the curve of her hips. Her old leather jacket was faded and worn and looked older than she was. It concealed the top half of her figure, but he knew what she looked like in a bathing suit— the pink polka-dot bikini at the lake in Jimmy's pictures.

"The Callohans used the loft when they were building their ranch house on the hill. There's no bathroom, but the old shanty is over there and still usable." She pointed to the wooden out- house not far from the barn. "If you decide you want to live in the loft, you'll have to shower at the hangar. The Callohans bathed in that old tub over there." She pointed to a stand of rusted working corrals.

He followed her, walking slowly, amazed that even an outhouse did not deter him from wanting to live here.

She stopped before going into the barn's tack room to point again at a place near the corrals. "See the tub?"

The old bathtub sat inside the corrals. The claw legs were gone. The tub's bottom rested in the mud.

"It's a water trough for the horses now," she explained.

"How did they do it?" John was confused.

"Do what?"

"Did they take a bath out in the open?"

She finally smiled. "They bathed under the stars, but here closer to the barn." She pointed to a place nearby.

"Really? That must have been cold in the wintertime."

"They built a fire under the tub to heat the water. Jimmy said it wasn't so bad once you were in and staring up at the big ole sky filled with stars. It was nice as long as you were the first one to get the clean water and were careful not to burn your butt on the bottom of the tub. I'll show you the room now. You might change your mind once you see it." She turned and headed into the tack room.

He followed her, shoving down the urge to tell her he missed Jimmy too.

By the time he had trailed her up a ladder in the corner of the tack room, through a hole that led into the loft, his heart was aching. He needed to tell her the truth. Needed to give her the letter. He couldn't let this go any further.

He began forming the words in his mind, sentences that seared his soul and left his tongue twisting the truth around, trying to figure out how to say it. Sweat broke out on his brow. He wiped it away and tried to calm down.

They climbed through the trapdoor into a room that ran the entire width and length of the barn. Swampy stood with her back to him as they stared at the place Jimmy had lived as a boy. The loft was open-beamed wood that smelled old and dusty but sure looked fine. Like the inside of a cabin. The sinking sun's rays came through two windows at the south end of the barn. Dust danced across the rustic room, glinting like diamond shavings in the sunlight.

Swampy raised her hand to capture the bright little particles floating in the light.

"I need to tell you something." John wiped the perspiration forming on his forehead.

She turned around. Her eyes sparkled with tears. There was so much sorrow on her face it completely silenced him. He couldn't say it. He stepped over and drew her into his arms, his heart beating in his throat. He swallowed hard and managed, "I don't want to replace anybody in your life, Swampy. I'm just looking for my own spot in this world. Just following the road signs, hoping to find my way home."

"Where is home for you?" The tears brimming over her lashes spilled down her cheeks.

He hadn't expected her tears. Her sudden vulnerability brought out every protective instinct he had. She was broken too. He could see that clearly now. What wasn't clear was when and how he would tell her who he really was. He captured her tears with his thumbs and wiped them from her cheeks, holding her face gently in his hands.

How could he tell her what he'd done?

He didn't care if it was too soon to hold her. Everything in life came too soon. Birth, love, death—they all did. He felt as if he'd lived just one lousy day without her, a day that had lasted his whole life. When she closed her eyes and shook with quiet sobs, he pulled her against his chest. What he felt terrified and thrilled him. She was made for his arms.

"We lost a lot of good men in Vietnam we shouldn't have," he whispered hoarsely into her hair. "I'm so sorry about Jimmy." He could no longer speak.

He was a coward.

But he was holding her.

"The last time I was here, Jimmy was with me. He loved this old barn." She leaned back in his arms and looked up at him. "Have you lost someone you loved, John?"

"Yes, I have." He swallowed hard.

She smiled through her tears and pulled away to walk wordlessly around the loft.

He quietly followed her, and they explored reverently, the way people walk through museums. Here was a life before easy living, when comforts were appreciated, not expected. A life of oil lamps and black cast-iron stoves that gobbled wood painstakingly chopped on cold winter mornings. A simple life enjoyed by the Callohans while they built their rambling ranch house on the nearby hill where Swampy lived alone now.

He stopped in front of the bear rug spread out before a dusty little stove, imagining himself there barefoot, his toes buried in the dense fur as he listened to the nighthawks in the fields and the coyotes in the hills and the cattle milling near the barn—and most of all just listening to the night. A hundred years ago here, the night probably sounded just like it did today. The loft had no TV to drown out the quiet, no noisy appliances to scare away the peace. Half-burned candles and a few oil lamps were scattered around the room.

"This place is perfect," he told Swampy, ending the companionable silence.

"I'm glad you like it." She finally smiled again.

"The loft doesn't have electricity," she said apologetically. "Mr. Callohan wired lights on the end of the barn for me a few months before he died. I used to ride my horse as long as I could in the evenings, that way I'd miss the six o'clock news."

John understood what she meant about the news. "I haven't watched the news in years. It just hurts too much to see our boys in Vietnam bleeding all over the TV."

He didn't say more, and she let it go and turned toward the trapdoor. "I'll be back in a minute."

After she hit a switch downstairs, floodlights, positioned very near the windows of the loft, spilled light across the room.

She climbed back up the ladder and said, "The floodlights help up here. You can keep them on as long as you want. All night if you want." She stepped over to the windows, looking out at the bright lights hanging on the side of the barn.

"I don't think I'll need them all night." He moved up beside her. "What are your plans for this evening?"

"This is about the time I sit on my porch swing and look down the hill and imagine that old flatbed Ford driving up the road. It rolls in slow and quiet because that's the way Jimmy always drove it, and I sit on the porch pretending he parks it right there."

She closed her eyes, pain all over her face.

The guilt he lived with every day rose up like a wall between them that he couldn't see over the top of. He closed his eyes too, listening to her talk about Jimmy.

"He's there in the front yard, and he comes through the gate, and he isn't wearing that damned uniform anymore. He belongs to me now, not Uncle Sam."

John opened his eyes.

"And we make babies that look like Patrick and Gracie, and …" She opened her eyes, shining again with tears. "I miss him every day. And every night. Especially at night." Wiping her eyes, she moved away from John. "I'm sorry," she said softly. "I never talk about it. I can't believe I'm telling you this stuff."

"No need to be sorry. Everyone needs someone to talk to." He shouldn't be here without telling her who he was and what had really happened in 'Nam. For a moment, he closed his eyes and said a prayer. More and more lately, he'd been talking to God since hitting that low in New Mexico. Sometimes he read the

Bible. Sunrises and sunsets moved him. He no longer took life for granted. It was hard to stay alive when you thought about dying every day. But here with Swampy, he wanted to savor every moment, even these really painful moments with her. He followed her down the ladder into the tack room and then out to the Camaro.

"When do you want to move in?" she asked at the car, her voice throaty.

"I'd like to move in tonight if that's all right."

"Tonight?"

"It doesn't have to be tonight."

"No, tonight's fine. Do you need to go somewhere to get your belongings?"

He shook his head, embarrassed to tell her everything he owned was in the trunk of his car.

She looked toward the barn and pointed to the floodlights. "I'll leave the lights on for you and let you settle in." She began to walk up the dirt road that led up the hill to the house.

"Where are you going?" he called after her.

"Home."

"I'll take you home." He shifted, uncertain if he should follow her on foot or get into the car and drive her the rest of the way up the hill.

"I am home." She kept on walking.

"See you in the morning." He waved, his hand lingering in the air. He didn't want her to go, and knew he shouldn't stay. A good man would give her the letter and drive away. But he wasn't a good man. Not anymore. Not since Jimmy died.

Watching her leave, he felt himself slipping into that old abyss of guilt and loneliness and regret. He should tell her who he was right now. She deserved the truth.

He tried to call her back, even opening his mouth, but realized she was probably too far away now to really hear him. Especially since he could hardly speak past the lump in his throat. He stood there until she disappeared under the big cedar trees that surrounded the white two-story house on the hill, and then he went to his trunk to gather up his things.

Setting himself up in her life this way, pretending to be some random pilot just looking for work, was wrong. But he wanted to help her. She needed an experienced pilot. Someone she didn't have to pay much to dust for her. He could do that. He threw his duffel bags over his shoulder, grabbed his sleeping bag, and headed for the barn.

He built a little fire in the small black stove in the loft and stood for too long staring out one of the windows at the house on the hill, where a single light glowed in an upstairs room. Memories engulfed him and then began to eat him alive. Jimmy had turned to Jesus in 'Nam. He'd gone regularly to prayer services, asking John to go too. John always had an excuse for Jimmy because he believed what the Colonel always said: *"Religion was for weak-minded men."* Still, deep down, John was conflicted about religion. His mother had dressed him up every Sunday for Mass, but the Colonel would never go, except on Christmas and Easter. His father didn't think much of church. He especially didn't like his own mother taking his son to her Methodist Church, but those memories with his grandma at her sweet little country church when he was young were some of John's fondest. He'd even been baptized in the river with his Methodist cousins when he was ten years old, but they'd all kept that a secret from his parents. Since he'd returned from the war, he'd often thought of going back to church. Hymns still moved him, now more than ever. When he began to hum "Amazing Grace," it comforted him. He didn't care that he was now a weak-minded man. He got down on his knees and prayed.

# Chapter Fourteen

Swampy built a fire in the living room stove and sat in Mr. Callohan's old leather recliner, staring at the flames licking around the oak logs. Jimmy and his dad had split these logs over a span of years, and the once large woodpile behind the house was small now. She didn't know what she'd do when the wood finally dwindled away, maybe by the end of this winter.

Her rambling ranch house felt colder and lonelier than usual. Gadget was curled up on his old sheepskin near the stove. He was a short-haired little mutt and shivered whenever the weather dipped below sixty degrees. She'd learned to live with a little fire and a lot of loneliness, but tonight with John Reno taking up residence in her barn, the emptiness of her home was amplified.

She popped open a beer and picked up the shoebox on the floor beside her chair. The letters were not in any order. She just pulled them out and read them at random. If she'd recently read one that she grabbed, she'd stick it back in the box and choose another. Tonight, she chose this one:

*October 15, 1969*

*Dear Swampy:*

*The rainy season is here. All it does is rain with the monsoons. Everything is wet. There's no way to stay dry. Guys get fungus between their toes. The rain comes down sideways with the wind. The rivers are overflowing. The stench is awful. That's the thing about Vietnam. It smells like crap over here all the time. They burn our dung in human-waste buckets. Diesel fuel and excrement creates an unforgettable smell. Now the slow, muddy rivers are flooding, and the stench is overwhelming. It can drive guys crazy.*

*The living conditions are pretty uncomfortable too. We sleep in canvas-covered bunkers sandbagged up about six feet above the ground. There are six of us in our bunker. All pilots. The pilots here are very concerned that all crew members know how to fly, so they teach their door gunners and crew chiefs basic flight techniques. Some of the crew chiefs and gunners are just kids. Barely eighteen. I'm teaching three boys to fly right now. They all graduated high school this year, got drafted, and are eager to learn how to fly. Nobody wants to be in a helicopter without knowing what to do if something happens to the pilots.*

*We sure appreciate your care packages, honey. I never thought Ritz crackers, canned oysters, sardines, and your cookies could taste so good. The Kool-Aid is a big hit too. I built a little wooden shelf above my bunk and keep my care packages from you up there, and the funniest thing happened yesterday. A little spider monkey with a black face and big green eyes tore your latest package up. He opened the*

*Kool-Aid and was sticking his paw in to eat it off his fingers when Luke and I returned to the bunker and caught him in the act.*

*Luke declared war on the monkey. He dropped his flight bag and dove after the little bugger. The monkey jumped off the shelf and became entangled in my mosquito netting like a fish in a fishnet. We all have mosquito nets. You can't sleep without them. The monkey was screeching like a wounded animal. It was so entangled Luke had to pull out his survival knife and cut an opening to get the monkey out of the net. I thought Luke was going to kill the monkey—he hates monkeys—but he let it go. The monkey made a hasty retreat into the jungle just outside the camp's perimeter with red Kool-Aid on his fingers.*

*I asked Luke why he let the monkey go and he said, "Because it looked at me with those big green eyes like Swampy's." That made me laugh. I told Luke your eyes aren't really green. And they aren't really blue. They're somewhere in between. So we looked at your pictures and tried to decide if your eyes were green or blue. Luke says green. I say blue. I think Luke needs a wife. He loves your care packages. Nobody sends Luke care packages. I don't understand it because his parents are rich. But that's the thing, money can't buy you love. We're not rich, Swampy, but we have love. That's a lot more than many of the boys have over here. A lot of the guys get Dear John letters from their girlfriends, breaking it off. Some of the guys even cry. They get drunk and cry like babies. It's kind of heartbreaking. And if they get wounded, those boys yell for their mamas. They also get attached to the mama-sans who take care of us here.*

*The mama-sans do our wash. We pay them a few dollars, and they bring our laundry back to us clean and dry. I don't know how they do it in this rain, but they do. They are older women with families of their own in the nearby village. I miss you something awful. Just a couple more months and I'll be home. I can't wait to get back to you. Please tell Dad I miss him too. He's probably doing a lot of duck hunting this time of year. Ask him to make me some duck jerky and send it over. Luke wants to taste it. He's only had duck pâté. Who eats duck pâté?*

*I miss eating Dad's barbequed ducks. I miss hunting with Dad. I miss making love to you. I miss holding your hand in church. I miss the smell of spring and a blooming almond orchard. I miss flying the Stearmans. Helicopters are fun, but not when you're trying to land in a hole in the jungle under enemy fire to pick up wounded men. I'm ready to return to dusting.*

*Are you riding the horses? Please give Duke an apple for me. That big old buckskin likes his apples. Are you still getting tomatoes from the garden? What I wouldn't give right now for a bacon-and-tomato sandwich.*

*Well, I need to hit the hay. Hoping no mortars wake us up tonight. Don't worry, they're never close. Just close enough to rouse us out of bed. Hoping to stay in the sack tonight and have sweet dreams of you. I love you, Swampy.*

*Always yours,*
*Jimmy*

# Chapter Fifteen

The first rays of dawn touched the barn gently, slipping through the window of the loft with the golden light that photography people loved and religious people loved even more. It shone on John's face as he rolled over on the bearskin rug, slowly coming awake with the realization sunlight shimmered through his eyelids. When he heard the barn door slam downstairs, he jumped to his feet, combing his fingers through his hair.

Swampy called from the tack room. "John? You awake?"

"I'm up, boss," he answered in a raspy morning voice.

"Well, let's get going. We're burning daylight."

*"We're burning daylight."* A now familiar saying and a now familiar voice. He smiled as he pulled on his Levi's. "Sorry, I fell asleep in front of the fire last night."

"You've got one minute to brush your teeth. I'll meet you at your car. We've got three orchards to spray today. We need to get going."

John and Swampy sprayed the fields together cutting the time in half. Most companies ran Ag Cats now. It took two trusty old Stearmans to do the job of one Ag Cat.

Blue flagged for them, along with a very sullen Lucy. Patrick played a few hundred yards away in the bed of Blue's pickup. Lucy insisted on wearing an old WWII gas mask that made her pretty face look like something out of *The Twilight Zone*. She said the spray was hazardous to her health.

Blue thought she was crazy. He held his flag high as John began spraying at his end of the field of almond trees. A labyrinth of power lines skirted the orchard. Flying *Molly*, John slipped gracefully beneath the wires and then began laying the spray swath as if the old plane glided down an invisible line. His plane never vacillated a foot's variation in heading or altitude. At the end of the run, John made a swift, unspectacular turn and was back running another swath just as perfect as the prior one.

Blue whistled through his teeth. *Nevada is a real duster after all.* He turned to the other end of the orchard, counting out his steps, moving toward the distant figure of his sister-in-law. In the distance, she looked like the Creature from the Black Lagoon with her gas mask and dark baggy coveralls.

Swampy flew the same job more aggressively, executing some daring moves that made Blue think she should be in an air show instead of spraying this orchard. John continued flying his impeccable swaths. Blue grinned, watching John spray the orchard as only the pros sprayed them. Not one mistake, not one deviation, not one dangerous turn or wasted air promenade. Nevada flew like he was kissing daisies. Thankfully, the power lines were on John's side of the field. Nevada treated the wires with respect. He didn't dive under them like Swampy would do. John eased under them from a ways back. Everything he did up there looked calculated yet as natural as a bird.

Blue was impressed.

When he and Lucy finally overlapped their flagging steps, they watched John and Swampy fly the last two swaths side by side. It was a beautiful display of airmanship. Swampy set the speed, and John broke another perfect run to fall in beside her, synchronizing his Stearman next to hers. At the end of the run, both planes pulled up over the wires at the same time, heading back to the hangar, side by side like swans.

"Don't think I've ever seen anything that pretty in my life." Blue watched the Stearmans whine away across an endless sky.

Lucy took off her mask and dropped her flag on the ground. She removed an old faded gray felt cowboy hat—Billy's favorite piece of clothing—then shook out her long blond hair.

"Except you, darlin', of course." Blue winked at her without smiling.

"Why don't you take that flag you're holding and stick it up your skinny ass, Blue." She stomped away toward the Chevy, slapping Billy's hat and the mask against her shapely thigh, not bothering to take her flag with her.

"Hey, that's a great idea!" Blue laughed. "But I think it would fit up your ass much better. Everyone knows you got a friendly ass, Lucy."

"Go to hell!" she hollered over her shoulder. She broke into a run toward his pickup, where Patrick played in the bed with a box of Hot Wheels cars.

*She wouldn't.*

Blue bent down to pick up her flag. He watched her really kick it in gear, dashing for his truck like hounds were after her.

*Damn her! That's just what she plans to do.*

He sprinted toward the Chevy, but Lucy was running well ahead of him now. His keys hung in the ignition. He always left them there. She was counting on leaving him out here in the middle of nowhere. He was surprised she could run that fast with her hourglass figure. He thought he would catch her, but carrying the two long-poled flags, flapping noisily, slowed him down.

She scrambled into the cab and had the engine roaring just as he jogged up. Patrick screamed when his mother gassed the Chevy, sending him rolling against the closed tailgate. Little Hot Wheels clattered all over the truck bed as Lucy spun out in the gravel, spraying Blue with stinging rocks as she sped away.

He flung both flags onto the gravel. He'd been about to leap in the bed of the truck but had hesitated, afraid he'd land on his nephew. Though Patrick was probably banged up anyway with her wild departure.

Watching her carelessly endanger his beloved nephew made Blue hate her even more.

*I know better than to tangle with that she-devil,* he chastised himself as he began walking toward the hangar ten miles away.

Lucy was the longest-clawed cat he'd ever come across. She was one of those clever little kitties, and he'd acted like a big dumb dog around her. She'd get him ready to eat her alive, and then she'd scurry over the fence and trot home with her tail in the air as he beat his head against the fence in a spit-flying fury for an hour or two. Just like now.

# Chapter Sixteen

John and Swampy flew toward the hangar, the wind roaring against their faces, the wing wires singing in the Stearmans. They waved to each other several times, smiling beneath their goggles. When they neared the hangar, John fell in behind, letting Swampy take the runway first. Looping around as she landed, he touched down a safe distance behind her. Single file, they rolled to the loading rig, where Billy stood on his crutch, holding Gracie in one arm.

Swampy taxied her Stearman right up next to the rig so she could refill the hopper. John shut down his plane and climbed out, removing his goggles and placing them in the cockpit for when he returned. He walked over to Billy.

"Can I help you?" Though he'd watched Billy do things amazingly well for a one-legged man on a crutch carrying a baby, he wanted to offer to assist filling Swampy's plane.

"Hold Gracie for me." Billy handed him the little girl.

John awkwardly accepted the child. When Gracie frowned, as if to say, "You're not holding me right," he tucked her up against his chest as he'd seen the other adults do. She smiled and began to make little bird noises. He smiled back, delighted the baby seemed to like him. Seeing that Billy had no problem working the filling rig by himself, he walked over to where Swampy sat in her Stearman. She was overseeing the spray poured into her hopper. He didn't say anything for a moment, just held Gracie as he stared at her in the open cockpit.

Her goggles hung around her neck. She hadn't removed her helmet. A few stray wisps of hair had escaped the old brown leather. The strands clung to her wind-reddened cheeks. In those baggy coveralls, sitting in her plane, she looked happy as could be. He hated to bring up what was on his mind, but the way she flew that plane bothered him to no end.

"Why do you fly like that?" he asked when she finally met his gaze.

"Like what?" She cocked her head, appearing to take him seriously.

"Like you've got the wind by the tail and you'll hang on if it kills you."

"Do I fly that way?" A grin split her lips.

"You fly like you've got to prove you're a good pilot, when in fact you are a good pilot and there's no need to prove it to anyone. Especially not to me."

"Well, thank you, sir." She took off her helmet, shaking out her ponytail. "But I do need to prove it. I'm not some licensed aviator like you. I'm a self-taught woman doing a man's job in a man's world, and I've got to do it better than any man or I'll be forced out of this business by some hotshot duster like you."

"I doubt there's a man alive who could force you out of that plane." He admired her moxie—it was her daredevil flying he wanted to tame. "Who taught you to fly?" He bounced the baby in his arms, making Gracie grin.

"Moby was a WWI ace fighter pilot. He crop dusted around here for years. He was Jimmy's grandpa's best friend. Moby was the only man who would take me flying. None of them good ole boys thought I could cut it as a duster. But Moby believed in me. We only got a few lessons in before he died. I taught myself the rest."

"Didn't you worry about needing more training?" His gaze traveled over her face, memorizing it. She was so spirited. Her smile dauntless. It didn't seem like she could ever crash. But he knew how death came, rolling out of nowhere, taking people in an instant. He could still see the men's faces. Jimmy. Lieutenant Daniel Lancing. The best gunner he'd ever seen, Tommy Rideout. CW2 Mike Morrison. Lieutenant Larry Beatty. Crew chiefs Andrew Manning and Michael Clay—those crew chiefs still just kids. He could go on naming men they'd lost in Vietnam. He drew a deep breath.

Her smile eased away. "I didn't care about anything after losing Jimmy. Flying became the only thing that mattered. If I lived, I lived. If I died, I died. Jimmy died flying. That's what they told me. I figured I may as well die flying too."

John kissed the baby's fingers poking at his lips. Gracie giggled and grabbed at his mouth some more. He captured the baby's hand so he could speak. "Do you even know how to fly safe? Do you realize what your limits are up there?"

"I fly the only way I know how. I go by my gut." She slid a hand through her ponytail. "One time I blew a turn at the top of my climb. I wasn't dusting. I was just up in the sky, hoping I'd crash so they could bury me beside Jimmy. I didn't have a headwind. Instead of coming around in the turn, I stalled in an inverted climb. I went into a spin I thought would kill me, but without doing a thing to make it different, I came out of that spin and wound up in a lazy-daisy dive. All I had to do was pull back on the stick."

Billy hobbled up on his crutch.

Swampy stopped talking.

John gently rubbed Gracie's back. She quit poking at his face and watched her daddy come toward them.

Blue's truck came roaring down the road and squealed into the parking lot. Patrick's head bobbed up and down in the bed of the truck.

Billy propelled himself on his crutch into an awkward run toward the pickup. Swampy scrambled down off the plane, sprinting toward the Chevy as well. John trotted after them, holding Gracie close.

"What happened?" Swampy raced ahead of Billy, who struggled to get to the truck as fast as his crutch could carry him.

"I've had it!" Lucy screamed. "You're all a bunch of lunatics! I'm leaving!"

"Lucy, that's enough," Swampy said sternly as she rose up on tiptoes to look in the bed of the truck. Patrick was crying but appeared unhurt. Hot Wheels cars were everywhere.

"It's not enough!" Lucy sprang from the pickup, slamming the old metal door shut with a bang. "I hate Blue and you too! You work us night and day like those broken old planes you're flying into the ground! We're people, Swampy! Flesh-and-blood human beings with needs and wants and feelings! At least I am."

"Honey, calm down." Billy went to her.

"And you! You're not a man! You haven't been a man since you came back from that godforsaken war with your leg blown off! You think making love to me is enough! But it ain't! I need more than that, Billy." Her wail trailed off to a pitiful whine.

"Don't say these things, Lucy. You'll regret it tomorrow." Swampy's voice was soft but steely.

"No, I won't," Lucy said bitterly. "I gave Billy my youth. I gave you all beautiful babies. All you've given me is hard work and loneliness. You're all the biggest bunch of losers I've ever met." She settled into a soft, broken voice. "You work. You work. You work some more. You never go out, Swampy. Don't you ever long to go dancing?" Tears streamed down Lucy's face. "I haven't danced since Billy came home from Vietnam like this."

"Well, at least he came home. I'd give up a lifetime of dancing just to have Jimmy back without any legs." Swampy's voice was throaty with grief.

"Would you?" Lucy snarled with unexpected fury. She looked at John, holding her baby. "Even now that you have him?"

"Enough, Lucy." Billy had tears on his face too. "Just go ... Find someone to dance with. You've been wanting that for a long time."

She turned to her husband, and her whole body shook with heaving sobs. Billy looked as if he would fall over on his crutch, as if that one leg could never hold the weight it held now.

"It's all right. You can go, Momma," Patrick said from the truck. "Aunt Swampy will be my mom."

After looking at Patrick like he'd broken her heart, Lucy stumbled away. Billy hobbled after her. John walked over to the truck bed. Moving the baby to his left arm, he lifted Patrick out with his right. The little boy wrapped his arms around John's neck and hung on for dear life. In that instant, John lost his fear of kids. He wanted to do everything he could to protect Patrick and Gracie from their parents' sorrow. He knew what it was like to live with unhappy parents.

Swampy soothed Patrick's hair down with trembling hands as she said to John, "She must have left Blue out at the Huber farm. We better go get him."

John followed her to his Camaro, where he helped load Patrick into the backseat. He handed Gracie to Swampy and opened the passenger door for her. She slipped into the seat, settling the baby on her lap.

John closed Swampy's door as quietly as he could and then walked around to his side to slide behind the wheel.

Ten minutes later, they pulled up alongside Blue, who was tromping down the road, carrying two flags that flapped in a wind that blew from the west and smelled of rain.

# Chapter Seventeen

The busy days of winter flew by on the wings of the red-and-white Stearmans. John and Swampy fell into a comfortable but grinding existence of flying together until they were exhausted. Blue did their flagging and Swampy hired a kid named Tommy to help flag. They shared rides to and from the hangar, mostly in John's car, but they rarely talked about anything other than crop dusting, until the 24th of April.

"I can't believe Lucy didn't even call today," Swampy said as the Camaro carried them home to the ranch an hour earlier than usual. Blue and Billy and the kids would follow later so Swampy had time to prepare for Gracie's first birthday party.

"Maybe she's on her way home now." John took his eyes off the road for a moment to look at Swampy. It seemed strange to be driving toward a horizon lit by twilight. Usually they were just landing the Stearmans as the sun went down.

She shook her head, staring out the window at the beautiful gloaming. "Lucy probably doesn't even remember what today is. Patrick's birthday was the day after New Year's. Only heaven knows where Lucy was then. Probably with Rex or some other poor man who didn't know what hit him until she twisted through his life like a Texas tornado."

It surprised him that she was finally opening up. For nearly four months now, all she'd talked about was work. In the beginning, he thought she was obsessed with crop dusting, and in a way she was, but he soon realized the company was how she provided for her family; if it went under, they'd all be out on the street. It was also how she escaped her own humanity. Swampy didn't have to be human as long as she functioned like a machine. When it came to running Callohan Dusters, Swampy was amazing, but when it came to relationships, she usually ran people right into the ground. He'd learned she didn't want to deal with people's feelings. Her own feelings most of all. This was the first contemplative mood he'd caught her in, and he wasn't about to let the soft side of Swampy slip away.

"Did you ever like Lucy?" He wanted to keep her talking.

She turned back from the window, looking bemused for a moment. "Billy liked her, so Blue and I tried to like her too. But Lucy will never be happy where there's real happiness. It's not about liking her. It's about understanding her. I'll never understand a woman like Lucy."

"You can't understand her because you'd never leave the people you love." He knew Swampy well enough to realize she'd never abandon her brothers, let alone Patrick and Gracie.

"How can she leave her babies? I'd die in a second if someone made me walk away from Patrick and Gracie."

He remembered all the people he'd walked away from in the past several years. The last thing he wanted to do was dwell on that fact. "I don't know. Maybe her heart shuts off." He'd been shutting his heart off for a long time. It was how he survived.

During the past months, he'd watched Swampy's devotion to the children grow. In another month, if Lucy did come home, she was going to have a fight on her hands. Those kids were Swampy's life now. Little Gracie already called her "Mama." And when strangers in town assumed the children were hers, she no longer corrected them. She'd just smile and say thank you, and then gather them up like a mother hen, tucking Patrick against her leg and Gracie to her chest, appearing so proud to be their mama. Seeing Swampy embracing motherhood, unlike Lucy, unlike his own mother, made him all achy inside. He couldn't remember his own mother ever holding him like Swampy cuddled the kids or playing with him like Swampy did in the evenings at the ranch, rolling around with Patrick and Gracie on the living room floor. Watching Disney movies and *Wild Kingdom* on Sunday nights like there was nothing better in the world than that bowl of popcorn they all shared. He always made the popcorn and was more than grateful when Swampy invited him for Sunday night television with the kids.

He couldn't help but smile because Swampy was all soft and tender with the children like a mother should be. But she also flew that old Stearman like the Red Baron, declaring war on bugs and rot and anything else that might ruin a farmer's livelihood.

"Why are you smiling?"

"Am I smiling?" He pressed his lips together. "I'm not smiling. I'm exercising my mouth. I want it in top shape for tonight's dinner."

"What dinner?"

He had assumed she would invite him up to the house tonight to join the celebration. He'd even saved the stuffed white kitten he'd gotten for Gracie to give to her at the party, though he'd wanted to present it to her the moment he'd purchased it two days ago at the drugstore in Live Oak.

"Gracie's party." He suddenly felt foolish and turned his attention back to the road.

"Oh, that. I didn't think you wanted to come."

He looked at Swampy. She appeared serious. "You bet I want to come. Why would you think I wouldn't want to come to Gracie's party?" He returned his eyes to the road but glanced back at her in disbelief. *How could she think that?*

She grinned, and he realized she was teasing him. First, she talked reflectively about her family, and now she teased. He laughed in awe of her.

"What's so funny?"

"You."

"Why am I funny?"

*"I was just thinking about The Invasion of the Body Snatchers."*

They pulled up in front of the ranch's gate, but Swampy didn't spring out of the car to open the entrance like she usually did. No longer grinning, she waited for him to explain.

"I'll get the gate," he said when she didn't open her car door.

She grabbed his arm. "What about the *Body Snatchers?*"

He looked at her fingers on his forearm. Her hand was small and dirty and eager, like a boy's hand. When he looked into her eyes, he no longer found humor in what he was about to say. "Never mind. I'll get the gate."

"Don't change the subject. Come on, tell me what's up with me and the Body Snatchers?"

"I thought maybe the Body Snatchers stole the real Swampy. You're talking about things other than crop dusting. And about how you don't like your sister-in-law. If Lucy returns, I'm afraid you'll beat her up. You're a human being like the rest of us."

She jerked her hand away. For a moment, she looked hurt, then she tried to laugh, then she climbed out of the car and opened the gate without another word.

He drove the Camaro through the opening and then stepped out of the car. He walked over to help her secure the gate.

"I don't need your help," she said, her tone short.

"I know but let me do it." He tried to take the gate from her to slip it into its wire harness.

For a moment, she held on to the post, but she finally let it settle into his grasp. When he finished securing the wire, he turned to her. "I'm sorry. I didn't mean to hurt your feelings. How 'bout we go on a date? I'll take you to dinner tomorrow night, and we'll talk about what makes you human like the rest of us."

On Saturday nights, they often took the children to eat pizza or Chinese food in town. Blue sometimes went along. Billy even went a time or two, but never had Swampy spent an evening alone with him.

She walked back to the car without answering him.

He trailed after her, regretting asking her out. He was here to work for her, not romance her. She climbed in her side, he climbed in his, and they drove up the hill in awkward silence. He stopped the car in front of the house where he always dropped her off, and left the engine running.

She opened her car door. "Consider tonight our date. Be back up here in an hour for Gracie's party."

"Do you want some help getting ready? I cook a mean macaroni and cheese."

She got out of the car, closed the door, and spoke through the open window. "I did most of the dinner prep this morning. I just need to stick the chicken in the oven and set the table."

"What time did you get up this morning?"

"Three thirty." She finally smiled a little.

"That's not morning. That's still night." He returned her smile.

"Three thirty, four thirty, what's the difference?"

"Three thirty is the middle of the night. Four thirty is almost morning. I think crop dusters should take up banking hours; let the bugs get their beauty rest before we kill them."

Her little smile disappeared. "Bugs don't sleep."

He laughed as she stepped away from the Camaro's window and walked toward the house. He called after her,

"I feel sorry for all the bugs around here."

She turned around. "I don't feel sorry for bugs. I kill them."

He drove down to the barn, chuckling at her bug vendetta. An hour later, he walked back up the hill carrying the stuffed white kitten and knocked on her front door.

Patrick threw the door wide open. "John's here!" he howled.

"Dinner's ready," Swampy yelled from the kitchen.

John tucked the stuffed animal under his arm as he reached into his pocket to pull out a piece of gum for Patrick. "Save the gum until after dinner."

Patrick closed the door while sticking the gum in his pocket, and then headed for the kitchen.

Blue, Billy, Swampy, and Gracie were in the kitchen. Gracie sat in a highchair, and Blue and Billy were seated at the table. Swampy plunked down a homemade whipped cream-covered cake and then looked at John. Red icing on the cake read, "Happy Birthday, Gracie and John."

He stared dumbfounded at his name on the cake.

"Happy birthday, John." He could hear the pleasure in Swampy's voice.

Blue and Billy clapped. Gracie banged a spoon on her high chair's tray.

Patrick snickered at John's astonished reaction, scampering away from his side to climb up onto a chair at the table.

"How did you know tomorrow's my birthday?" He was embarrassed. And then delighted. And then embarrassed some more.

"I saw it on your driver's license when I hired you. Just a day after Gracie's, so I remembered." She motioned for him to take a seat at the table. Before he did, he walked over to Gracie's high chair.

"Here you go, Miss Gracie." He handed her the stuffed kitten and gently ruffled her wispy blond hair.

Gracie dropped her spoon and reached for the plush animal. She held it with both hands, pulled it straight to her mouth, and began to chew on its nose.

After that, they ate the fried chicken and mashed potatoes and gravy as if half-starved. When dinner was over, Swampy stuck two candles in the cake, and they all sang happy birthday to Gracie and John. He finally blew out the candles after Gracie nearly burned her fingers on the flames trying to grab them.

Once the dishes were washed and Gracie and Patrick were tucked into bed, Blue and Billy drove back to the hangar in Blue's pickup, dropping John off at the barn as they went down the hill.

John carried with him a new shirt. He'd been given grander gifts in his life, but running his hand over the sky-blue silk shirt, he couldn't remember what those other gifts were. Though the shirt came signed from everyone, he knew Swampy had picked it out for him. She'd also given him the day off tomorrow.

He'd argued with her, saying he didn't care it was his birthday, but she had insisted. He climbed into bed, thinking about how he didn't want a day off. He would much rather go fly with Swampy.

Which got him thinking about the reason he liked working with her seven days a week from dawn to dusk and why he'd asked Swampy out to dinner at the gate. Hours later, still wide awake, he felt so guilty he couldn't stand himself. He should tell her the truth. There was no doubt he loved her. He'd given up the idea of leaving once she found another duster. The thought of going away killed him. He wanted to build a life with her, help her raise Gracie and Patrick if Billy didn't snap out of his depression. He imagined what Swampy's and his own babies would look like. Would they have her blue-green eyes and stubborn disposition?

He hoped so.

The night spun out as he paced the loft and stared out the window, watching her bedroom light on the hill. She always left her porch light on too. The moon moved through the sky as if it hung on an invisible wire. Everything seemed to hang on an invisible wire in this world. The sun rose and set. The seasons changed. Eagles shed their feathers and gained new ones and flew higher. He'd once believed in evolution, but he didn't anymore.

How could a fish become a man?

How could he be with Swampy after what he'd done in Vietnam?

He desperately longed for forgiveness. He walked over to the nightstand beside his bed and picked up the Bible Jimmy had given him in Vietnam. Mr. Callohan had sent two Bibles to Jimmy—one for John. Even at the time, when John wasn't interested in religion, it had deeply touched him that Jimmy's dad sent him a Bible too. Tonight, it moved him even more. In the words written in red, he searched for relief from his guilt and grief.

# Chapter Eighteen

After a morning of running errands, Swampy returned to the hangar to find Blue missing along with *Molly*. At two in the afternoon, Billy appeared well on his way to a drunken stupor. He staggered around on his crutch, tinkering with *Old Dan*. When Swampy barked his name, he spun around and slammed his face into the plane's big metal propeller.

"Ohhhh," he groaned, throwing a hand over his injured forehead. "Damn, that hurt."

Swampy strode over and grabbed his arm, yanking his hand away from his forehead. An egg-size welt swiftly formed on the center of his head. "You'll live." She didn't care if he lived or not. She was so mad at both her brothers—Billy for being drunk and Blue for disappearing with *Molly*.

"I don't think I will." Billy hobbled around her and plopped himself down in Blue's tattered lawn chair, holding his hand over the bump on his head. Swampy wondered for the hundredth time what John was doing today. Nowadays, she depended on him more than she cared to admit. And she loved being with him every day.

Billy was rarely in any condition at night to care for the kids since Lucy had left. She was glad she'd dropped Patrick and Gracie off at Mrs. Larson's that morning instead of leaving them with their father.

"I miss Lucy." Billy looked at her like a puppy who'd just had the wind kicked out of him by an abusive master.

Squatting down beside him, she touched his arm. "I know." She tried to be sympathetic, an emotion that didn't come easy to her. Billy was pitiful. He hadn't bathed in days. His eyes were so red they reminded her of those photos when flashbulbs gave people's gazes an albino glow.

Billy motioned toward his missing leg. "She left me because of my leg. If I was still whole, Lucy would still love me."

She stared at Billy's absent leg, her empathetic gaze growing stony. "A lot of men lost more than a leg over there, Bean."

"Maybe, but did they lose their hearts? Because I did. I lost mine in the Ia Drang Valley." Billy put a hand against his chest as if he searched for something there.

He'd brought up that valley a hundred times before, and Swampy always changed the subject. She didn't want to hear about Vietnam. But today, for some inexplicable reason, she encouraged him to tell his story. "What happened over there?"

For a time, Billy remained silent. Just as she was about to leave him alone and try to salvage what was left of the day, he began to speak.

"We were headed for landing zone Albany, just smoking and joking and stumbling through that sharp old elephant grass. They ambushed us. It was bad. Real bad." Billy wasn't looking at her any longer. He had a thousand-yard stare gazing through the hangar wall toward a distant field an ocean away.

"They were all over us. We were fighting like hell. The LT went down first. No one was in charge. You could only see a few feet in front of you. I started running. I was just so scared I started running like a damned rabbit. I fell over this log. The log was my buddy Jenner. There wasn't a whole lot left of him. I knew it was Jenner because he always wore this macaroni necklace his daughter made for him. Then I heard the gooks. They were all around us. I crawled under Jenner. One of those son of a bitches used me and Jenner to steady his weapon. He thought I was dead too. He started firing. He was killing my friends. I didn't move. I was such a coward I didn't move. I let that gook kill my friends."

"It wasn't your fault, Billy. You were just a kid. What were you supposed to do?"

He kept his eyes on that distant field as he watched the battle play out there. "I was supposed to save lives. I was the medic. But I was so scared I froze. Someone came along and emptied their magazine into that gook's head. I still didn't move. I wanted to be dead. Whoever killed the gook must have thought I was dead too. The jets began howling overhead. It was so bad we'd called our own air strikes in on us. I remember staring at the bellies of them planes, just praying they'd drop a bomb on me. They started dropping napalm. The grass around me was curling over from the heat. I passed out. Next thing I know some dumbass private's dragging me through the elephant grass. I held on to my medic bag but lost my gun. Then that dumbass private stepped on a Betty. Blew us both sky high."

Billy fell silent.

"It was war." Her fingers curled into claws around the arm of his lawn chair. "People do terrible things in war. It doesn't make it right, but it makes it bearable. It has to, Bean."

Billy's face was stoic. "You know what our government said about that battle? They said it was a success. Just light to moderate casualties. Half our battalion was wiped out. A success? I was there, and I still don't know what the hell we were fighting for."

Swampy grabbed Billy's hands. "We're trying to help those people over there. We're fighting to give them the same freedom we have here. To give them a democratic country. Something like that. Is that so wrong, Bean?"

Billy stayed silent.

"Is it?" She demanded in a choked voice. "'Cause if it is, Jimmy's death was in vain. Your friends' deaths were in vain. All those boys who cross that ocean and never come home—I can't believe their deaths are in vain, Billy. All those boys dying for nothing … I just can't believe in nothing. I hate the war more than anyone, but I can't say it's being fought for nothing. We're fighting for something. I lost Jimmy for something. You lost your leg for something, Bean. Believe in something because if you believe, then life matters. A belief will keep you breathing, and if we're breathing, then we have hope, right?"

Billy stared at her, a lamentable smile flourishing on his face. "I've never heard you talk that way about 'Nam. I thought you didn't agree with the war."

"I don't agree. But I believe in America. If our government believes this war is helping those people and our soldiers are dying over there and being torn apart here because of what they've gone through over there, well, then I have to trust in that. If I don't, I'll go crazy. I'll lose hope. And I can't let myself lose hope."

The rumble of John's Camaro pulling up alongside the hangar ended their conversation. She let go of Billy's hands and stood up beside the lawn chair as John stepped through the hangar door.

"I thought I gave you the day off." That funny feeling—like she'd swallowed a gallon of dragonflies—hit her harder than usual.

"You said you might dust the Bufford farm this afternoon. I thought I could help." He stared at her for a long moment before looking at Billy. "Hey, Bill, you okay?"

"Hey, John. I'm okay. You okay?"

The sound of an incoming plane sputtering and stalling captured everyone's attention.

"That's *Molly*." Billy staggered out of the chair. "Something's wrong with her engine—"

Swampy and John beat Billy out of the hangar. They ran to the airstrip, then stood there helplessly as the Stearman struggled to reach the runway. When *Molly* finally landed safely, they all rushed over to the clanking plane.

Blue killed the banging engine and stood up in the cockpit. He smiled as if he'd just taken the Studebaker for a Sunday drive. He climbed out onto the wing, hopped down to the ground, and staggered a little as he walked toward the front of the plane. "She sounds stove-up, don't she?"

"What did you do? What's wrong with *Molly*?" Swampy marched over to Blue, ready to kill him.

John and Billy followed her.

"Hit some big-assed birds." Blue stood in front of the Stearman's engine, swaying slightly and smelling like alcohol. The only thing stronger was the smell of scorched duck. Blue began pulling feathers out of the greasy nooks of the motor.

"Are you trying to ruin us?" Swampy rose on her tiptoes to peer through the propeller blade at the smoking engine.

"Calm down, LG." Blue's rumpled camouflage fatigues reeked of cheap perfume. From the look of him, wherever he had gone had been a place with a lounge beside the runway.

"Don't tell me to calm down, Blue Donovan." Swampy stomped her foot so hard it hurt her heel. "We need *Molly*."

"I had a flashback." His hand was full of oily feathers. "I headed home as soon as I snapped out of it, but I ran into those damned birds."

Billy came up beside Blue and began to help pick bird pieces off the hot engine.

Swampy shoved her way between her two brothers to get a better look at the smoking engine. Billy, already unsteady on his crutch, stumbled, nearly falling when she pushed him.

"Take it easy." He hobbled out of her way. "I'm crippled, remember."

"The only thing crippled is your brain. You and Blue need to go root yourselves a place in the mud like two hogs until you sober up." She strained higher on her tiptoes to inspect the smelly engine.

John stepped up beside her in front of the plane. "We can finish the Bufford farm before dark. I'll fly *Old Dan*. I just need you to flag for me. Billy and Blue can get to work on *Molly*."

Swampy looked to John. She was ready to scream in frustration. Her cheeks were hot with indignation. John gave her a reassuring smile. She didn't say anything, just whirled back to her brothers.

"Don't either one of you touch this engine until you sober up. And I want it fixed before tomorrow morning." She strode away, her ponytail swishing.

"Guess you boys better make some coffee," she heard John say. He followed her to the Studebaker, where she stuffed her flag in the backseat.

She swiped a hand across her eyes as he reached the car, not wanting him to see her angry tears. "Let's get the Bufford farm done before dark."

"Don't be too hard on your brothers. They're bleeding all over themselves right now."

"They've been bleeding since they got home from Vietnam. What am I supposed to do? Those aren't my brothers over there. My brothers were good boys who would never have acted like those pitiful jackasses." She looked toward the plane, where her brothers loitered in front of the damaged engine.

"Billy didn't even drink before he went to Vietnam, and Blue never touched dope until the war hooked him on that stuff. I've given them all I can, and they've only gotten worse. I don't think I can save either one of them." Her voice was soft and throaty, torn from somewhere deep inside of her.

She climbed behind the wheel and rolled down the window. When she turned to face him, he leaned in and pressed his lips to hers.

He kissed her gently but thoroughly, swallowing her sorrow. He moved his hand to the back of her neck, under her ponytail. The skin under her hair prickled beneath his fingers. He deepened the kiss when she opened her mouth to him. She flung her head back against his hand, surrendering completely, losing herself in him, forgetting her troubles, forgetting everything but John's mouth on hers. The Studebaker revved up as her foot pushed against the gas pedal. If the car hadn't been in neutral, John probably would have lost his head.

She laughed nervously against his lips as she jerked her foot off the gas. He didn't give up on the kiss, not letting her nervousness get in the way of his passion. The Studebaker's engine settled back into a sputtering chug as his kiss lasted a bit longer.

"Tell me that made you feel better." He removed his hand from her neck to run a finger lightly along her jawline.

"That made me feel better," she softly admitted.

"Go on a date with me, please."

"This is such a small town. People will talk." She bit her bottom lip still throbbing from his kiss.

"There's always talk in two-bit towns. Do you think they haven't already talked about us? We've probably been the topic of conversation down at the Curb Café since you hired me."

She knew he was right, but it hurt to imagine it so. The Curb Café was Jimmy's favorite restaurant. She didn't want anyone thinking she had replaced him. Especially now that she owned Callohan Dusters and the ranch. The Callohans were all gone. Here she was, a poor girl from the South, with everything they had. She may lose it all, but for now it was hers. She owed Jimmy so much, but she couldn't stand another night alone on the porch swing, staring at the barn, longing for John's company.

"I guess we could do something, but only if Billy and Blue sober up. The kids have to be picked up at Mrs. Larson's by five thirty tonight."

"Don't worry. I'll take care of it. I'll meet you at the orchard in ten minutes. We'll have the farm done in no time. After we're finished, you head back to the ranch and get cleaned up. I'll pick up the kids and make sure they're taken care of with Billy and Blue or Mrs. Larson."

"You mean I can't go out looking like this?" She glanced down at her coveralls and then grinned at John.

"I'll take you any way I can get you. If you want to smell like the inside of a hopper, that's fine by me."

"Well, if I smell like the inside of a hopper, it's because you flew your swaths too wide and sprayed me."

"I never fly my swaths too wide."

"You must have. Smell my coveralls."

He leaned through the window, pressing his face against her shirtfront. "You smell like a hopper, but you feel like a beautiful woman."

"John ..." Her hands trembled as she pushed him away. She'd been wanting this so much, but now that he was finally kissing her, she didn't know what to do.

"I'm sorry, I can't help myself." His gaze softened. He looked like he'd kiss her again.

She began rolling up the window. "You have a field to spray, and I have a date to get ready for. Let's get going."

# Chapter Nineteen

John was thrilled she'd finally agreed to go on a date with him. Smiling, he stopped her from rolling up the window. She tilted her head sideways, smiling at him. It struck him how happy she looked. A flash of memory scorched his mind: Swampy, smiling this exact same way in a photograph. He had stared at that picture a million times since that fateful morning nearly four years ago. His heart constricted as he realized she'd once smiled this identical way for Jimmy.

He recalled that morning in Vietnam when he and Jimmy had talked about a dream Jimmy had the night before.

"It's spring," Jimmy had said, his voice plaintive. "Do you know how pretty California is in springtime?"

"No. Is it prettier than Swampy?"

"No, but the ranch is covered in wildflowers. Sweet Lord, I miss the ranch. I wouldn't miss it so bad if Swampy wasn't there. I see her standing on the porch in those big furry pink slippers she doesn't really like but wears because I gave them to her before I left in case she was pregnant. I wanted her to be pregnant. They say women's feet grow when they're pregnant. Did you know that, captain?"

"Nope. Never known a woman well enough to find out such things."

"You should find yourself a wife and find these things out when you're done with this war."

"I think I saw her—Swampy," John admitted. "This beautiful girl was leaving the Catholic chapel at Fort Rucker. I was walking behind her. She was heading out the door and suddenly remembered she had forgotten to dip her fingers in the holy water. She swung back, and we dunked our fingers at the same time. Her eyes met mine for an instant, then she was gone."

"Why haven't you ever told me that?" Jimmy demanded. "I've told you just about everything I know about Swampy. Couldn't you tell me you shared a bowl of holy water with her?"

"I don't know if it was her. I figure it couldn't have been Swampy in that Catholic church at Fort Rucker."

"It was her," Jimmy said sullenly.

"It wasn't her. Just a girl who looked a lot like her. Maybe Swampy has a Catholic twin somewhere?"

"It was her!" Jimmy jumped up from his seat on the jungle grass and glared down at John. "I flew her out there to see me!"

"Jimmy, take it easy." John started to rise, then decided to keep his seat, letting Jimmy have the height advantage for once.

"Oh, dear God, I need to see her." Jimmy sat back down beside John. His eyes looked tormented for a moment. "I had a dream last night."

"You want to tell me about it?" John leaned back on the grass, trying to appear relaxed, but he wasn't relaxed at all. Jimmy was really upset.

"I'm sorry I went crazy like that. I—the dream is really getting to me. I dreamed I was making love to Swampy. I mean really making love, looking into her soul like there was no tomorrow and then ..."

"Then what?" John urged when Jimmy fell silent.

"Then I was you."

"What?"

"I was you."

"You're kidding." John tried to laugh, but the laugh didn't come. It stuck in his throat and all but choked him.

"I'm not kidding. I thought maybe it was another fluke dream or something. Maybe some dumbass private was smoking dope next to my cot. But—I don't know. For a moment, I was you, then it was you with her, and I was standing there watching you. I looked at Swampy's face, and I saw how much she loved you." A tear streaked down Jimmy's cheek. He quickly wiped it away. "It really shook me up, John."

"John?" Swampy said, looking up, squinting through the bright sunshine at him. "Knock, knock. Is anyone home in that head of yours?"

"Swampy ..." He steadied himself on the window frame. He leaned his forehead against the top of the car, looking in at her. "I don't want to push you into anything you're not ready for. Maybe we shouldn't do this."

She stared into his eyes, and he could see she wanted him too. This was the point of no return. It would change everything. Maybe ruin everything.

He said, "You're my boss. Maybe we should just leave it at that."

"You just kissed me. Usually the kiss comes after the date, so the way I see it, you owe me dinner." She let go of his hand and grabbed the steering wheel.

He pushed himself away from the car. "Dinner it is. Step wide when I run my swaths. I think Billy has been tinkering with the spray valves. They're working better than we think they are."

"You just don't want to admit you fly your swaths too wide." She put the Studebaker in reverse and began backing out of the parking lot.

John put his hand over his heart, smiling for her. After she pulled away, all he could think about was Jimmy's dream.

# Chapter Twenty

Swampy put on another dress, turned around in front of the mirror hanging on the back of her bedroom door, and then took it off, tossing it onto the bed. It landed on a heap of other dresses as she turned back to her nearly empty closet. Only one dress left. A dress she didn't think she could bring herself to wear. It was a June dress. For a June day—the day Jimmy would have come home from Vietnam.

The dress was a white polyester knit, soft and sleeveless, with a short hem, the style in 1969. In a spacious Macy's dressing room, it had hit her mid-thigh. She remembered thinking she'd have to lie out beside the lake and get a tan before June. She'd paid a fortune for it, and it had killed her to do it. Spending that kind of money on a dress was ridiculous, she had decided then and decided again now. She'd never buy an expensive dress like this today.

She left it hanging in the closet to take a shower. Under the shower head, hot, pounding water washed over her, along with the memories. She let them come, something she rarely did, as she lathered her body with soap. She imagined her hands were Jimmy's, his hands leathered from hard work sliding over her body. Try as she might, nothing moved in her but tears so deep they felt embedded in her empty womb. She had so wanted to have Jimmy's baby, but it hadn't happened. It struck her that she could no longer remember Jimmy's touch. Only John's touch remained. His hands on her face, wiping away her tears.

Her hands fell heavily from her body. She kept her eyes closed, trying to stop the tears, turning into the spray, letting water slap her face. Had it been that long? Was that why she couldn't remember Jimmy's touch? Or was it that he just hadn't touched her enough? They'd still been newlyweds when he left. Vietnam had gotten so much of Jimmy, and she had gotten so little.

John's kiss was fresh in her mind. She couldn't even remember how Jimmy had kissed her.

She left the shower after washing her hair, scrubbing her scalp so hard it tingled. She found herself toweling off in front of the closet, staring at the white dress, one hundred and sixty dollars' worth of fabric she'd never worn. It didn't seem right to waste money that way. She took Jimmy's homecoming dress down and held it up in front of her, looking at herself in the mirror.

She couldn't picture herself wearing this dress at the San Francisco Airport anymore, couldn't imagine running to Jimmy in it, no longer saw the pleasure on his face when he saw her coming. How the soft white knit clung to her figure, how she looked like a woman in it, not a high school girl. She'd let her bangs grow out so she could pull her hair back in a French twist. The white dress was definitely a French-twist dress.

But standing in front of the mirror now, holding the white dress in front of her, she could picture none of it with Jimmy—because it hadn't happened. The day Jimmy had come home in a sealed box, she'd worn black. And black again at his funeral. The white dress had never been a part of their life together. She finally laid the dress on the bed apart from the others.

She dried her hair and then put the dress on. It fit her the same way it had in that Macy's dressing room the first and last time she had worn it. Pleased that it still fit so well, she pulled on nude colored nylons, then a pair of white-and-gold high-heeled sandals she'd bought to go with the dress. She walked around the room, stumbling here and there on the shag carpet. She hadn't worn heels since her wedding day. Maybe if she walked slower than normal, she wouldn't end up bouncing her behind on the ground.

She headed for the bathroom to finish getting ready. Using both hands, she twisted the bulk of her hair into a loose bun. Holding the bun at the back of her head, she pulled out the drawer beside the sink to grab a handful of bobby pins. She stuck the bobby pins in until the twirled hair held, then stared at her face in the mirror.

She hadn't worn makeup since Jimmy had left for Vietnam. The drawer with the bobby pins contained what was left of her cosmetics: black mascara and a tube of red lipstick. She put a small amount of lipstick on her cheeks, rubbing it in until only a soft blush remained. She did her eyes next. The old mascara clumped up badly on her abundant eyelashes. When she finished, her eyes looked like two black long-legged spiders had died there. She washed it off and tried again, dabbing mascara on her lashes more carefully.

Lastly, she put the red lipstick on.

The lipstick was too much of a transformation. Her lips looked too big and bright. She wiped it off as best she could with a handful of toilet paper. The crimson color had stained her lips, so she wiped a dab of Vaseline on them, producing the shiny touch that seemed to be the style these days.

The doorbell rang, and her knees began to tremble. She took a deep breath as she walked out of the bathroom. Suddenly, she remembered she hadn't put on any perfume. She didn't even own perfume. Kicking off her heels and picking them up, she raced down the stairs into Mr. and Mrs. Callohan's old bedroom. There on the big oak dresser was a small bottle of fragrance. She snatched it up, dabbing White Shoulders behind her ears and on her throat and wrists. She rushed back to the front door, slipping on her heels just before opening the door.

John stared at her as if he'd never seen her before.

She stared at him the same way.

He'd cut his hair short and wore a black sport jacket, the winged-collared blue silk shirt she'd given him for his birthday underneath. His western-cut Angels Flight pants fit him perfectly, and new cowboy boots were on his feet. He was unbelievably handsome. A pleased grin slipped onto her lips as she looked at his new haircut. "Are you going to come in, or are you going to stand on my porch all night, stranger?"

"Most definitely come in." His voice sounded more gravelly than usual. She could tell he was nervous too. He didn't take his gaze off her as he stepped into the house. She moved aside to let him step in and could feel him staring at her backside as she closed the door.

"If I had known you looked like this underneath, I would have burned those coveralls long ago."

"Well, if I'd known you could look so respectable, I would have taken scissors to you months ago. Your haircut looks terrific."

They stared at each other for an admiring moment and then she walked over and opened the closet door in the entry hall to pull out a light wool cloak. "I'm starved. Let's get going. How about Chinese food? I know a nice little place across the river in Marysville."

Before she could close the closet door, John closed it for her. The warmth of his big body so close made her dizzy. He smelled of sandalwood soap and a crisp woodsy aftershave. She wondered where he'd gotten such a stylish haircut—certainly not at Clyde's Barber Shop in Live Oak. Maybe a salon in Yuba City. She held the cape between them, balling and unballing the wool in her nervous fingers.

"You're beautiful." He ran his fingertip across her bottom lip. She all but melted, leaning against the closet door he had just closed to gain a little distance from him.

He devastated that distance just by leaning in. He didn't touch her. Instead, he rested both hands against the door above her head and bent down to kiss her.

*Oh no, he'll taste the Vaseline.*

He didn't seem to mind. His kiss left her trembling. He ended it too soon and took the cape from her hands to help her slip it on.

"We're not going for Chinese food. Sorry, Little General, you're just going to have to be my copilot tonight."

"You've been spending too much time with Blue and Billy."

"Little General fits you."

"Someone's got to be in charge. If you don't give people rules, they go all haywire on you and nothing gets done the way it should."

"You know you have a mind like a bear trap?" He smiled down at her.

"Does that bother you?"

"Not at all. I like a woman who knows her mind."

"Well, this woman is hungry." She wasn't about to tell him she hungered for him. Instead, she slipped from under his arms and walked out the front door.

He'd finally gotten the busted window fixed, and the Camaro was washed and vacuumed. They drove through a painted evening. The road twisted through pink and golden rays of a sinking sun. Those last rays shimmered through the windshield. A covey of valley quail scurried across the road, erupting into flight as John braked to let them cross into a berry patch along a ditch on the other side. Crickets played their supper music in the grassy fields. Though the wind from their open windows blew strands loose from Swampy's hair twist, she wasn't about to roll up the pane on such a lovely evening.

They drove through Live Oak's one stoplight, heading south on Highway 99. They passed a lumber mill and some barns, but mostly just fields and orchards along the road.

"Where are we going?" She finally rolled up her window when they reached the highway.

"Patience is a virtue." He gave her a smile and then turned back to the road.

"Not one of my virtues."

"Really? I never would have known." His laugh was deep and pleasant. She loved the sound of it.

She could see he wasn't going to give her an ounce of information, so she leaned back against the seat, watching darkness descend upon the poppy-filled fields along the highway.

# Chapter Twenty-One

Originally a Maidu Indian village, and later a steamboat landing, Yuba City had become a friendly farming community near the convergence of the Yuba and Feather rivers. Swampy rarely went there except for grocery shopping or an occasional trip to Sears because she worked all the time. John had chosen the finest restaurant in town. They walked into a brick building on Plumas Street and were seated at an intimate table with a white tablecloth and a candle burning between them. Tall green plants created privacy amongst the dining tables. Tastefully framed movie posters decorated the forest-green walls. A picture of Rick's Café Americain from the film Casablanca adorned the space above their heads.

After the waitress set down their waters and left, Swampy whispered over the top of her tall white menu, "I don't think you can afford this with what I pay you."

"Maybe you should give me a raise," he whispered back. He grinned, that easy smile she loved. She rarely noticed his scars anymore, but his dimples still delighted her.

"You make more than I do already."

"You're kidding." His smile disappeared.

"What are you ordering for dinner?" She returned her attention to the menu.

"I make more than you?" he insisted.

"After I pay the overhead and my brothers, yes, you make more than me. I think I'll order the chicken piccata." She didn't really want chicken, but it was the cheapest item on the menu.

"I can't believe you pay me more than you take home."

Because he seemed genuinely upset, she explained. "Callohan Dusters was a small company. Jimmy and his dad did all the flying. When Jimmy got drafted, Mr. Callohan had to hire another pilot. After Mr. Callohan died, I began running the show, and the pilot quit because I was a woman. The creditors about ate me alive before Mr. Callohan was in the grave. I barbed-wired the business back together with the money the government gave me for Jimmy's death, but by then I could hardly afford one pilot, let alone two. I knew the only way to keep the business was to do the dusting myself. But by the time I learned how to really dust, all our customers had gone elsewhere. I've had to come down on my fees to build a clientele back up."

She took a deep breath. This was getting depressing. "Folks decided from the get-go that I was a poor Southerner lucky to have married Jimmy Callohan, the town's football hero. Now I'm the crazy widow who flies his planes. The locals think Blue's deranged and Billy's disabled." She quit talking, realizing she was ruining the evening.

A solemn air hung over their table.

John reached across the white linen and took her hand. He smiled, squeezing her fingers.

"I'm sorry." She shook her head, embarrassed to have said all that. "I never did do well dating. Thankfully, Jimmy never cared."

"Well, you're not scaring me off. Together we'll make Callohan Dusters the most successful crop-dusting business in Sutter County. We'll have Ag Cats flying out our ears one day, wait and see. And you can cut my wages too—after I pay for this dinner." He grinned and her mood lightened.

She squeezed his hand and returned his brave smile. In no time at all, he'd changed her life completely. She stared into his eyes, marveling he'd come. John showing up in her life felt like a miracle.

She laid down her menu. "How 'bout I give you a bonus for this past month? I've flown your feathers off, and you just grin and bear it. And that way I can order something expensive on this menu, like the T-bone steak."

"Don't worry about a bonus. My bonus is spending every day with you. I'm ordering steak and lobster. How's that sound?" He stared into her eyes, stroking her hand with his thumb, rubbing the inside of her palm back and forth until she could barely breathe.

"Sounds good." She jerked her hand away when the waitress stepped around the wall of ferns.

"Celebrating something special tonight?" the waitress asked.

"Every night is special with Swampy." John gave her a look that made her cheeks heat up.

The waitress smiled at her before asking what they wanted to drink.

John said just water but told Swampy to get whatever she wanted. Because she'd never seen him drink, she ordered a Pepsi.

When the waitress left, he smiled apologetically. "I haven't had a drink in a hundred and twelve days. I hid in a bottle at night for years. When I got here, I didn't want to do that anymore."

She didn't know what to say. No wonder he no longer appeared weary and worn-out, like he had when he'd first shown up. He was so clean-cut and handsome now; she could hardly believe he was the same man who'd arrived in January. She realized she no longer drank beer every night, either. Having Patrick and Gracie most nights at the ranch had ended her lonely drinking on the porch swing. Now she bathed babies and read bedtime stories. She smiled. Life had changed for both of them.

After a tender pause, he asked, "What was it like growing up in Louisiana?"

"How did you know I grew up in Louisiana?"

He laughed softly, and looked down at his menu. "I just assumed ... Your accent and Cajun fire."

"I thought you already knew what you were ordering." Maybe he was embarrassed after admitting he'd had a drinking problem.

He studied the menu. The silence became uncomfortable. Finally, he set his menu aside and locked eyes with her. "How do you feel about honesty?"

"Well ..." His question surprised her. She took a deep breath. "I'll take honesty over just about anything. The only person I let lie to me is Blue. He takes after our mama. She'd lie for no reason at all. Guess it was just her nature."

John looked above their heads at the framed movie poster. Something guarded had crept into his countenance. Swampy could no longer read his face. She looked up at the movie poster too. *Casablanca* was one of her favorite films, but she hated the ending. She assumed he wanted to know about her past. Maybe how she'd met and married Jimmy.

She folded her hands on the table, squeezing her fingers together. How much should she tell him? She began slowly, "Mama moved us to California the summer I turned sixteen. Her third husband got a job out here. The girls at my new high school made fun of my name, my clothes, everything, but Jimmy stood up for me. He was captain of the football team, president of his class. Everybody loved Jimmy. When he said I had a good name, I had a good name. He asked me out for ice cream, and we hardly spent a day apart after that until he got drafted."

She gazed around the restaurant, viewing the other movie posters hanging on the walls, and pointed to *Gone with the Wind*. "Jimmy liked my Southern accent. He liked everything about me. I have no idea why."

"I know why. You're strong, like Scarlett. And beautiful like her too."

She blushed.

"What happened to your parents?" he asked gently.

Her voice was soft and achy when she answered. "Daddy died when I was still pretty young. He was a former Marine. Mama plunked him in the dirt as fast as she could, and everyone, including Mama's new boyfriend, got roaring drunk at his funeral. Mama drank too, but not like Daddy. I think she drank out of boredom. Daddy drank to drown his broken dreams. Mama died in a car accident my senior year of high school." She just couldn't bring herself to tell John her daddy had killed himself. She'd been given the flag that draped Daddy's coffin and slept with it for years. It became a blanket on her girlhood bed and grew faded and worn from Mama's careless washing.

After they'd handed her Jimmy's flag, wet from the rain at the graveside service, she'd wrapped herself in it on the porch swing and about froze to death that night after his funeral, thinking like Daddy's flag, it would become a blanket on her bed. But in the morning, she hung Jimmy's flag on the clothesline until it dried, and then tucked it away high up on a shelf in her closet with Daddy's worn out flag. She wasn't a little girl anymore. Sleeping with Jimmy's flag wasn't going to comfort her like Daddy's had.

The waitress returned to their table with a basket of bread and a Pepsi. Swampy was relieved to be interrupted from her sad thoughts.

John turned his attention to the waitress. "We're ready to order." He handed their menus to her. "Two steaks and lobster tails. Lots of melted butter on the side."

After the waitress left, John said, "I'm sorry about your folks."

She took a piece of bread from the basket, buttered it, and handed it to him. Something deep in her chest ached but sharing a little of her past with John helped her feel closer to him. "What about your parents?"

He took a big bite of bread. She could tell he didn't want to talk about his mom and dad, either.

"Are they still alive?" She tried to smile a little to encourage him.

He nodded and finished chewing. "Yes, but I don't see them anymore."

"Why not?"

"They live back East."

"Do you have any siblings?" She buttered more bread for herself.

"No. But I always had a dog. My father believed in bull terriers." He smiled ruefully.

"What was your favorite dog's name?"

"Boomer. Did you have a favorite dog when you were young?"

"Mama hated all dogs but poodles. She had a scar on her leg from a German Shepherd. I never had my own dog until I married Jimmy. Gadget is my first dog."

"Well, he's a good one."

She didn't like talking about her parents either. She took pity on him and returned to a safer subject: crop dusting. "I love flying with you," she admitted as their soup and salads arrived.

John reached across the table for her hand. "Growing up, we always said grace before dinner. Do you mind?"

She didn't mind and *wanted* to pray with him, which surprised her. She hadn't felt like praying since Jimmy died. Mr. Callohan had said grace before every meal. She took John's hand and closed her eyes against the sudden tears building.

He said a short prayer of thanks, and when she opened her eyes, he was staring at her. The look on his face made her stomach drop to her toes.

"I love flying with you too," he said.

She blinked away the moisture in her eyes and tried teasing him. It felt safer than letting the moment deepen. "I don't scare you anymore?"

"Sometimes you scare me." His eyes grew serious.

"You never say anything about my flying anymore."

"I figure if we crash into each other, we'll die together."

"I won't crash into you. I always know where you are in the sky."

When had he become her whole world? She couldn't imagine flying without him. They rode together to and from work most days. Patrick and Gracie adored him. She didn't want to face how much she'd come to depend on him, so she switched to small talk.

When their dinner arrived, he said, "I hope you like lobster."

"I've never eaten lobster," she admitted.

He grinned. "Well, you're in for a treat. Let me see your plate." He reached over and took her lobster, removing the meat from the shell and then the claws, then did the same to his own.

They laughed as lobster juice sprayed the table. John dipped the first piece of claw meat into the butter and handed it to her.

"It's wonderful," she said after tasting it.

A band in the nearby lounge kicked up and began to play Mac Davis's new hit, "Baby, Don't Get Hooked on Me."

*Oh, dear Lord, she was hooked on him.*

After dinner, John led her into the lounge. The band was now playing Patsy Cline's "Walkin' After Midnight" surprisingly well. She felt awkward in her slingback heels. The white polyester knit clung to her hips and breasts, making her self-conscious. She pulled the hem of the dress down, trying to gain more coverage on her thighs. In her work coveralls, she felt confident as could be, but in the dress, she felt vulnerable. John's hand on the small of her back, guiding her through the crowd, reassured her. There was a presence about John that made people stop and stare when he passed by. She felt safe and yet not safe at all with him tonight. Her heart was in trouble, that was for certain.

They slid into the booth at the back of the lounge where the music wasn't vibrating the tables. He touched her shoulder as she sat down. In the sleeveless dress, his warm hand on her bare skin made her shiver. She didn't look at him. Inside she was melting into a mess. A warm, wonderful mess.

The lounge's wooden walls were dark and polished. Above the wood, brick climbed to the tall ceiling. A long mahogany bar graced one wall with mirrors running the length above it. The place reminded Swampy of an old saloon.

"What can I get you to drink?" John asked.

"Do you mind if I have a beer?" Maybe it would help her relax.

"You don't want one of those foo-foo drinks that comes with a little umbrella? A piña colada or margarita, something like that?" He smiled.

"No, just a beer."

"Beer it is." John smiled and then walked over to the mahogany bar.

Swampy watched the couples tangled together on the dance floor during a slow song, and her knees began to tremble. Would John want to dance? She hadn't danced since that last night in the kitchen with Jimmy, when they'd tried to dance the pain of his leaving away.

John returned with a beer and a clear and bubbly drink for himself. Swampy guessed it was a soda, probably 7 Up. The band finished playing Patsy Cline and moved on to "Lean on Me."

John handed her the beer, then took a seat beside her. "I love this song," he said over the music. "Reminds me of the places I've been." He took a sip of his soda.

"Do you miss someone in one of those places?"

"I do."

"A woman?"

"A friend." He took a sip of his soda.

"Tell me about your friend."

"It's a sad story," he said with soft intensity. "I'd rather talk about it some other time. I brought you here to dance."

She shifted in her seat and looked at the dance floor, then back at John. "To be honest, I can hardly walk in these heels, let alone dance in them."

"I'll hold you up."

"You'll probably lose a few toes. I've never been a great dancer."

John stood up and offered his hand. "I'm a great instructor. Come on, dance with me." His voice was full of confidence. The change in him since he'd arrived at Callohan Dusters astounded her. The bearded, blue-eyed drifter of those early days was gone. In his place stood a natural-born leader with bright eyes full of promise. Farmers called the hangar now asking to speak to John about their dusting jobs. These same men had refused to do business with her because she was a woman, but they were back, wanting John to fly for them. Billy and Blue now looked to John for their work orders too. When she would tell her brothers to do something, they would say John had told them to do it yesterday or that John had already taken care of it.

She spent most of her time dusting now, which made her happy. She loved flying. It was so much better than fighting with Blue and Billy at the hangar or haggling with farmers over the phone who talked down to her like she didn't know anything about dusting because she was a woman.

John was still standing there, waiting for her to take his hand. She didn't set her beer back on the table until it was empty.

"Thirsty?" His eyes brimmed with humor.

She covered her mouth to stifle a little burp.

"I could have sworn I came in here with a lovely lady." He grinned. "How did I end up with my crop-dusting boss?"

"Am I really the boss anymore? Billy and Blue listen to you. The farmers ask for you. All I do is fly now."

He sat back down beside her, no longer smiling. "I thought you wanted to fly. I'm just trying to help you with the other stuff."

She locked eyes with him. "I don't need you or anyone else to take care of me. I can run my own business."

"I know." He smiled and didn't look away. He wasn't deterred by her petulance at all. He looked determined to overrun her defenses. To take over her life, not in a way she hated but in a way she loved. Without him, Callahan Dusters would probably already be closed by now. He had saved her business and swept her off her feet. He'd come out of nowhere, looking like a man with nowhere to go. Now all she could see was a future with John.

How on earth had that happened?

The band drifted into "Stand by Me." The lead singer had a soulful voice and put his heart into the song. Swampy closed her eyes. John could go as easily as he'd come. Quietly, on an ordinary afternoon, when she least expected it, he could just disappear. What if he drove away one day? Or died, like Jimmy, in one of her planes? She wasn't strong enough to survive another heartbreak.

He cupped her cheek with his hand.

She opened her eyes.

He searched her gaze. "Can we continue this conversation on the dance floor?"

"What do you want me to say?"

"Say you'll dance with me." His hand ran from her cheek, lightly down her neck, over her shoulder, and down her arm until he linked his fingers through hers. "It won't hurt a bit. I promise." He smiled and tugged her up out of the booth.

She tripped a little as her trembling knees made her high heels even more treacherous when they stepped onto the wooden dance floor.

"I've got you," he breathed in her ear, wrapping his arms around her and cinching her up against his chest. "You smell so good. And feel so right." Then he swept her around the floor in a slow waltz that utterly surprised her.

John could really dance.

# Chapter Twenty-Two

They danced for hours and then drove home under a midnight moon. Swampy sat pressed against him with his arm around her. When they turned onto the dirt road leading up to the ranch, he felt her body stiffen.

"I had a wonderful evening." She scooted to her side of the seat, looking out the passenger window toward the oak trees standing in the field like sentinels.

"Me too." John kept his eyes on the barn up ahead.

"I thought maybe we could take the day off tomorrow. Sleep late. Go on a picnic or go fishing?" She turned back to him, her voice uncertain.

"Are you giving me another day off?" All he could think about was stopping at the barn, not driving the rest of the way up that hill and walking her to the door of her big, lonely ranch house.

"Only if you spend it with me." She didn't smile. Her desire was tangible.

When the road forked near the working corrals, John turned the car toward the barn and the loft. He didn't care if this was right or wrong. All he could think about was loving her. He parked in his usual spot near the big oak tree.

She didn't wait for him to open her car door but got out and met him as he came around the vehicle. Somewhere in the distance a coyote howled, and for a moment the crickets and bullfrogs quieted. The night stilled. She stepped into his arms and pulled his head down for a deep, throbbing kiss that robbed John of reason. That made everything hot and wild and worth it.

He began to tremble the way she was trembling. Without ending the scorching kiss, he scooped her up and carried her into the barn, setting her down in front of the stairs to the loft, where he ended their breathless embrace.

She shivered, and he rubbed her upper arms. "I'll get some firewood. You go on up. I'll be there in a minute."

He turned on the outside floodlights as she disappeared up the ladder. Then he gathered an armload of wood from the stack behind the barn. He knew it was wrong to keep hiding his past from her. He searched his soul but found no courage to tell her the truth.

Maybe he would never tell her.

Maybe he would burn Jimmy's letter.

Feeling like a coward but wanting her so badly, he carried the firewood to the loft and built a small fire.

She sat on the bearskin rug without saying anything, the firelight flickering from the stove's open door onto her face. She looked so vulnerable. So beautiful. So timeless.

He removed his boots and then squatted in front of her. "I'm nervous too," he whispered. He ran a hand through his hair, looking deep into her eyes. "I don't want Jimmy's place in your heart. I want my own ground."

She rocked a little, turning her gaze to the stove, where flames leaped and danced around the stacked logs.

He captured her chin and tilted her face back to his. "I've loved you from the moment I first saw you." He stroked a finger across her lips, then reached out and slipped his hands into her hair, gently working the pins loose.

Her hair tumbled around her shoulders as firelight danced in her eyes. He wrapped his fingers in her hair and kissed her like there was no tomorrow, like he would die against her lips—and a part of him did. The part that could be honest with her about Jimmy and Vietnam.

The next morning, they awoke in each other's arms as the sun streamed through the windows. It was a beautiful day, but John and Swampy stayed in bed. They shared a Pepsi from the ice chest he'd bought at the Sears in Yuba City. He cooked grilled cheese sandwiches on the small camping stove as Swampy watched him from the bed. He turned on a little battery-operated radio, and they listened to an Elvis Presley special after lunch. The song "Love Me Tender" found them making love again.

They drove up to the ranch house that afternoon. The day was warm and sweet with the feeling of spring. Swampy was barefoot with the little white dress folded in her hands. She wore his red flannel shirt, which covered the tops of her thighs, and her hair hung loose down her back. She looked so pretty he could hardly stand it. The phone was ringing when they entered the house.

John could hear Billy at the other end of the line.

"Swampy, where the hell are you? Blue's on his way out to look for you and John."

She assured Billy they were fine and then ran upstairs to her bedroom as Blue's Chevy barreled up the driveway.

John walked out onto the porch and sat down on the swing, as Blue slid into a dust-flying stop in front of the house. Patrick's small head bobbed in the cab of the truck, along with Gracie's blond one bouncing up and down. Blue left the kids in the truck as he loped up to the porch.

"Where's Swampy?"

"She's in the house. She needed a day off."

"You're an amazing man." Blue grinned. "My sister's never taken a day off in her life."

Swampy came out onto the porch wearing jeans with John's shirt knotted at her waist. She looked so inviting he wished they were alone so he could untie that knot. Her hair was pulled back in her normal ponytail, a look of business on her face.

"Did you and Billy get the birds out of the Stearman?" she asked Blue.

"We were up at dawn pulling feathers from *Molly's* valves. I flew her this afternoon. She purred as pretty as you probably did for Nevada."

"You've got a foul mouth, Donovan." She looked past her brother at the little faces pressed against the window of the truck. "How are the kids?"

"They miss their mama today. Lucy called from Abilene. Guess she met some trucker headed for Texas," Blue said with disgust.

Swampy walked to the truck to see the children.

"How's your brother?" John asked, leaning forward on the porch swing. He felt so bad for Billy.

Blue rested a combat boot on the porch steps. "He's back at the hangar getting drunk. But he's better off without her. We're all better off. I hope we never see that she-devil again."

Swampy left the pickup and walked back to the porch. "I told the kids they could spend the night." She looked at John with a question in her eyes.

That surprised him. She usually took charge and didn't care what others thought about it. "Let's go get them." He rose from the swing and walked to the Chevy with her to retrieve Patrick and Gracie.

Blue's truck was down the hill before they took the children into the house. They spent the evening eating spaghetti and rolling around the family room, where a stuffed elk head hung over the fireplace. Gracie went down for the night before the stars came out. Patrick lasted an hour after dark.

John helped Swampy clean up the kitchen and then sat on the porch swing with her. The front door was open and the screen door shut so they would hear if the kids stirred.

Moths fluttered against the screen, drawn by the lights inside the house. A gentle breeze whispered through the cedars in the yard. Frogs and crickets stirred in the fields. Gadget wouldn't leave Swampy's feet. She petted the dog for a while and then leaned back on the swing and rested her head on John's shoulder.

"I used to sit on an old sycamore stump and pretend it was my front porch," she said. "I painted that old stump white when I found some paint in my grandfather's shed. Blue and Billy teased me about it. They even stole a rocking chair off someone's veranda and left it on my stump. I'd rock for hours in that chair, pretending I had a house full of young'uns. I've always wanted lots of kids. But not like this. Patrick and Gracie need their daddy."

"Maybe he'll get better."

"What if he doesn't?"

"Let's take it one day at a time." John squeezed her knee.

"Is that what we're doing here? Just taking it one day at a time?"

"No." He paused, letting the words sink in for her—and himself too. "I want a lifetime with you." He took her by the hand. "I love you. I'll do whatever you want me to do. I'm not going anywhere." He reached for her other hand, hoping she'd say she loved him too, that she wanted a lifetime with him too, but she didn't.

# Chapter Twenty-Three

Swampy settled into taking Patrick and Gracie home with her at night since Billy was in no condition to care for the kids come evening. They hadn't heard a word from Lucy since she'd called from Texas, and Billy wouldn't stop drinking. The kids grew attached to John and so did she, but she wasn't about to admit she needed him. In a way, it felt like a betrayal to Jimmy. John helped with the children, and they'd quickly become a little family. The truth was she'd never been this happy in her life.

Summer in California tended to be a dry, dusty time, but the first week of June it rained. John, Swampy, Patrick, and Gracie picked strawberries on Sunday afternoon anyway and ate half of them as they drove home with bugs pelting the windshield along with the raindrops. Patrick's and Gracie's faces were stained with strawberry juice. Swampy gave them a bath while John put the few remaining strawberries away and fixed supper.

The June rain kept Callohan Dusters crazy busy. Rot hit the fields after the summer storm, and dusters worked overtime. Swampy and John flew twelve-hour days. They climbed into their planes at sunrise and rarely left the fields and orchards until dark. If they didn't have the kids, Swampy slept in the loft with John, but most nights Patrick and Gracie came home with them. John always returned to the barn after tucking the kids into bed and then spending an hour with her. Sometimes they'd sit on the porch swing if they weren't too tired. She still couldn't bring herself to make love with him in the house where she and Jimmy had begun their marriage.

By August, they had fallen into a grinding rhythm of flying every day. One morning, she had only a few runs left—dusting an aphid-plagued farm–when the temperature began to climb. It was too hot for the diffused sulfur they were spreading. The sulfur had a low flash point, and she knew it, but she was determined to finish the farm.

Heat waves danced up from the airstrip as John guided *Old Dan* down the runway. Billy was already refilling Swampy's hopper with sulfur by the time John taxied up.

"What are you doing?" John demanded as soon as he'd shut down *Old Dan's* engine. "I'm going to finish the job." She fanned herself with Billy's old gray cowboy hat, which he'd handed her before pulling himself up into the filling rig, as she waited in the shade of her plane.

John climbed down from *Old Dan* and walked to where she stood. "It's too hot. We'll have to wait until tomorrow morning when it cools off to finish the job."

She tossed the gray hat back to Billy. "It will only take a few more runs." She put her leather helmet back on even though it was too hot for it. "I'll be done in no time."

Blue rambled over to join them as John wiped perspiration off his brow. He wasn't smiling like usual. He unzipped his coveralls down to his waist. His white T-shirt underneath was soaking wet with sweat. "I knew a crop duster in Texas who crashed his burning aircraft into a lake in a last-ditch effort to survive after spreading sulfur in a hundred-degree heat. He didn't make it."

"I'll be fine." Swampy braced herself for a battle. John sounded calm but the intensity of his piercing gaze took her aback.

"Is anyone listening to me?" John turned to Blue. "The pilot baked himself." He swung back to Swampy. "You can't spread sulfur in this heat. It's too dangerous."

"I know it's dangerous. That's why you're done for the day. I promised Jack Blevins I'd save his crop, and that's what I plan to do." She turned to Blue. "Go get the fire extinguishers and head for Tucker's runway. It's close enough to the Blevins' farm that if I get into trouble, I can land there."

"Nevada's right, LG. It's too damned hot to run sulfur. Remember how you boogered *Molly* up last year spreading sulfur? It took Billy a week to get her back in the air."

She glared at Blue. He didn't need to say that in front of John.

"You've landed a burning plane before?" John's voice grew as steely as his eyes.

When Swampy didn't answer, he asked Blue, "Has she?"

Blue opened his big mouth. "Last year. Billy and I didn't know she was flying such volatile stuff until she landed *Molly* nearly on top of us. I saw her comin' in puffin' yellow smoke like a chimney. Billy and I ran for the extinguishers. Next thing you know, she'd taxied that smokin' plane through the hangar door."

"It wasn't that bad." She swiped at the sweat running down the back of her neck. The helmet felt like a heater on her head. She hollered, "You about done, Billy?"

Billy's answer was to back the rig away from the plane.

"I'm not going to let you do this." John zipped up his coveralls and stepped in front of her.

"Who's the boss here? Blue, go get those extinguishers and get on over to Tucker's airstrip." She backed away from John.

"All right, boss," John growled, "if it has to be done, I'll do it." He moved to get in the Stearman.

She grabbed his arm. "No. You're sitting this one out, hotshot."

"To hell if I am!" He shook loose of her hand.

"Yes, you are," she said in a determined voice. "It's my company and my Stearman."

"I don't care if you own the whole damned county." He was nose to nose with her now and lowered his voice. "The only way you'll fly *Molly* is over my dead body." He stepped around her and then vaulted into the plane.

Blue jogged up with the fire extinguishers, sweating profusely.

"You're fired! Now get out of that plane, you big jackass," she yelled at John.

He cranked up the engine. The roaring motor drowned out the rest of her tirade. When she attempted to climb up into the cockpit with him, Blue dropped the extinguishers and grabbed her around the middle, dragging her off the wing, away from the rumbling Stearman.

"Let me go! Damn it, Donovan! I'll fire you too! Billy!" she screamed. "Billy, help me!"

Billy had parked the filling rig and hobbled over. He stood there silently, watching her struggle in Blue's sweaty arms.

"You're fired too, Billy! All of you are fired! Let me go!" she screamed over the reverberation of *Molly's* engine.

After John taxied *Molly* down the runway, Blue released her.

"John could die!" she cried.

"Now you know how Nevada feels. He wasn't gonna let you fly that powder keg for the same reason you don't want him flying it. He loves you, fool that you are. You're crazy to spread sulfur in heat like this. Now Nevada is risking his life because you never listen to reason, LG."

She took a deep breath, trying to calm down as John rumbled away, heat waves dancing in his wake on the airstrip. When sucking hot air didn't make her feel any better, she balled up her fist and punched Blue as hard as she could in the stomach.

"If he dies, I'll kill you!" She grabbed two of the fire extinguishers and ran for John's Camaro, hoping he'd left his keys in the ignition.

Blue held his gut, letting out a string of curses, and then picked up the other fire extinguisher and chased her to the Camaro.

# Chapter Twenty-Four

John didn't think about anything except getting the farm done before it grew any hotter. He was no longer angry, just grateful he'd kept Swampy from crawling into this powder keg. *Molly* was holding her own, sailing along as he began dropping sulfur dust on the field. Halfway through his load, he began to relax. When he finished the field several swaths later, he was smiling. He still had a quarter of a tank of sulfur when he turned toward the hangar. The pop and hiss of the sulfur igniting actually surprised him. He hadn't really expected the plane to catch fire.

Tucker's airstrip was only a mile away. He hoped Blue and Billy had stuck to the plan. Swampy had been furious when Blue scooped her off the Stearman's wing as he rolled away. Maybe she'd decided to let him burn to death and nobody would be there to rescue him.

He thanked God when he saw his Camaro and Blue's pickup parked beside Tucker's short dirt runway. Yellow smoke boiled out of the front seat hopper, blowing into his eyes, making it hard to see the airstrip. Flying on instinct and functioning on pure adrenaline now, he pulled down into his landing, aiming the plane at his car.

As he landed, Blue and Swampy ran alongside him, spraying *Molly* with fire extinguishers. Billy did his best on his crutch to help too, finally catching up to the smoking Stearman and blasting his extinguisher on the plane as well.

John removed his foam-coated goggles and stepped out of the cockpit, covered in white froth but smiling. Before he could jump off the wing, Swampy threw down her extinguisher and climbed up onto the plane to wrap her arms around him.

"Next time you steal one of my Stearmans, I won't fire you, I'll have you arrested." She dragged his face down for a passionate kiss.

"There won't be a next time," he said after kissing her. "Sane dusters don't spread sulfur in a hundred-and-three-degree heat."

He jumped down from the wing and then helped her off. She was smeared with fire-eating foam now too.

Blue and Billy set down their empty extinguishers, laughing and slapping John on the back in relief.

Tom Tucker, a retired crop duster who now piloted only his yellow dune buggy, cruised up and parked beside the foam-covered Stearman. "I thought my eyes were foolin' me when I saw that blazin' Bull Stearman headed for my runway." The old man slapped his knee. "I'll be damned!" He got out of the buggy and reached for John's hand. "That was some cool-headed flyin', son. I haven't seen a duster comin' in hot since 1952. Don't you kids know better than to lay sulfur on a day like this?"

John, Blue, and Billy looked at Swampy.

She bristled like a cat caught in a rainstorm. "The aphids were about to ruin Blevins' crop. He's raising five kids on farmer's luck. He needs all the help he can get."

John wrapped an arm around her indignant shoulders. "That's my girl. She's saved more farmers than Roosevelt."

Everyone laughed but Swampy. She leaned against John, and he could feel her shaking with relief. He was relieved too. He hadn't survived Vietnam to die in one of her Stearmans.

John and Swampy returned to the ranch and hosed the fire repellent off each other in the yard. They stripped away their soaked coveralls, but the clothes they were wearing underneath were all wet, too.

"Do you want to take a shower?" Swampy had a strange look on her face. Her hair dripped water and her pale blue T-shirt was plastered to her body. He tried not to look at her wet shirt. There was only so much a man could take.

"Sure. I think I have an outfit in my car." Because he often changed at the hangar, he usually had a clean set of clothes in his trunk. He wondered what she was thinking looking at him that way.

"Okay," she said softly. She watched him walk across the yard to the Camaro. He came back with a pair of jeans and T-shirt, along with rubber flip flops he'd worn to the New Jersey shore with his parents after his graduation from the Point. He also carried a tiny white box he'd tucked into the pocket of his clean Levi's.

"Follow me." She headed into the ranch house with her quick gait of all work and no play that he was so used to at the hangar. The house felt like a sauna, the air thick as a thermal blanket inside. The kids had stayed with Billy tonight. So far, Billy was sober this evening, which was pretty rare, since he was usually drunk by dinnertime. Patrick and Gracie practically lived at the ranch now. John didn't mind. He loved those kids.

When they reached the master bathroom, Swampy didn't say anything. She just pointed him through the door. He didn't know what to say either. They were crossing a line she'd drawn months ago. She never let him loose in her house, other than the kitchen, laundry room, and bathroom. And the living room where they often played with the kids at night. Once she left, he closed the door.

He stripped off his wet clothes and showered quickly, trying not to think about anything but getting clean after his brush with a burning Stearman. When he heard the shower door click open and she stepped into the spray with him, still in her wet clothes, he was shocked. She didn't say a word, just wrapped her arms around his waist and held onto him under the pounding water.

"Are you okay?" He felt a little vulnerable, considering she was dressed and he wasn't.

"I'm sorry," she whispered loud enough to be heard over the spraying water.

"Sorry for what?" He stroked her wet hair with his hands.

"I almost killed you flying that sulfur." She kept her cheek pressed against his chest.

His heart was beating hard. It must be pounding in her ear. He knew the apology didn't come easy for her.

"Well, I'm still here. You're stuck with me," he said.

She turned her face and pressed her lips against his skin.

He reached over to grab the bottle of shampoo from the shower shelf, squirting some into her hair to clean away any fire repellent still there. The shampoo smelled sweet, and he realized this was why her hair always smelled so good. He began to massage the shampoo into her scalp, and she tilted her head back to make it easier for him. Her eyes were closed. Her dark lashes spiked with water against her wet cheeks. He stared at her face as he washed her hair. She was so beautiful it made him ache. After rinsing her hair, he bent down and kissed her with all the love and desire tangled inside him.

"Will you marry me?" He pulled the white box from his pocket as they sat on the porch swing, watching the sun go down. She was dressed now in a yellow terry cloth tank top and cutoff denim shorts. Her feet were bare and her toenails painted red. That was eye-opening. He'd never imagined she'd take the time to paint her toenails during dusting season. She'd never looked more beautiful to him as she did tonight.

He'd purchased the ring at Sears last week. He knew a diamond wouldn't impress her, but still got one that was expensive. He'd never seen her in jewelry except Jimmy's wedding band, which she'd quit wearing before their date in April.

He was holding her hand in his, and when he brought out the ring box, their hands began trembling at the same time. He put the tiny box on top of their clasped hands.

"Marrying would change things," she finally said, taking the little box from him, her eyes full of doubt.

"Are you talking about changes like your name?"

"I own Callohan Dusters. I'm the only Callohan left. I don't want a new name." She didn't open the box.

"So, don't take my name." That hurt, but he understood. Jimmy Callohan would always be a part of them.

"You could live with that?" Her voice softened, she sounded surprised.

"I could live with anything, as long as I'm with you."

"People will think you're marrying me because I'm a rich widow." She played with the box in her hands.

His heart began to sink. She'd let him into her home and given him her body, but he could see he wasn't going to get all the way into her heart. Maybe he never would. And that would have to be okay. A part of his heart had died with Jimmy in Vietnam and maybe hers had as well, but when they made love, nothing was between them at all.

"We both know I'm not rich, but I own a ranch. And a dusting company. And two planes . . ."

"So around here, you're rich," he finished for her.

"In a lot of places, I'd be rich. Where I come from, this is filthy rich. Maybe where you come from too."

She was talking straight, like she always did, but he didn't feel good about what she was saying. Money didn't matter to him. It never had—surely, she knew that. The horizon was pink and gold now with the sun dying on the California coast range. Such a beautiful night. Gadget slept at their feet under the swing. Mourning doves cooed in the nearby cedars. "Things are different where I come from," he admitted.

"How different?" She sounded curious.

She'd made it easy until now to hide his past. "Different enough." He looked away.

"If you're asking me to marry you, I deserve to know more about you, John." He heard a smile in her voice.

He started slowly, keeping his eyes on the dragonflies gliding over the grass. The lawn was full of them tonight. Dragonflies were fantastic pilots. Nothing flew like a dragonfly. When he was a boy, he'd loved catching dragonflies. "I was born in Virginia but have lived in a lot of different places. I'm a military brat. My parents still reside in McLean."

"Sounds different." She reached for the box in his hand. A blissful breeze arose out of the stillness. The cedar trees began to whisper. "May I have it?"

He caught his breath. "Really?"

"Yes, really." Swampy smiled with the tiny box in her hands. "What's your mama like? Is she bossy like me?"

He laughed. "My mother is in control of everything but my father, the Colonel."

"Do they have a happy marriage?"

"They are well-suited for each other but not happy."

"Why do you think they married each other?"

"My mother's father was my father's commander. I think their marriage was army-issued."

He could see the wheels of her mind spinning. His stomach was in knots. Wiping sweat off his brow, he looked back at the golden sunset.

"Your family really doesn't matter. My mama was something else. I hope nobody measures me by her." She opened the box. Her sigh of delight wasn't what he expected.

"I measure people by their own actions," John said. "I used to compare myself to my father and never did measure up to him. Trying to be like my old man wasn't worth the effort. I see that now." He watched her take the ring out of the box and put it on her finger.

"Can we just talk about us?" His throat grew so tight it was hard to speak. He owed her the truth about 'Nam but everything inside him held it back—like a dam trying to stop a raging river that would drown them both.

"I don't need to know anything else." She touched the ring on her hand. He could see she was pleased with it. "Let's just start over with us." She reached up and ran her fingers over the scars on his cheek. "I won't ever ask how you got these because you don't want to tell me." Then she pulled his face down for a kiss that consumed him.

He wrapped her in his arms and never wanted to let her go. "I love you," he said hoarsely against her lips. "Thank you for not asking about my scars. My mother hates them."

"I love your scars," she answered and then kissed him with everything she had.

# Chapter Twenty-Five

The loft was hot. John had run an extension cord from the barn's exterior electrical outlet into the room so he could run a fan. The fan blew warm air over their bodies, cooling their damp skin. The steady hum of the blower drowned out the sounds of pigeons settling in the rafters outside the loft's thin plank walls. With the windows open, they could hear the coyotes howling in the lonely hills and a nighthawk calling for a mate out in the darkness.

"I never thought I'd feel this way again." Swampy told him as they lay on his bed. She wore his engagement ring and nothing else.

His warm breath blew past her ear as he ran a hand down her ribcage.

"I never thought I'd feel this way at all. Marry me tomorrow."

"Before or after we spray the peaches?"

"After. We'll drive to Reno. Chapel of the Bells, I drove past it on my way here. Sweet little church with a white picket fence sitting back off the road in the biggest little city in the world. That's what the sign says downtown near the church."

"You're serious."

"I've never been more serious in my life."

She reached up with both hands, capturing his cheeks. He was smiling, staring deep into her eyes. She saw love on his face she could never have imagined for herself after Jimmy died. "Well, we can't go wrong with something so certain."

"Tomorrow," rumbled deep from his chest as he leaned in to kiss her.

"Tomorrow," she answered against his lips.

She awoke at her normal time, an hour before dawn. The room was dim, but no longer dark. She slipped from underneath John's arm to slide out of the bed, then put on his T-shirt and walked around to his side of the bed to shut off the alarm clock on the nightstand. She'd wake him after brewing a pot of coffee.

She turned off the alarm and noticed a small square of paper beneath the clock. She picked it up, turning the blank square over in her hand. It was an old photograph, but the room was still too dark to get a good look at the picture. She set the photo on the counter and lit the lantern on the table. While she put on the coffee, she glanced at John sleeping. Maybe it was a picture of an old girlfriend. The photo must mean something to him if he kept it beside his bed. She'd never noticed it there before, but then it was so rare that she stayed with him in the loft these days with the kids always at the house.

Once the coffee was brewing on the camping stove, she picked up the photo and sat down at the scarred oak table, smelling the coffee as it warmed on the stove. She placed the picture under the soft glow of the kerosene lantern. In the flickering light, the photo was as tattered as a child's well-loved blanket. A familiar-looking girl stood there.

Her heart settled in her throat as she recognized her own face, the smiling girl she'd been before Vietnam. It was Jimmy's favorite photo, taken during their honeymoon in Tahoe. It had disappeared with him in Vietnam. Her hands began to shake so badly she had to grasp the picture with both hands.

"Jimmy gave it to me."

She nearly tipped over the lantern at the sound of his voice. The perking coffee sounded loud in the silent room. John stood in his boxer shorts, a shattered look upon his face.

"Jimmy?"

He grabbed his pants off the chair and threw them on before answering. "Jimmy was my best friend in 'Nam."

"What?" Everything in her unfurled, like a hangman's rope sliding her toward eternity.

"Would you like a cup of coffee?" He walked to the counter. The coffee boiled over, sizzling as it splashed onto the hot stove. He turned off the burner, poured two cups, and returned to the table. He set a cup in front of her and sat down in the other chair. "I was with Jimmy the day he died."

She closed her eyes. It couldn't be true, but she knew it was. She whispered, "You're Cool Hand Luke."

The bottom was falling out of her world.

"My name's John Luke. The men in my family all go by their middle names. I never went by John until after the war."

"Oh, God." She opened her eyes, knitting her fingers together on the table, her knuckles turning white as she squeezed them together.

"I'm sorry." He looked so devastated.

"You lied to me. Were you going to marry me without telling me you knew Jimmy?"

He put his head in his hands.

She could see he was grief-stricken and ashamed, but anger poured through her. She began to shake with indignation.

"Why?"

When he finally looked up, the pain on his face made her catch her breath.

"Jimmy died because of me."

As he began to tell her what happened in Vietnam, she slipped his ring off her finger.

# Chapter Twenty-Six

*Vietnam, 1969*

John maneuvered the Huey over the jungle canopy. A crew of three accompanied him. A young crew chief sat in the rear of the aircraft. Glancing over his shoulder, he could see the baby-faced boy—brand new to his air cavalry platoon—was deathly scared and too damned young to be in Vietnam. John wished the kid wasn't in his chopper.

He turned his attention back to the jungle, but his thoughts remained with the boy. A month from now, that soft-skinned kid would look different. He would learn. They all did. He glanced at his hard-faced gunner, at his brooding copilot, and then back to the boy. Nobody remained young in 'Nam. The war had a way of crushing that out of you.

His gaze was on the boy when the leg of the kid's chair took a hit. The seat collapsed. The boy unbuckled and fell against the aircraft's vibrating floor. He landed on his face, busting his lip wide-open. He spit blood as he shouted into the mouthpiece of his helmet.

"Sir, sir! We're taking fire, sir!" The boy sprang to his feet like he was going to run somewhere.

"Damn it, kid! Sit down! Don't get in the gunner's way," John bellowed into his mouthpiece as the boy bear-crawled toward the front of the Huey. "If my gunner wastes a bullet on you while you're heading for my lap, it'll really piss me off! We got the North Vietnamese Army all over down there to catch those bullets, son! Get out of the way!"

The gunner, not much older in years than the terrified crew chief, sat in the gunner's well in front of the missing door. He fired into the jungle at enemy tracers popping through the canopy of trees like flaming footballs. He ignored the fear-crazed crew chief and John's barking commands and concentrated on his shooting— as if he sat at a firing range on a sandy hill at some US Army post instead of being propped in the wind tunnel created between the door openings. Bullets busted into the metal of the aircraft, pinged off the skids, and every now and then whizzed into the chopper, bouncing around with the hysterical crew chief.

"I'm hit! I'm hit, sir!" The boy's cries locked into the aircraft's intercom system, tearing through John's ears like pieces of hot shrapnel.

"Lieutenant, is he hit?"

"I can't tell, captain," Lancing said as he watched the crew chief thrash about. The boy wrapped himself in the cord of his headphones the way a frantic fish wraps itself in the line that has caught it.

"Rideout, is he hit?" John shouted to his wiry gunner, who was clinging to his M60 machine gun.

"No, sir! Just busted his lip on the deck, sir!" The gunner continued to launch bullets into the trees. He was all soldier, with nine months of battle under his belt. The gunner's eyes were flat and emotionless, a cool-headed marksman, John was thankful to have him protecting the ship.

"Private, you're not hit. Now sit your ass down, or I'll shoot you myself." John slowed the aircraft, flying lower, looking harder at the ground below.

A Long Range Reconnaissance Patrol (LRRP) team had run into an unexpected pocket of North Vietnamese. Six of the eight-man team were wounded. A fierce firefight was still in progress. A veteran commanding officer with two Distinguished Flying Crosses, John remained clearheaded as he scanned the jungle for the downed Americans. *Just another walk in the park. Just another peaceful day in Vietnam*, he told himself.

The crew chief finally found another seat and buckled back in, but not because of the order to do so. A bullet had ripped off the toe of his boot. His face was white with shock.

"This doesn't look good, captain." Anxiety filled Lieutenant Lancing's voice, though he rarely showed emotion.

They'd been through numerous firefights before and had flown back to base with holes all over their aircraft. They would be fine.

John turned his attention away from his flight crew. Americans were down in that jungle bleeding to death—soldiers whose lives rested in his hands. He alone would make the decision to get them out or abort the mission. He'd never left an American at the mercy of this small elusive enemy or their big deadly jungle before. He wasn't about to leave any today.

"Snake Man, pop smoke now," he growled into the radio to the gutshot recon soldier on the ground.

"We've … got … smoke," a weak voice at the other end of the line answered.

John spotted the billowing red smoke wafting up from the green jungle in the near distance. "Roger, smoke. I see red."

"We've … got … red," the voice responded.

"Duster, we've found our boys," John radioed Jimmy, who was piloting the second rescue helicopter.

There was a long pause at the other end of the radio.

"Duster, do you copy?"

"Roger, Nevada," Jimmy finally radioed back. "I don't know. Things don't feel right to me. I think we've got a cow on the wrong side of the fence here."

"Negative, Duster. Our little doggies are ready to be rounded up. Everything looks good. Go pull 'em out."

"It might be an ambush, captain." Jimmy sounded hesitant.

*What the hell was going on? Was everyone losing their cojones today?*

"Damn it, Duster. We've got no time for waiting. Things are hot, but I see no flames! Get down there! That's an order!"

There was another long pause at the other end of the frequency and then a strong affirmative. "Yes, sir."

"Be careful, Duster. We've got more enemy here than fleas on a Hanoi rat."

"I trust you, Nevada."

Jimmy's helicopter ended its low recon over the burned-out hole of jungle and hovered in with noticeable caution.

No sooner had the skids of his aircraft hit the ground than the jungle opened up with fire that came out of the trees like the breath of hell. Glowing tracers streaked from the wall of tangled vines, tearing into the landing helicopter. For every yellow and orange tracer observed, four unseen rounds exploded against the Huey. A wave of flames erupted inside the helicopter, spewing out the missing doors. Seconds later, the Huey exploded into a fireball.

"No!" John cried. He hovered dangerously low, his eyes locked on the burning aircraft. Next to him, Lieutenant Lancing opened his mouth, but no audible words came out. John closed his eyes for an instant. When he opened them again, he could hardly see through his tears.

"They're gone, captain! Let's get out of here before we go down too!" The gunner shouted.

No heroes here. Only men. Horrified mortal men.

"Where are your hands, LT? Why aren't you on the controls?" John yelled into his mouthpiece as their helicopter pitched sideways.

"He took a round, captain. The LT's dead," the gunner's voice came soft and strained over the intercom.

John finally focused on his copilot. Lancing's head hung forward. Something warm slipped down John's chin. He put his hand to his cheek, and it came away bloody. He hadn't felt what hit his face as he watched two burning men tumble out of Jimmy's helicopter. *Jimmy ... be on your way to heaven, buddy. Oh, Jesus, take him home.*

"We're going down, captain. A round hit the engine. Autorotate, captain! *Autorotate!*" the gunner yelled.

The sky swirled as the helicopter sledge-hammered the earth with a force that threw the gunner into the jungle. Plexiglass shattered. Sheet metal ripped. Then a stillness settled over the crash like the eye of a storm.

John tore his way out of the smoking rubble. He grabbed the dazed crew chief by the nape of his flight suit, dragging the boy along, diving into a muddy cavity in the ground nearby. Then he lay there in shock, staring up at an endless indigo sky as black smoke streaked across the blue.

"Captain! We gotta get out of here! The mortars! Captain, I hear mortars coming!" The crew chief's desperate voice bounced off a grooved-out wall of earth—a bomb crater that offered some refuge as the nearby helicopter, now twisted and smashed with skids buried two feet deep in the soft jungle mud burst into a fireball.

Rat, tat, tat. Rat, tat, tat. M60 gunfire. The terrified crew chief perched over the banked earth, firing at anything and everything in the jungle. Muffled explosions thumped in the distance. The ground trembled. The LRRP team bombed into oblivion as friendly red smoke sputtered away last seen by enemy eyes.

"Captain! The mortars! Charlie's gonna get us! Snap out of it, captain! Charlie's coming!"

The young crew chief's words barely penetrated John's thinking. The mortar rounds taking out the LRRP team were dull thumps far away. The bombing meant nothing now. John felt like he'd been sucked into a void. A great black void. He lay in the bomb crater, stared at a smoke-filled sky and vaguely heard his terrified crew chief praying and cursing and firing into the jungle.

"Captain! Damn it, captain! Don't you have some
for? I've got a wife! I've got to live for Anne!"

It was the word *wife* that John finally heard—somewh
and abiding in his heart—and in the air. And it was not the    w
chief's young, shrill voice he now heard. It was Jimmy's voice
that came to him quietly, like the black smoke drifting across the
sky: *"Live for my wife. For Swampy. Get up. Get moving. Hide in
the jungle."*

Then another voice rumbled out of the lingering softness where
Jimmy's had come from, a heavenly command that filled John so
deeply not one corner of his mind, body, or soul felt empty any
longer. *"Get moving."* An invisible hand on his shoulder, pulling
him up and pushing him out of the hole. He knew what he had to
do. He couldn't die in this burned-out hole in the jungle where two
helicopters flamed away in popping white fire. Burning choppers
and a best friend turned to flame, then to ashes, then to the smoke
twisting into the sky.

He needed to disappear in that jungle and save the boy beside
him sobbing and firing a bloody M60 at an enemy that for some
reason had disappeared back into the jungle. And John knew why
the enemy had disappeared. It was only temporary. The young
crew chief begging him to move was right. The mortars would hit
at any moment.

"Get up, son! Hit the jungle and head east! *Now!*"

John jerked the boy out of the crater as exploding mortar
rounds suddenly rained down. The ground erupted in great fire-
filled masses around the burning helicopters twenty yards away
as John shoved the stumbling private toward the wall of endless green foliage that was their only chance. When the mortars

stopped falling, the North Vietnamese Army (NVA) would return. Helicopter pilots meant nothing to the NVA. If the mortars hadn't finished everyone in the choppers, the NVA soldiers would kill any survivors when the mortaring ended.

Private Joey Tanner had only been in Vietnam for a week. In John's flight platoon for three days, but long enough to hear the stories the men told. In his two tours, John had been shot down three times, downed behind enemy lines twice before, and had found his way out of the jungle no worse for wear. He'd eaten wood rats and vipers, drank water off of leaves, and escaped from enemy territory. Since he had taken command of Bravo Troop, John hadn't lost a man—not one single soldier on the booby-trapped ground or in the bullet-riddled air. Now Joey Tanner followed him through the jungle, feeding off his captain's ferocious will to live.

"Don't make a sound, private. Get on the ground," John growled. "I don't want to hear you breathe. You do what I do. You do it when I do it. How I do it. Exactly like I do. Understand?"

Joey nodded his head as they hit the dirt and crawled side by side on their bellies through the foliage-littered jungle floor. John whispered instructions between mortar rounds. He had his .45 pistol in one hand and his survival knife in the other and moved forward on bloody elbows ready to kill or be killed.

The gunner's M60 was back in the crater because John had jerked Joey out of there so suddenly the boy had dropped it.

"Get under the brush. Now!" John whispered, hoping the boy would do exactly what he said. He could hear the enemy as he burrowed into the earth like a hedgehog. The ground was a foot thick with leaves and sticks and vines, and Joey Tanner earned the nickname "Gopher" because the boy burrowed better than John at a moment's notice.

The NVA Army walked right by them as they lay barely breathing under a layer of leaves and vines. And the NVA passed over them again and again because they had found the M60 in the crater, where amazingly no mortars had hit, though the bombs had landed all around their hole.

The enemy soldiers dressed in their green NVA uniforms chattered in their brisk language as they looked for the survivors who had left their blood and the big American gun behind. The NVA soldiers smoked American cigarettes, probably found on a dead LRRP soldier, and tromped around in their northern jungle, making all the sounds a confident army makes on home ground. Laughing and jousting and calling to each other as two men lay for hours like the dead men they may yet be, listening to their blood roar in their ears long after the NVA moved on.

When night fell, the jungle became as black as the pupils of a serpent—as alive as that same serpent's tongue. Writhing with bugs and snakes and tigers and a whole host of other animals not nearly as dangerous. And morning came soft and shimmering through the triple-canopy jungle.

John and Joey hid by day and traveled by night through that jungle.

Then they saw the tiger. A great, graceful killer that watched John and Joey freeze and stop breathing as the revered hunter sniffed the air, intrigued by their bloody human bodies. For a long moment, the tiger inspected them there beside the creek before turning to walk away, as if he had better things to eat and more attractive things to kill than two bloody men staring at it across a rotten log on a singing jungle morning.

"So, Gopher, tell me about Anne. What's she like?" John said, his first real words, spoken a day after the helicopters went down.

"Well, captain," Joey said as they huddled under a deep root ball of a giant tree, waiting for nightfall so they could travel, "she's my brown-eyed girl. She's got these big brown eyes that look at me like I hung the moon. Her hair is blond. Real blond. She works in a beauty shop and bleaches it herself. She wears too much makeup, but dang is she pretty."

"That's nice, Gopher. Real nice." John stared at the menacing jungle that might still kill them.

"Well, don't worry, I'll get you out of this jungle. How does a few days of R & R in Saigon sound? You can call your brown-eyed girl and tell her you love her when you get there."

"You married, captain?" Joey's face looked like it was cracking and breaking when he talked because of all the dried mud and blood there.

"No." John didn't want to look at his crew chief as he thought about Swampy receiving the news of Jimmy's death, so he stared up into the snarled guts of the century-old tree. A tree that had probably seen French soldiers huddle beneath it too. And Vietnamese soldiers and Chinese soldiers and British soldiers. A jungle that had known soldiers for years and years and still more years.

"Me and Anne got hitched a few months ago. And it was high time too. That girl wouldn't let me touch her until I put a ring on her finger. She's Catholic. I love being married. You should get married, captain."

"I'm not your captain anymore. I'm nobody's captain." John's voice split and bled like his wounds. Everyone calls me by my middle name at home. I'm just Luke."

Joey Tanner nervously cleared his throat. "Sure, captain. Sure, you are. You're a hero, captain. A real hero, sir—"

"No!" John grabbed the front of the boy's flight suit and held on with desperate strength for a minute. "I'm not your captain. I'm not a hero, Joey Gopher from North Carolina. I killed my best friend and five other men's best friends, and I don't know where I'm going now. All I know is this jungle wants to eat us alive and spit us back out while we're still crawling and kicking and breathing our last breath, just so it can eat us alive again."

Joey looked up into the root ball and didn't say anything more for a long time.

Several days later, having trekked sixty miles, they turned their muddy faces up to a blue sky to find helicopters honing in on a nearby American airbase. John and Joey hugged each other before walking toward the place where they'd seen the helicopters disappear into the dense jungle canopy.

They sang "Brown Eyed Girl" in loud, clear voices so no nervous infantrymen would shoot them thinking they were Viet Cong as they came in, avoiding the trails that might be booby-trapped, picking the roughest terrain to traverse through, wearing the jungle mud and leaves and smell, having almost become the jungle themselves.

# Chapter Twenty-Seven

John's hands shook, sloshing coffee over the sides of the cup he held. It took a moment for that thousand-yard stare to leave his eyes. He appeared so anguished, but Swampy felt no sympathy for him. Her world had just collapsed as surely as if he had dropped a bomb on it. She said nothing when he finally focused on her, so he continued telling her about Jimmy and 'Nam.

"He talked about you all the time. Before long, I felt like I knew you. After months of listening to Jimmy day after day, I thought about you more often than I cared to admit. I don't know, Swampy, I just don't know ..." He set his coffee down and picked it back up, then set the cup down again without taking a drink. He ran a hand through his hair, then both hands, holding his head as if in pain.

"The first time I saw your picture, I felt something ... Hell, I felt like I'd been hit by a falling star. Jimmy was fresh off the boat. He was smoking a cigarette and staring at a picture of you. I don't even smoke, but I did that day. I wanted a closer look at that picture he was holding."

"What kind of cigarettes did Jimmy smoke?" Swampy asked. How could this be happening? From seeing her future in John's eyes to hearing he'd killed Jimmy. It was her worst nightmare come true.

"Marlboros. Jimmy only smoked Marlboros. Then he gave them up after a few prayer meetings and began carrying a Bible around."

She flinched but didn't say anything more, so John continued, "We flew search-and-recovery missions together. By the time Jimmy died, I knew everything there was to know about him ... and you.

"The day it happened, the day Jimmy was killed ..." John's voice trembled. "Like I told you, the NVA popped smoke when our guys did. Those lucky bastards came up with the same color. Jimmy knew something was wrong. He thought it was an ambush. I didn't think so."

John paused, struggling to speak before going on. "I believed nothing could touch me—or my men—I thought I was lucky, but six men died that day. Those men went home to their families in boxes because I screwed up." John's eyes begged for compassion, forgiveness—any ounce of understanding she could give him.

But she had nothing left to give him except his ring back. It lay on the table in front of her. She slid it over to him.

He covered the diamond with his hand.

"Jimmy didn't want to land that day, but I told him to get down there and pick up those wounded soldiers. I could have just as easily landed my own ship to make the rescue, but I didn't. Jimmy was scared. I could hear it in his voice over the radio. Maybe I was scared too. Maybe that's why I ordered him down instead of going down there myself. There's a fine line between courage and cowardice in war. I crossed that line."

John paused for another agonizing moment. "A million times I've gone over it in my mind. Why didn't I land first? It should have been me. Nobody loved me. My parents don't really give a damn about me. I should have died in 'Nam instead of Jimmy. I'll never forgive myself."

For a moment, overcome with emotion, he seemed finished, but then he regained control and ended his story. "After Vietnam, all I could think about was coming here. Finding you. I think Jimmy knew before it happened that he was going to die in that jungle and I was going to end up here with you."

Tears rolled down Swampy's cheeks. She didn't feel the wetness until they dripped onto her hands that gripped the edge of the table.

"I have a letter for you. Jimmy asked me to deliver it in person if he died." John leaned across the table, reaching for her hand, but she grabbed her cup, throwing coffee across his fingers.

"Don't touch me," she whispered. Her life was shattering into a million pieces.

He pulled his dripping hand off the table and leaned back in his chair.

She set her empty coffee cup back on the table so hard the mug cracked. "Did you plan this? Was it the planes you wanted? The dusting company? The ranch? Or just everything that was Jimmy's, including me?"

"I didn't come here for anything you have. I came because of you. *You.* Nothing more."

He stood up slowly, as if a thousand pounds lay across his broad shoulders. Swampy had never seen this John Reno. Coffee dripped from his hands, but he didn't seem to notice. He looked at her searchingly, as if memorizing her features.

She felt like screaming in agony as she stared back at him. He had to go. There was no way he could stay now. He had destroyed everything.

"I'll spray those peaches before I go. I'll pack up and leave after I finish the orchard," he said.

"I don't want you in my Stearmans. I trusted you. I never trust anyone, but I trusted you." She began to sob.

He walked around the table, lifting her out of her seat. He held her close, burying his face in her hair. "I love you," he whispered fiercely. "I'll always love you, Swampy."

Crying raggedly, she began beating his chest with clenched fists until he let her go.

"Please, Swampy. I could leave tomorrow, or the next day. Maybe after the dusting season ends. . ."

"No." She shook her head, slowly at first, then more vehemently. "Just go!"

He released her, and she collapsed back into the chair. Sunrise had arrived sometime during their confrontation. The room sparkled with thick amber light. John took a step back, then another. He looked around, as if not knowing where to begin.

Swampy sat at the table, crying.

He began packing his belongings. He'd come with so little that in minutes everything he owned was in his worn army duffel bag. She sat at the table like a piece of petrified wood, like that old stump she'd daydreamed on as a girl.

"I'll send a postcard when I end up somewhere."

She didn't respond. She stared at the flickering wick of the lantern, her picture beside it on the table.

"Swampy, look at me. Just look at me one last time, please."

She turned to him. He stood beside the trapdoor, with his bag in hand, no shirt on, and his bare feet stuffed into his cowboy boots. She raised her chin and stared at him as tears rolled down her face. She didn't say anything. Neither did he. They just stared at each other for a moment that seemed to last a lifetime.

"I'll get the letter from my car, and then I'm going."

He disappeared for several minutes and returned to hand her the letter. She took it but didn't open it. Instead, she laid it down beside her picture on the table.

"I'm sorry, Swampy." He'd put a shirt on, one of his flannels. He was so striking. A man other men admired. And other women wanted. She could clearly see now he was Cool Hand Luke. Of course, he was the Luke from Jimmy's letters. How could she have been so blind?

"I don't ever want to see you again."

He nodded, and tears spilled out of his eyes, running over the battle scars on his cheek. Scars he'd gotten the day Jimmy died.

She laid her head down on the letter on the table and sobbed.

# Chapter Twenty-Eight

*Dear Swampy,*

*If you're reading this letter, I'm sorry I'm gone. I knew Luke would keep his promise and bring it to you. If he's with you now, please tell him thank you. He's come a long way to see you. I've never met a finer man than Luke Reno. I think you'll like him. I had a dream I just can't shake. I know dreams can be strange. And I've never put much stock in a dream before. But this dream still haunts me, so I'm writing you this letter hoping you never read it. I'm still hoping I'm coming home to you.*

*First, I want to tell you I've met the good Lord over here. I now see how real and true Jesus is, and I'm praying that you will be saved too, that someday I'll see you again in heaven. Life is short even if you live a long time. The Bible says a thousand years is like a day and a day like a thousand years. In a thousand years, I will still love you. And it won't be here on earth. Go to church, honey. Listen to the pastor. Or a priest if you want to return to the Catholic church, the way you grew up. It's not about religion, it's about loving the Lord, living for Him. I'm praying you meet Jesus. He's so good, honey.*

*And please give Luke a chance. Tell Dad to put Luke to work flying the Stearmans if he's left the army. He's the best pilot in the world. I'm sure he could dust with his eyes closed. Dad will love him.*

*So, about my dream. I dreamed I died, and you ended up with Luke. Am I jealous? Dang right, I'm jealous. I want to spend the rest of my life with you. Have babies with you. Grow old with you. But the Good Lord knows what's best. We just need to trust Him.*

*I want you to have a good long life. A beautiful life. I want this for Luke too. There's no two people I love more than you and Luke, except Mom and Dad. When Mom died, I didn't understand how Dad could accept it the way he did. He told me Jesus knew what was best for us, and all that did was make me mad. Now I understand. If you're reading this, I'm with Mom, so tell Dad not to worry. We'll be waiting for him when he gets here. I spent my life watching Mom and Dad love the Lord. Don't know why it took me so long to make my peace with Jesus. But I have, so don't worry about me.*

*You and Luke take care of each other. If Luke has to bring you this letter, I know he'll be hurting. He still thinks he's in charge of life and death over here. He believes he's lucky, but there's no such thing as luck. I'm praying Jesus takes good care of you both because he's in charge of everything.*

*I love you, honey. When you get to heaven, I'll be wait-*
*ing for you here.*

*Always yours,*
*Jimmy*

She reread Jimmy's letter several times, trying to accept it.
A week went by. Then two. She flew the Stearmans. She rocked
on the porch swing. She drank beer until she got the hiccups and
began to cry. She fought with Blue and Billy. They were angry at
her for sending John away. Billy was convinced John had come
with good intentions and wouldn't leave her alone about bringing
him back. Blue held his tongue until he did his homework, and
then he came to her with what he'd found.

"John didn't come here for anything you have," Blue told her
as she crawled out of her plane after a long day of flying. He held
a paper in his hand, pushing it in front of her as she slid off the
wing to the ground. It was a copy of a Virginia newspaper article.

"The man's a war hero. He graduated from West Point. His
father's a colonel at the Pentagon. But this is the cherry, LG—
Nevada's rich. The guy was born with a silver spoon in his mouth
and he won the Silver Star too."

She stared at the paper Blue held two inches from her face.
Grabbing the article out of his hand, she pushed him aside and
strode past him toward the hangar.

"Look at it!" Blue trailed her across the runway. Dust devils
blew about in the nearby field, little wind funnels Swampy had
always admired because they seemed so random. Like God's hand
stirring up the ground. A warm wind rustled the paper in her fist.

"His family lives in a historic mansion in McLean, Virginia. A mansion! Are you listenin'? Hell, LG, he gave up a mansion for you! He gave up a heroic military career for you. The man was a decorated army major. What does he need with our little rinky-dink dusters out here in the middle of nowhere?"

Swampy spun around in the parking lot. Blue had been trotting to keep up with her brisker-than-normal stride and nearly slammed into her when she stopped to face him.

"Quit pulling on my ear!" she said. "I'll look at the paper when I'm good and damn well ready to look at it!"

"Don't be so stubborn." Blue glared at her. "That stubbornness is going to ruin you, LG. That's your big downfall. You're so bull-butt stubborn you'd rather let Nevada go than admit you're wrong."

"How do you know I'm wrong? How do you know, Blue Donovan? You've been so loaded with booze this summer, you don't know your butt from your brains. Billy too. I've never seen such worthless pieces of work as you two drunkards."

"I know Bill and me have been backslidin', but damn it, LG! You didn't need us anymore. You had Nevada. He flies like a bird in those dusters. I've never seen anyone like him. If you let him go, you're a bigger fool than I think you are. You're so determined to make it on your own that you won't let anyone help you. That's a fool. In this world, we all need a little help."

"I've got you and Billy and the kids. That's all I'll ever need."

"What about love?" Blue jumped up and down, his boots pounding the pavement. "You need love just like most women. Swallow your pride. Ask John to come back. If you won't do it for yourself, do it for Nevada. That man needs all the stubborn love you've been hoardin' in your heart since you lost Callohan.

I know you're pissed you didn't get to love your husband for the rest of your life, but damn it! I saw you with Callohan, and I've seen you with Nevada. I know you loved Callohan, but you belong with Nevada."

"You don't know nothing, Blue! Nothing! What do you know about love? You've never loved anyone. You bed 'em and leave 'em, and you're telling me how to love?" Her eyes stung with tears she wasn't about to shed in front of her brother.

"I know a hell of a lot more than you think I know," he growled. "I loved a girl once so much it about killed me. It would have killed me if I had gotten to her in time."

"What are you talking about, Blue?" She reached out and touched his arm. His eyes shined with that look that scared her.

He sat down right where they stood in the middle of the parking lot with the late-August sun glaring down. Swampy kneeled beside him, her hand locked on his arm.

His hair blazed red as the sun lit the fiery strands. The cement was burning hot. Blue didn't seem to notice. "Prettiest thing I ever laid eyes on. We were gonna marry. The only time I ever felt at home was in her arms. I never felt it before, and I ain't felt it since, and those son of a bitches killed her. Her own damned kind mortared the village because of a buffalo!"

"Take it easy, Blue." Swampy grabbed him by the shoulders.

"Just a buffalo the village gave us to roast one night because we were tired of eatin' C-Rations! She died because of a stupid *buffalo!*"

"Blue ..." Swampy shook him. He had always claimed to have flashbacks, but she'd never truly believed him. Now she could see he was somewhere far away, back in time on a terrible day.

"I held her in my arms all day and all night. She was burned so badly I wouldn't have known her if she hadn't been wearing the bracelet I'd brought her back from Saigon. She never knew what hit her. She died in her hut with her sister and nieces, a bunch of little girls those bastards murdered. I found her before the second mortar hit. They got her on the first mortar round. The first damned round."

"Blue, I'm sorry. So sorry." She held him as he sat cross-legged in the parking lot.

Billy came out of the hangar and hobbled up to them. "What's wrong?"

They both looked up at Billy standing in front of them, a one-legged shadow blocking the sun. Billy's arrival snapped Blue out of his anguish.

"I'm okay," Blue said, and he suddenly sounded okay.

"Are you sure?" Swampy was shaking.

Blue rose to his feet, pulling her up with him. "My ass is on fire. Damn, that asphalt is hot!"

Swampy and Billy looked at him with concern.

"What's y'all's problem?" Blue grinned. "We got each other, don't we? Hell, we got a little mule—that'd be Swampy. We got a pretty flamingo standin' on one leg—that'd be Bill. And we got a rabid dog—me. We had a fine eagle here too—that'd be the decorated army officer in that picture you're holdin', LG. Read the article. It will tell you just how much Nevada gave up coming out here to these lonely old farm fields to find you."

Blue's smile faded. He stared at her in a hard way. "Some of us get our chance. If we're lucky, we get a second chance to love again. You and Nevada are meant for each other. You're half the people you can be without each other. *Half.* You have what he needs, and he has what you need, and if you throw that away, if you give it up because of that stubborn nature of yours, you'll never, ever love like this again. I guarantee it."

Blue walked toward the hangar, leaving her and Billy staring after him.

"He's right," Billy said softly.

Swampy remained silent, but inside she was reeling. Blue had loved a girl killed in Vietnam. No wonder he couldn't get over the war. She never knew he was grieving. Was she that blind with Blue's heartache too just like she'd been blind to John's pain?

She didn't want to see other people's anguish. It reminded her of her own heartaches and that was just too much to process. So Blue acted crazy sometimes. Like Daddy had flipped out after becoming a Marine and going off to war and then coming home half the man he'd once been, Mama said. Other folks' pain was too costly. Swampy could barely afford her own sorrows. Daddy's suicide was locked in a box inside of her and nobody opened that box. Nobody. And she didn't want to open other people's boxes of pain. Didn't want to know why John would never tell her where he'd come by those scars on his cheek. Didn't want to know why Blue and Billy numbed themselves with marijuana and booze after 'Nam the way Daddy had drank down his disappointments too. Life was hard enough. She was barely getting through each day now without John.

Billy wrapped an arm around her shoulders. "Blue just misses John, like we all do."

"Did you know he loved a girl killed in the war?"

"Yeah, I knew."

"Why didn't I know?" She asked but she already knew the truth. It was because she couldn't handle other people's troubles.

"You'd lost Jimmy. We didn't want to make it any worse. Blue told me I couldn't tell you."

"Since when do you listen to Blue?"

Billy squeezed her shoulder. "Sometimes I do."

"All we really need is each other." She put her arm around Billy's hard, thin waist as they walked back to the hangar, her baby brother moving along on his crutch in a slow, graceful way. She'd said the same thing to Billy and Blue after Daddy died. All they needed was each other. They'd all agreed they would be fine, just the three of them.

When they entered the hangar, she wadded up the newspaper clipping Blue had given her and tossed it into the trash without looking at it. Billy watched her do it but said nothing. She held on to him more tightly after throwing away what Blue had worked so hard to find.

After Swampy left the hangar to head home to the ranch, Billy hopped over to the trash can, where he pulled out the small ball of paper, smoothed it out, folded it neatly, and then put it in the breast pocket of his tool-crowded coveralls. He had already read the article, a missing-persons ad sponsored by John's wealthy family. A number of soldiers came home from the war only to disappear in America's turbulent landscape. Many Vietnam veterans were not welcomed home. They were spit on and called "baby killers."

Most just wanted to forget they'd ever fought in 'Nam. Billy sure wanted to forget, but the war followed him every day as he walked around on one leg. The sound of a car backfiring would set his heart racing. He still had nightmares. And slept terribly without Lucy beside him.

Patrick came bouncing out from behind one of the Stearmans. "I'm hungry, Dad!"

"How 'bout potato soup?" Billy could barely get the words past the lump in his throat as he looked at Patrick. His son was getting so big. In better days, before things with Lucy had gone sour, he'd often made potato soup for his family. Patrick loved peeling potatoes, standing on a chair in front of the kitchen sink.

"Can I peel with a knife like you, Dad?"

"Nope, you'll use the peeler. You gotta grow a little bigger before you use a knife. Maybe when your head gets to about here." Billy pointed to a place on his crutch. "I think this is about the size of a boy who peels spuds with a knife."

Patrick scampered over to his crutch. He placed his head against the wood. He had a ways to go to reach his father's hand.

"You'll get there soon enough." Billy ruffled his boy's hair, and then headed for Gracie's playpen. "Time for spud peeling. Patrick, go wash your hands." He plucked a sleeping Gracie from her pen, shaking his head at the aircraft grease covering Patrick's hands.

"I was fixing planes!" Patrick exclaimed. "Like you, Dad!"

"Fixing planes, huh? Did you check the oil? You gotta check the oil each time the plane comes in. Oil's real important when it comes to aircraft."

"I checked." Patrick grinned proudly.

"That's good, but when you grow up, I want you to fly those planes, not wrench on them like your old crippled dad."

"Fly like John?" Patrick eagerly asked.

"Yep, like John." Billy smiled.

"Where'd John go?" It wasn't the first time Patrick had asked for John. Nobody knew what to tell him, so they lied, assuring Patrick John would be back. They just didn't know when.

"John left like Mama did," Patrick said, and Billy could see he was about to cry.

"No, not like your mama." Billy smoothed Patrick's cowlick out of his eyes. "Aunt Swampy asked John to go somewhere for her. He'll come back. Now go wash up so we can get to work on those spuds."

# Chapter Twenty-Nine

Swampy flew the dusters from dawn till dusk. An infestation of armyworms threatened to ruin this year's tomato, bean, and alfalfa crops. Rice farmers were battling a weed problem as harvest approached. The phone rang off the hook with farmers who wanted their fields sprayed yesterday. Swampy took every job that came Callohan Dusters' way and tried not to think about John, which was impossible with all the farmers asking for him when they called.

Inevitably, John would invade her thoughts, usually after hours of flying, when she grew too tired to ward off the daydreams that always began unconsciously. She'd find herself looking out across the Stearman's wing, realizing she was searching for John, remembering how they'd flown the fields together. Everything was always so blue out there beyond the singing bi-wing wires. So wide-open and empty.

Once in a while, she'd see another plane in the distance. A yellow Ag Cat spraying another farm or a distant airliner climbing out of Sacramento and turning west—headed for Hawaii or some other tropical paradise. Full of couples in love. At least that's what she imagined when she saw the big passenger planes. It was the airliners that made her ache, made her lonelier than she'd ever been. Even more lonely than losing Jimmy.

She could only imagine what went on inside those big shiny planes. The passenger jets represented romance, all those honeymooners going somewhere. She felt like the only person on earth without a lover as she pictured all those people seated in the planes, holding hands, so happy in love.

At least when she saw an Ag Cat or perhaps a rare Stearman still humming along out there in the blue, she knew the person flying that plane was alone. Maybe not achingly lonely like she was, but still alone—like everyone ultimately was in life. She couldn't help thinking she was paying for her sins. They should have done things right. John should have told her the truth when he arrived. Given her the letter. They could have worked through Jimmy's death together and then walked down the aisle instead of just shacking up.

She'd never let John spend the night up at the house with her and the kids, but that was just a formality. They'd become lovers, and she regretted that. Maybe it was her Catholic guilt. Her mother had insisted you marry a man before you sleep with him. No wonder Mama had so many husbands. What good had all those marriages done for Mama?

Thinking about it disheartened her all the more. She hadn't slept with Jimmy before marrying him. She'd been a virgin on her wedding day. Why had she fallen into bed with John? So much had changed in the world with the war.

After the Summer of Love in 1967, the beatniks said marriage was a symbol of the traditional capitalist culture that supported the war. The sexual revolution was in full swing, and John Lennon and Yoko Ono insisted, "Make love, not war." That sounded so good.

Why not free love? Why bother with wedding bands? But she knew the truth. Love wasn't free. After she and John became lovers, they'd become a part of each other. They could never go back to just working together, or even just friendship. Their souls had united along with their bodies and now this tearing away was tearing her apart. She'd never felt emptier in her life than she did now. Even losing Jimmy hadn't broken her this way.

Funny, she hadn't thought much about Vietnam since John had left. Like an exploding nova, the war had become a black hole in her life. It didn't seem important anymore. Somehow John's confession had been the catalyst to heal that for her. She just didn't care about 'Nam anymore. She thought about John all the time but didn't think about the war.

She thought about how John would smile at her in that easy way, his dimples so much bigger than his scars. How he always landed after she did, jumped out of his Stearman, and walked over to lift her down from the wing after a long day of flying.

How she'd wait for him, taking her time undoing her harness and removing her goggles, then fiddling in the cockpit until he came. How she would stand nonchalantly, as if it always took her ten minutes to finish in that dashboard cockpit. As if she had a hundred things to do before leaving the plane. She would laugh when he lifted her down, enjoying their sweet little game so much, but always a bit embarrassed since she'd climbed down from the Stearmans by herself a thousand times before.

This was how she passed the days without John—she'd spray the fields thinking about him, telling herself all love affairs ended, even the great ones. And wasn't it better to end a relationship sooner rather than later when your whole world had become so tied up in that person you didn't know if you were coming or going? Wasn't it easier to accept being alone today instead of tomorrow? Instead of when you were old and gray and not strong enough to eat soup by yourself. Let alone suffer through losing the love of your life to cancer or pneumonia or some blue-haired floozy in the old folks' home who still had all her marbles when yours had long since rolled away and you no longer recognized the man you'd spent fifty years loving?

Her mind ran like this as she worked herself to exhaustion each day just so she could sleep at night. And all thoughts, every last notion that skittered through her head, circled back to John. Was he flying right now? Driving the Camaro? Running a hand through his sun-streaked brown hair? Was he missing her? Was he sick with longing like she was? Was he in a Stearman somewhere, reaching down to open the hopper door to drop spray across a field the same way she was doing at this very moment? Did his plane feel like it was light as a feather, floating through the air some five feet above a vast green alfalfa field?

Swampy finally noticed how light *Molly* felt. Glancing around, she realized she'd flown several swaths across the alfalfa without dropping anything more than the tears she'd shook from her goggles. She pulled up steep in the middle of her run, the kind of vertical climb that made John crazy, and looped back home, pushing the memories of him once more to the furthest corner of her weary mind.

Ten minutes later, she landed the plane and taxied it over to the filling rig for one more load to finish the field. She glanced around, noticing how quiet things were at the hangar with nobody in sight. For the first time since she'd started the business back up after Mr. Callohan's death, she had enough income to hire more workers. Tommy she'd picked up awhile back, and now Mick, to flag and help around the hangar. John had made that possible. He'd flown for pennies on the dollar, and they'd done three times the normal business in the past eight months. The company was humming along now, out of the red, actually turning a profit.

She knew she needed to hire another pilot, but the thought of replacing John twisted her up so bad she felt like dying. Out of desperation, she was letting Blue fly some dusting jobs here and there, trying to keep up with the workload, but she'd already gotten several calls from irate farmers due to Blue's antics. The first call was over Blue repeatedly buzzing a house to check out the farmer's daughter sunbathing in the backyard; the other calls addressed Blue's spraying abilities. Three days ago, he'd emptied half his hopper on a barn full of chickens. The chicken farmer said he'd sue if his birds turned up sick.

As she climbed out of the plane, Patrick ran out of the hangar to greet her. He wore more aircraft grease than clothes. She wondered if the hot cement bothered his bare feet. It didn't appear to. Patrick hadn't worn shoes since the weather had warmed up. She recalled her shoeless days. Her feet had turned to leather, and she'd run through thistle fields and across fiery asphalt without a care. Growing up, she, Blue, and Billy received a new pair of shoes each autumn that had to last all year. Patrick owned more than one pair of shoes but ran barefoot because nobody bothered to keep shoes on him.

The muggy evening hummed with mosquitoes. She felt so worn out that she didn't even swat at the annoying bugs. She scooped Patrick into her arms, smelling insect repellent on him. The bug juice seemed to be working because his dirty little body appeared mosquito free.

"Hi, Packy. Where is everyone?"

"Dad's in the hangar drinking beer. Uncle Blue's flying. Tommy's flagging for Uncle Blue, and Mick went off to chase women down at the Corner Club." Patrick looked pleased after reporting everyone's whereabouts.

She cringed upon hearing Blue was out flying. The last thing she needed was another lawsuit threat. She gave Patrick a tired smile. "Let's go talk to your dad." She put him down—he was getting heavy—and headed for the hangar, her nephew trailing after her.

"How do you know Mick chases women at the Corner Club?" she asked as they walked the short distance to the big tin building.

"Uncle Blue told me. Why does Mick chase women? Is he trying to scare them?"

She looked down at Patrick's earnest little face as he waited for her answer.

"Well, he isn't trying to scare them. Maybe he's playing tag."

They entered the hangar, and she was relieved for once that Billy played the radio so loud. She could see Patrick's little lips moving, asking more questions, but his words were drowned out by Elton John's "Rocket Man"

Billy yelled from where he sat on a stool in front of the long workbench.

She heard John's name, but that was about it. She walked over and turned off the radio. "What did you say?"

"I said we need John. We're behind on our jobs. Blue went to finish the Sillman rice farm. Mr. Sillman called three times today. He's mad as hell. You told him his rice would be done yesterday. He says the weeds are about to ruin his crop."

"I'm doing the best I can." She tucked some of her hair, which had escaped from her ever-present ponytail, behind her ears. She waited for Patrick to scamper off before she hissed, "I miss John too. As a duster, he's irreplaceable. But Jimmy died because of ..." She couldn't bring herself to outright blame John for Jimmy's death. She swallowed the sorrow choking her. "Who knows what he came here for."

Billy wiped sweat from his brow with the back of a grimy hand. "He came for you. Can't you see that? I'd give up my other leg if Lucy would look at me the way John looks at you."

"He lied to me, Billy. He lied to all of us."

"Hell, Swampy, so the man told a lie. Blue lies all the time." Using his crutch, Billy stood up from where he'd been sitting in front of a mess of aircraft parts and empty beer cans.

Her composure dissolved. Pushing through the heartache was wearing her thin. "Lord, Billy, don't you think it killed me to send John away? Don't you think I'm dying every day without him?"

"Then call him back. Ask him to come home."

"I can't."

"Sure you can. The first time's the toughest. It gets easier. Once you love someone long enough—hard enough—that old pride just starts withering away like a sour grape. Pretty soon your pride becomes this little bitty raisin." Billy held up his hand and measured with his fingers. "It's about this big, and you pop that old pride in your mouth and swallow it." Billy grinned. "Eating those raisins has kept me alive."

Something that resembled a smile twisted onto Swampy's lips. "I hate raisins. I couldn't eat one if I tried."

Billy reached out and rested his hand on her shoulder. "You'd be surprised what you'll eat once you grow hungry enough."

She shook her head, biting her bottom lip for a moment before whispering, "I'm the type of person who starves to death, Billy."

Billy's hand fell away from her shoulder. "Suit yourself," he muttered. "Go back to being a bossy, lonely little mule—because that's all you are without John."

Swampy bristled. "Don't start on me. We tolerate each other's faults. That's what families do. Who's flagging for Blue?"

"Tommy. That boy is a worker. You should have hired him on full-time instead of Mick. Mick just wants to get in your pants. It's the only reason he's working for us." Billy hopped past her on his crutch.

"Mick is a good flagger. He stays right with me. I never have to look for him in the field—he's always beneath my plane."

"I bet he is." Billy pulled a wrench from his greasy coveralls.

"When did Blue leave? It will be dark soon."

"About an hour ago. Tommy met him over at the rice field."

# Chapter Thirty

*Old Dan* felt sluggish. Blue regretted putting so much spray in the hopper, but he was anxious to get the job done for Swampy. During his first pass over the field, he located Tommy waving his flag at the end of the run. The field was a tight one—the Sutter Buttes cradled three sides and power lines draped on the west and east ends of the rice paddy. The first swaths went smoothly. Blue took his time until *Old Dan* lightened up and began to fly easier. By then, dusk was coming on, and Blue began having visibility problems.

Flying toward Tommy at the east end of the field was fine, but each time he pulled up and turned west, the sun blinded him nearly all the way across the field. Instead of flying into the sun, a cautious pilot would have looped around for each pass, flying every swath in an eastern direction, but Blue wasn't a cautious pilot. And he sure as hell wasn't going to waste time and fuel backtracking every other swath so he could see the runs better.

After several swaths, Tommy began waving the flag at him, indicating something was wrong. But Blue couldn't figure out what the boy meant. On both sides of the field, the tall wires offered plenty of clearance. Blue dove under the wires and then climbed up into his turn. Tommy was pointing his flag across the field, motioning for him to get down lower.

*Smart-ass kid.* Blue didn't need his help.

He knew what he was doing. He flipped the boy the bird as he looped around and headed back into the sun.

Squinting to see the wires at the west end, Blue was about to dive under the electrical lines when the plane jolted sharply. The Stearman came to an almost abrupt stop in midair and then began to vibrate wildly.

He'd flown into the wires.

"Oh hell," he said as the wind blew upward against his face as *Old Dan* spiraled toward the ground. He yanked his shoulder straps tight right before the plane plowed into the rice field.

The Chevy roared up to the hangar, skidding tires screaming away the silence of the setting sun. Swampy ran out to see what had happened, with Billy several steps behind her, struggling on his crutch.

Tommy sprang from Blue's pickup. Swampy almost plowed into him as they converged in the parking lot.

"Blue crashed!" Tommy said. "It's bad. I got to the plane as quick as I could, but Blue was gone! He just disappeared. Like smoke."

"Slow down—tell us where Blue is," Swampy said sternly, her heart stopping, and then pounding wildly.

"I don't know where Blue is." Tommy had tears in his eyes. Only seventeen, his youth was apparent at the moment.

"Billy, call an ambulance," Swampy cried. "Tommy, get in the truck. Show me where Blue crashed."

"I'll be right behind you in the Studebaker," Billy yelled as he hobbled to the phone.

Swampy sprang into the Chevy, pushing Tommy over to the passenger seat. He gladly gave up the driver's side. Fifteen minutes later, they ran across the top of a rice paddy levee toward the crash site.

The plane had gone down at the base of the Buttes. The sun lay behind the small mountains now, darkening the rice field. Tommy tripped over a thistle patch growing on the narrow levee. Swampy kept on running.

The crash was eerily quiet. The plane lay upside down at the end of the rice field. It sat in a foot of water. Green rice shoots blanketed the water's surface, looking like black lawn in the waning light. Swampy plowed into the water, circling the plane, frantically calling Blue's name.

"We can't search anymore tonight, Mrs. Callohan. We'll start at first light," the sheriff said, standing in the glow of Swampy's flashlight. He was a tall man, paunchy around the middle—large and in charge—but Swampy was fit to be tied.

"My brother is out here in these buttes. He's a war veteran, probably thinking he's back in Vietnam. He's a little crazy. We have to find him."

"I'm sorry, Mrs. Callohan, but that's all the more reason to wait until morning. Them Vietnam vets go a little nuts sometimes. I don't want one of my deputies getting hurt."

"We found his gun in the plane. How's he going to shoot one of your deputies without a gun?"

"Calm down, Swampy." Billy stepped over. "Blue's alive. We'll find him."

Swampy shifted in agitation. Five flashlights moved when she did to keep her in the light. An ambulance, and two police cruisers were parked on the dark hillside.

"It's midnight, Mrs. Callohan," the sheriff said. "We've looked for hours. We believe he's hiding in those hills."

Her voice rose with anxiety. "Have you looked at that plane, Sheriff? My brother is probably in bad shape, and you're telling me you and your deputies need to go home?"

"Swampy, take it easy." Billy placed an arm around her shoulders.

"No!" she cried, spinning out from beneath his comforting touch. "Blue could die tonight. He might be bleeding to death right now."

"He doesn't want to be found." Billy looked certain. "He probably hit his head and thinks we're the enemy. Sheriff Sanders is right. Blue is in a dangerous state of mind. We need to wait for daybreak so he can see that we are looking for him."

Swampy finally began to cry. Billy moved to put his arm around her again. This time she leaned against him.

"I'm sorry, Mrs. Callohan," the sheriff said. "We'll all be here at first light to look for your brother."

The flashlights moved off Swampy and Billy as the rescuers headed for their vehicles.

Billy held Swampy tight. "It'll be all right. Blue will be fine. He escaped the North Vietnamese twice. There's nothing in these buttes that's gonna hurt him tonight. We'll find him in the morning."

Swampy looked up into Billy's silhouetted face. She still had the flashlight on in her hand. The round spot of light danced on the dry grass of the hillside as she moved the light up to Billy.

"Blue's a survivor. He's probably cooking himself up a rattlesnake right now in some cave he's jungled up in. When he snaps out of it, he'll come out." Billy smiled.

Swampy tried to return his smile but couldn't. "What if he doesn't snap out of it? What if he really has gone completely crazy?"

"Blue's always been crazy. Remember that time he hid us in the swamps because Mama busted your lip for getting into her makeup? He took good care of us in the bayou. Don't worry, he'll be fine."

The next day, when the search party couldn't find a trace of Blue, hounds were brought in. It didn't take long for the dogs to pick up Blue's scent, a trail that ended at the base of a high cliff near the summit of the buttes.

Swampy, Billy, and the other rescuers looked up the sheer rock bluff, amazed a man could climb it with only his bare hands. Blood was smeared on the face of the cliff. The hounds jumped and bayed, springing up on their back legs and propping their forepaws on the rock wall as they howled into the sky.

Swampy's head pounded with a headache. She'd hardly slept. She wanted to kick the dogs into silence. Instead, she turned to the animals' handler. "Can you please shut those dogs up?"

Everyone dripped with sweat. A hundred-degree heat and bloodthirsty mosquitoes tormented the tired group. When the trainer yelled at the dogs, the long-eared animals plopped onto their haunches and began to whine.

"He can't be up there," said an arrogant young deputy Swampy hadn't liked from the minute he'd given her a suggestive once-over.

"He's up there." Billy stared at the deputy in challenge.

Swampy knew Blue was up there but couldn't believe Blue had climbed that cliff while bleeding that badly. Billy leaned on his crutch, sweat dripping into his eyes. Swampy stepped up to him and wiped the sweat off his brow with a Kleenex she pulled from her pocket.

"Blue picked a perfect spot for a slick to come in and pick him up. Look." Billy pointed to a smaller ledge above the big one they stared up at. "There's just enough room for a slick to land on the flat top of that peak."

"What's a slick?" the young deputy Swampy didn't like asked impatiently. He slapped at mosquitoes, appearing uncomfortable in his sweaty uniform.

"A Huey."

"A helicopter?" The young deputy laughed. "You gotta be kidding me? There's no way a helicopter's coming in here to pick up this lunatic."

She stepped up to the young deputy and poked her finger at his chest. "My brother's not a lunatic. He's a tax-paying citizen, and he deserves the same kind of respect you'd give any other injured person."

"Is that right, sweetheart? Well, other injured folks don't lead us on a wild goose chase like this one." The deputy smirked at her.

"Look, my brother fought for his country. He's a decorated Marine." She took a deep breath, trying to tamp down her temper, but before she could continue, the tall, paunchy sheriff stepped between them.

"I'm sorry, but Deputy Riley's right, Mrs. Callohan. I don't see how we can call for a helicopter in this situation. A rescue chopper is only used in dire emergencies."

An older deputy, a thin, graying man who had remained quiet throughout the search, finally spoke up. "I might be able to arrange something, sir."

All heads turned to the graying officer. A smile grew on his weathered face. He was middle-aged but appeared in good shape. He talked around a wad of chewing tobacco in his mouth.

"What do you have in mind, Max?" The big sheriff propped his hands on his hips.

"Tomorrow is my drill weekend. My National Guard medevac unit in Sacramento has several training flights scheduled. I don't think it would be a problem to buzz by here and see if we can help."

"You're a helicopter pilot?" Hope filled Swampy.

"Yes, ma'am. I was shot down in Korea. I know a little about what your brother is going through right now."

"We'd sure appreciate your help," Billy said.

"Happy to do it. We'll be up here about six thirty tomorrow morning. If we find your brother, we'll drop him off in the flats where the cars are parked." The deputy pointed down the hill to the parking area.

The next morning, Swampy and Billy arrived at the parking area just as the sun crested the horizon. They cut the Studebaker's engine and waited, drinking strong black coffee out of a dented thermos. When they weren't glancing at their watches, they scanned the lightening sky for the incoming helicopter. At exactly six thirty, the distant drum of a Huey brought smiles to their faces.

"The sound of freedom." Billy's eyes grew misty.

It was a good five minutes before they spotted the aircraft in the breaking dawn.

"There's nothing in the world like the sound of an inbound Huey." Billy's eyes were locked on the incoming helicopter.

"It sounds beautiful." That rhythmic thumping reminded Swampy of cavalry hooves. The Huey flew closer, the pounding blades echoing through the buttes like thunder as they climbed out of the car.

Two police cruisers drove up and parked beside the Studebaker in the dry grassy field. The sheriff and three of his officers got out of the vehicles. Swampy was relieved to see the young deputy she didn't like was not among them.

"Our Huey's right on time," she announced, speaking loudly to be heard over the helicopter's pounding rotor blades.

Billy leaned against the side of the Studebaker. Swampy and the officers joined him, clustering around the black car. The officers held Styrofoam cups steaming with coffee. The sheriff and one of the deputies munched on apples as everyone watched the helicopter fly toward the summit of the Buttes.

The Huey hovered down until it disappeared into the hills, but the thumping blades only grew louder.

"Looks like they're going to land. They must have found him," the sheriff said around a mouthful of apple.

Billy and Swampy exchanged weary smiles and then looked anxiously back to where the helicopter should rise out of the peaks soon. Moments later, the Huey appeared and flew toward them. It landed some twenty feet away in the field. Swampy covered her ears against the reverberating noise and squinted into the wind kicked up by the rotor blades.

One of the pilots climbed out of the aircraft and walked toward them. He wore a green army flight suit and matching helmet. Swampy didn't recognize the deputy until he pulled his helmet off.

Max yelled to be heard over the noise. "Your brother's in the helicopter. We're going to fly him to the hospital. Would you like to see him before we go?" He smiled. "He's happy as hell to be out of that jungle."

Swampy eagerly came forward. Billy did too and asked, "Blue thinks he's in Vietnam?"

"We've assured him he's in California, but I don't think he believes us yet. Maybe seeing you two will convince him." Max motioned for Swampy and Billy to follow him under the winding blades where dirt and grass blew into their eyes as they climbed aboard the chopper.

# Chapter Thirty-One

A few weeks later, Billy drove to the hospital to bring Blue home. When he got to Blue's room, a small, pretty Vietnamese girl who worked as a nurse's aide sat beside Blue on his bed. She and Blue chattered back and forth in Vietnamese, smiling and giggling. Billy had met the girl several times when he'd come to visit Blue. She was fresh out of Saigon, a war refugee, the sister of a Vietnamese woman who'd married an army doctor working at the hospital. Several weeks of medical care had healed Blue's body, but this girl, Lan, with her brave eyes and butterfly touch, had healed something in Blue's soul. He was different now. Blue was in love.

After Blue said good-bye to Lan and they arrived back at the hangar, Blue put on coveralls, instead of changing into his military fatigues—to Billy's surprise.

The next day, Blue wore coveralls again. He didn't ask for his shotgun back, though he did tuck his knife inside his boot. Each day more tools settled into the pockets of Blue's mechanic suit, and every afternoon he drove to the hospital to pick up Lan when she got off work. He no longer spent his nights drunk and stoned, patrolling the hangar or heading into town to raise some hell. He spent his evenings with the brown-eyed girl from a war-ravaged land. Blue even told Billy he was going to marry Lan. That made Billy sad and happy—sad that Lucy had never come home but happy that his brother had finally found someone to settle down with because Blue really needed a good woman.

Swampy flew constantly in *Molly* as Blue and Billy did what they could to repair *Old Dan*. Blue amazed Billy on a daily basis with his mechanical skills as they put the mangled Stearman back together with parts they scrounged out of every junkyard within a hundred miles. Blue had never wanted to work before, but he was a changed man. And like their daddy, could fix just about anything he set his mind to when he was sober. One hot afternoon as they worked on *Old Dan* in the hangar, the phone rang. Billy hobbled over to pick it up.

"Hello," he said, hoping as he always did that Lucy would be on the line to tell him she was on her way home.

"Hey, Billy." The deep voice belonged to John. "How are things going down there?"

"Not as good as when you were here." Billy dragged a battered lawn chair close to the phone and sat down. "Blue crashed *Old Dan* and spent a couple of weeks in the hospital. He's recovered, but *Old Dan* is still a mess."

"Are you sure Blue's all right?" The concern in John's voice made Billy smile.

Billy glanced over at his brother, working diligently under the battered plane. "After getting his brains rearranged, Blue's better than he's ever been. *Old Dan's* the one in bad shape." Billy heard John's chuckle and the sadness behind the laugh.

"How's Swampy?" John asked.

"LG's the same old stubborn mule." Billy closed his eyes, hurting for John and hurting for himself because of Lucy. "It's her loss, John."

Billy waited during the long pause at the other end of the line before John said, "I've taken a job with the forest service fighting fires up north. I'll be in California a few more months." After another long pause, John's voice sounded steady and resigned. "I'd like to leave an address and telephone number in case Swampy wants to reach me."

"You bet. Let me grab a pen." Billy jumped up and hobbled over to get a pen and paper. He came back to the phone and wrote down the information John gave him.

"Well, you and Blue take care of her for me," John said softly.

"You bet. We miss you, John."

"I miss everyone." John sounded far away, like on some pay phone out in the wilderness.

Static hit the line.

Billy hung up the phone and sat in his chair for a while, watching Blue work on the plane. He felt hopeless again today. Every day was hopeless. He looked down at his missing leg. After staring at the stump for what seemed like forever, he forced himself out of the chair.

"I'm going out to get the mail," he called to Blue as he grabbed his crutch and hobbled out of the hangar. It wasn't until he came back into the hangar that he finally looked through the stack of mail in his hand. He stopped next to his cluttered workbench when he saw the pink envelope postmarked in Dallas. He tossed the other mail on the wooden slab and stared at the letter.

The smell of Lucy wafted up to him. She always sprayed her letters with Wind Song. The scent left him trembling. Closing his eyes, he finally put the envelope up to his face and inhaled deeply. The love he still felt for her nearly buckled him. Unable to stand the painful suspense any longer, he tore open the envelope and read the note, and then grabbed up a wrench and threw it through the hangar window.

"What in the hell's the matter with you?" Blue yelled from under *Old Dan* when he heard the wrench crash through the window. When Billy didn't answer, Blue crawled out from underneath the Stearman and walked over to him.

He handed Blue the letter. "She wants a divorce," he said brokenly. "It's that damned Texas trucker. She's gonna marry him."

Blue reached out and took hold of Billy's shoulder. "Damn her." Blue's consoling touch helped Billy regain some composure.

"I told Mrs. Larson I'd pick the kids up early today." Billy's voice strengthened as he spoke. "Could you swing by and get them for me on your way to see Lan? And then drop them off at Swampy's tonight? I could really use some time alone."

"Are you sure you want to be alone?" Blue squeezed his shoulder.

Billy smiled as he balled up the letter. "I just need to get it together. I didn't expect this ..."

"I'm sorry, Bean." Blue only called him Bean when it meant something.

"Thanks. You're a helluva brother. Don't worry about me. We're better off without her, right?"

"Hell, yes," Blue said with feeling. He headed for the door.

Billy followed him out of the hangar into the hot sun, leaning hard on his crutch. Grime from working on *Old Dan* coated his

cheeks. Blue's face was just as filthy. Lan wouldn't mind—she'd
be happy to see Blue. Billy wished he still had a wife happy to
see him. When he'd first returned from the war, Lucy had been
so happy. But it hadn't lasted. She couldn't stomach his missing
leg. Neither could he, so he'd taken a hit of this and a hit of that
to make it through the day. He'd spent the last handful of years
making it through each day by medicating himself with drugs and
booze.

"You sure you're okay, Bill?"

"I'm starting to feel pretty good." Billy looked past Blue, suddenly interested in the world around him. He'd always liked these
quiet farm fields, but missed the swamps. All the trees draped with
Spanish moss in Louisiana. The still waters full of every living
thing. He looked toward the Sutter Buttes—Spirit Mountain to
the Indians. A few ranchers called the place home, but mostly the
buttes were uninhabited. Wild animals and livestock roamed the
hills. Did spirits walk there too?

"Me and Lan will take the kids to dinner before taking them to
the ranch. When you talk to LG, tell her I'll have the kids home
by bedtime."

"Tell Patrick and Gracie I love them." Billy swallowed hard
and tried not to think about tomorrow.

"Sure. I'll tell 'em." Blue gave him an encouraging wave.
"Things are gonna be better, Bean. You wait and see."

Glancing at the sun, Billy knew it would be a good two or three
hours before Swampy returned. She would fly until she ran out of
daylight. The sun was high in the sky and hotter than hell.

"Why don't you head on into the hangar and have a beer?
I've got a joint hidden in the spare nuts and bolts drawer if you

feel like takin' it easy." Blue grinned, and Billy returned his brother's smile.

"You get going. Old lady Larson will chew your ass if you're late picking up the kids."

"That's why my ass is so small," Blue called as he headed for the Studebaker. "Mrs. Larson's been chewing on it for the past three years."

Billy laughed and then watched the Studebaker roll out of sight on the lonely country road. Inside the hangar, Roberta Flack's "The First Time Ever I Saw Your Face" drifted from the radio.

The number one tune played several times a day. The song added to Billy's despair. It always set him aching over Lucy. He thought of their children living with Swampy now at her ranch. At the moment, gripped by a tenacious summer that sizzled away September, the buttes were brown and dry right now, like Billy's soul. But he imagined the small mountain range in an eternal spring, blooming with wildflowers, Patrick and Gracie running through the green fields of the ranch.

He remembered Lucy, the little blond girl with precocious blue eyes and rosy lips, perpetually smiling. They'd met in second grade. She had taken his hand and walked him to the edge of the playground, where she'd kissed him, a swift smacking on the lips he'd never gotten over. She had become a part of him that day, all those years ago, and though she'd tried other men, she always came back to him. Even after the war, after he no longer had a fine strong body to offer her, she'd given him Gracie, the baby born out of their unending love. And there was Patrick, the son of his youth, when he'd been whole before the war and Lucy couldn't get enough of him.

He just couldn't believe she wasn't coming back. She always came back. But not anymore.

"Ain't No Sunshine" came on the radio, and his crutch slipped from under him as he sank onto his knee in front of the hangar, still staring toward the Sutter Buttes, a landmark for anyone who lived in the Sacramento Valley. The little mountains reminded Billy of a castle. His children would grow up at the ranch. Patrick and Gracie would never remember him as a one-legged drunk who'd made their beautiful mother run away. It just seemed to work out that way. When someone died, you never remembered the bad things about them. It was always the good things you remembered. It just seemed to work out that way.

Billy smiled, his bittersweet thoughts getting the best of him as Bill Withers sang exactly what he felt. The mosquitoes were already coming out, anticipating evening. Several anchored onto his arms, filling their tiny little bodies with his blood. He was about to swat them away and then decided against it. He might as well let the thirsty little bastards enjoy their last meal. He'd read somewhere that mosquitoes only lived for a day. One day. A single day to love. No wonder there were so many mosquitoes; all they did was make love and eat and make love some more. Sounded like a pretty good way to spend your last day.

After looking toward the Sutter Buttes one last time, the hills and valleys of sunshine and spirits, he limped into the hangar to write several letters. He'd gotten into it with Swampy this morning. She just couldn't understand why he was so depressed, and then they'd argued over John. "You need to forgive him," Billy had told her. "How can you let a love like that slip away? Bring John back."

"Jimmy isn't here because of him," she'd stubbornly said.

"I used to think it was my fault guys died in 'Nam. But I've come to realize bad things happen in war and it's not anyone's fault. You've never been in battle. You've never seen how fast things can go wrong in 'Nam. Are you going to hold that against John for the rest of your life?"

She'd stood there, staring at him without answering, before climbing into her plane and flying away. He'd watched the old Stearman disappear into a blood red sunrise, wondering what it would take to change her mind.

Maybe this would do it.

He felt bad for Swampy, but she needed to learn.

He wrote two letters, found a stamp in Swampy's office, and then left one letter on her desk and walked the other one out to the mailbox. Then he returned to the hangar and closed the big double doors.

# Chapter Thirty-Two

John stepped into the small country church and found a pew to sit down in for the Sunday service. He had the day off, which he hated. Too much time on his hands. Too much time to miss Swampy and the kids. Too much time to remember he was the reason six men were dead. Swampy was a widow because of him. Some of those men had also been husbands. And fathers. Children were fatherless because of him. And these days he felt fatherless too. Since the moment he'd dumped his oak leaf into the Colonel's drink, he'd been alone in the world—until Swampy had climbed out of that Stearman and looked into his eyes.

The pews were packed inside the church. He kept his head down, not wanting to interact with anyone. He just needed a place to lay his burdens down.

How long had it been since he'd gone to church? Before Vietnam for sure, back when he still believed church was part of being a good person. He'd long since come to the conclusion he wasn't a good person, so he'd stopped going to church. But then he started reading the words written in red in the Bible before he went to sleep at night. And in one verse, Jesus said nobody was good but God. That had stuck with him because he'd been earning his way all along. But he was learning people weren't inherently good—they were inherently sinful, said the Bible. And somehow those words in red were setting him free.

When the pastor started preaching about forgiveness, John's heart sped up. It began to pound in his chest like a sledgehammer until he thought he was having a heart attack.

The pastor kept talking: "We long for other people's forgiveness, but we must start by asking God to forgive us."

John's heart couldn't beat any harder.

"Come on up to the altar if you need forgiveness," the pastor said. "Christ died for your sins. Every last one of them. Come on up to the altar, Son. Accept the Lord's forgiveness so you can forgive yourself."

It was as if the pastor was speaking directly to him. The Colonel had always called him Son. Never Luke. Never John—always Son. His heart was pounding like a drum. It throbbed in his ears, and he felt hot all over. Shaky and on fire.

When he rose to stand, he realized several other men were standing too. Slowly, they made their way to the altar. John followed them. All the men knelt down. It felt surreal. The pastor waited. The organist began to play, "It Is Well with My Soul."

"What a joyful day," the pastor said over the soft music. "These men are washed in the blood. Their sins are forgiven. They can go in peace today." The pastor put his hand on each man's head and quietly prayed for a moment with each man.

When he came to John and placed his large, gentle hand on the top of John's head, tears dripped down John's cheeks. His heart slowed and settled into a steady rhythm. After the pastor's hand left his head, John felt lighter—free of his burden. A rush of thankfulness hit him. Jesus had died for what he'd done in Vietnam. He was forgiven. He knew it. He felt it deep in his soul. And, in that moment, he was able to forgive himself.

He didn't rise from the altar until the older woman at the organ finished playing the hymn. By then, people were filing out of the church. John fell in among them. He was out the door before an older gentleman stopped him by placing a hand on his shoulder.

"Son," said the man, "I just want to tell you that you have a Father in heaven who is going to help you now." The old man smiled, and John's eyes filled with tears again. "I served in the Navy in World War II. Men died on my watch." The old man's smile didn't waver. "Jesus died on that watch too. He died with each one of those men. And he died for you and for me. And when we die, the Lord will be there to take us home. Now go on with your life. Go in peace, Son." The old man squeezed his shoulder and then turned and walked toward the gray-haired older woman in the purple dress who'd played the organ so sweetly.

The old sailor took her by the hand and led her across the parking lot, where others were getting into their cars. Most of the folks were about their age. John's grandparents' age. The sun was warm on his face. A sigh escaped him. When he breathed in after the sigh, it felt like someone else breathed on his face.

The breath of God renewing him.

He made it to his Camaro and sat in his parked car, feeling stunned. His Bible, the one from Mr. Callohan, was on the passenger seat. He'd meant to carry it into the church but was so nervous about going inside he'd forgotten it. He picked up the Good Book and clasped it to his chest, so grateful for all those words written in red that had led him here. To this day, to this church, and to the pastor's sermon on forgiveness and the old man's benediction of peace. John longed to tell someone he was forgiven. Swampy immediately came to mind, and he prayed for her.

Swampy landed *Molly* and stood up on the seat, wiping sweat from the back of her neck as she looked around for Billy, Blue, and the kids. The Studebaker was missing from the parking lot, which she found unsettling. The only time Blue or Billy drove it was to take the kids somewhere. There was no reason the kids should be gone this evening.

She wondered if Patrick or Gracie had gotten hurt. Blue's pickup was parked in its usual spot. She called for her brothers to come help her pull the plane into the hangar, but no one answered.

The sun had settled behind the Sutter Buttes. Pink, silver, and golden rays streaked out of the horizon like angel's wings spread wide and feathery in a beckoning fashion. Swampy stared at that magnificent sunset, her unease swelling fast. The last time she had seen a twilight like that was when Jimmy died.

She jumped down from the wing and ran to the hangar, her goggles slapping against her breastbone to the rhythm of her wildly pounding heart. She threw open the hangar door and called for Blue and Billy but was hit by silence.

The lights were off, the big doors closed. She froze in the doorway, terrified to switch on the lights. When she finally did, she let out an agonized cry and ran toward the body hanging from the rafters.

"God, no. No, Billy, no …" She wrapped her arms around his leg. "Oh no, Billy, no, no, no … please, no." A ladder lay tipped on its side nearby.

She knew he was dead, but she hung on to him anyway, using all her strength to push his weight up so the rope wasn't choking him. Mosquitoes swarmed her, a cloud that hummed like a miniature chain saw. After what seemed like hours, she finally let go of Billy and left him long enough to stumble to the phone and dial 911, then she returned to hold his weight off the rope as she waited for help to arrive.

Billy's missing leg had never bothered her before, but now she cursed his lost limb. It was nearly impossible to hold him up with only the one leg to hang on to. Single-minded about what she had to do, she stood there raising her little brother up as best she could, propping his knee over her shoulder and pushing Billy's dangling body upward with all her strength.

"I love you, Bean. I'm so sorry you felt like you had to do this. Why did you do this? We need you. The kids need you. I need you. *Molly* and *Old Dan* need you! Who's gonna fix the Stearmans? Damn you, Billy! Damn you, Daddy! Damn both of you for doing this to us!" She sobbed and then yelled curses, and then sobbed some more.

When she was too spent to yell curses anymore into the empty hangar, she whispered, "Sorry."

*Sorry* was such a terrible word but she said it again and again.

"I'm so, so sorry, Bean."

# Chapter Thirty-Three

*Dear Swampy,*

*I've learned something about life and love. It is not living that is important, it's loving. I never understood that fully until I saw Blue with Lan. I started to understand when I watched you and John together, but I was so miserable over losing Lucy I hit the booze and let the understanding pass me by. You, Blue, and me have been living in the lonesome for too damned long. We've been wallowing in our pain like three pigs with just our eyes sticking out of the mud. Lucy tried to tell me we were sick, but I wouldn't listen. She said we were the most lonesome people she'd ever met because we fed off of each others' sorrow. I think we've all been sad since Daddy died and Momma kept marrying all those bad men.*

*I don't think you would have let John go if you didn't have Blue and me. You think loving family is enough, but it isn't. It wasn't enough for Blue, it isn't enough for me, and I know damned well it's not enough for you. You think on what I'm saying, Swampy, because you're going to be lonely all too*

271

*soon. Blue has Lan, I'm leaving, and you are going to be wallowing in your misery all alone for a change.*

*John Reno's a fine man. I've never met any finer. I think he'll be paying you a visit soon. Loving and living are like a man's two legs. Without loving, you're living life on one leg. It's hard as hell living that way. Lucy tried to love me after 'Nam, but I wouldn't let her. I felt a one-legged cripple didn't deserve Lucy. She was so beautiful. She was my everything. I can't go on without her anymore.*

*All I'm asking is that you give Patrick and Gracie a father they can look up to—John. The kids don't need me. They deserve better. And you're their mama now, Swampy. I know you'll do right by them.*

*I'm sorry to do this to you. I'm sorry we fought this morning. I know you'll probably be the one who finds me. But it's for the best. I don't want a funeral. I just want my ashes scattered someday in the Ia Drang Valley where I left my other leg. I want to be whole again.*

*Tell Blue thanks. He was a good big brother. We said our good-byes this afternoon. I love you, Silver. You've always taken good care of us. You are the grease that keeps our family running smoothly. Stop being stubborn and bring John home.*

*Love,*

*Billy*

Swampy sat on the porch swing most of that night after getting the kids to bed, reading Billy's letter again and again, hoping she'd wake up from this nightmare. Blue had offered to stay. Lan had been with him, her eyes brown and fathomless, a gentle, doe-like girl accustomed to the death and suffering she'd seen in Vietnam. Swampy knew the girl comforted Blue, so she'd sent them on home. Blue had his own apartment in town, and Lan would take care of him.

She read the newspaper clipping Billy had enclosed with his letter. It was the one about John she'd thrown away a month earlier. John's past didn't surprise her. The only thing that surprised her was that he had given up a life of wealth and privilege in Virginia to come out here and live in her barn.

She watched the moths flutter on the front porch screen. The coyotes came out, and their mournful howls reminded her of the sound a breaking heart would make. She could hear her own heart wailing in that wild plaintive way. She went and checked on the kids, then finally climbed into bed near dawn and cried until she fell into an exhausted sleep.

As Billy had requested, no funeral was held for him. His ashes were saved to one day be scattered over the Ia Drang Valley. For now, she and Blue wanted the brass urn that held Billy's ashes to sit where they could both look at him every day, so they agreed to place the urn on the hangar workbench where Billy always sat and tinkered when he wasn't under one of the Stearmans.

Two days after Billy's death, Swampy returned to flying. The days blurred together. A week went by hardly noticed. Lan quit her job at the hospital and moved into the hangar apartment with Blue, who said he couldn't live there alone after giving up his apartment in town. Lan took over watching the children during the day, and Blue went back to work on *Old Dan*. Blue seemed to be doing better than she was. He was so in love with Lan that even Billy's death didn't erase his newly found happiness.

Each morning Swampy climbed into *Molly* at sunrise after turning the kids over to Lan and Blue, jealous they were so in love and she was all alone. It made her miss John even more. His smile. His touch. His protectiveness over Patrick and Gracie and her. She missed his flying and his cooking. His help with the kids at night. His Juicy Fruit gum. She missed everything about him. The ache of missing him made her sick, especially when she watched Blue and Lan nesting up together in the hangar apartment where Billy had lived. How did they just go on with their lives when Billy was dead, and she was fading away?

Dawn surrendered to the rising sun as she took off into the air. When she returned to the hangar that afternoon, she was so tired her bones felt like noodles. A warm wind gusted out of the north. The big hangar doors were closed, and Blue, who usually came out to help her when he heard her plane coming in, was nowhere to be found.

When she opened the hangar's side door to find him, Blue hollered, "For cryin' out loud, Swampy! Close the damned door! The wind's blowin' Bill all over the place!"

On the ground, near the workbench, Blue knelt in front of a broken mason jar. He frantically scooped ashes into another mason jar.

She closed the door and rushed over to him. "What are you doing?" Her gaze scanned the workbench. Billy's shiny brass urn was nowhere to be found.

Blue finished collecting what was left of the ashes with a broken-handled broom. He looked devoted to the task, sweeping carefully into a dust tray and depositing specks in the jar long after all the ashes appeared to be accounted for.

"Poor Bean," Blue muttered, "he's probably missing his other leg now."

"Please tell me those aren't Billy's ashes." She bent over to look in the mason jar Blue clasped in his hand.

Blue set the broom and dustpan aside and screwed the lid on the jar filled with ashes. Pieces of the other broken jar lay on the concrete floor. He looked up at her with teary eyes and smiled before placing the jar on the workbench. He pushed it to the very back of the shelf so it wouldn't get knocked off again. "Billy's got a new home. A nice picture window he can see out of and watch us."

She stood there in stunned silence for a moment before asking, "Where the hell is his urn? I paid two hundred and fifty dollars for that brass bottle."

"Bill don't need no brass bottle. He ain't a genie." Blue pulled a stick of gum out of his pocket and popped it in his mouth, chewing fiercely for a moment as he gazed at the mason jar. After John left, Blue had taken up John's habit of Juicy Fruit gum. His gum chewing annoyed her to no end, and the sweet smell of Juicy Fruit left her missing John so much she ached. Blue probably knew that and chewed the gum just to spite her.

"Where's the urn?" She reached her hand into Blue's coverall pocket and grabbed his pack of gum. She pulled out a piece and popped it in her mouth, then stuck the pack back into Blue's pocket.

She closed her eyes, savoring the sweet taste on her tongue. It was the closest she'd ever come to kissing John again.

*She could almost hear his voice—"Have a piece of Juicy Fruit. It will make you feel better. Juicy Fruit always makes me feel better"—she opened her eyes.*

Blue was smiling at the jar Billy now occupied. "Bean likes the jar better, LG. I know he does. Now he can watch me workin'. He used to say he'd give his remaining leg to see me work."

Surrendering to the moment, Swampy laughed softly. Blue laughed with her.

"What did you do with the urn?" she asked, this time more gently.

"Patrick was in here earlier lookin' for a bucket to put some worms in that he'd found out behind the hangar. He's been diggin' in the dirt. Don't worry, Lan's watching him and Gracie back there."

A sick look settled over Swampy's face. "Do you think that's healthy?"

"I told Patrick to wash his hands after playing with the worms."

She shook her head and started laughing again. "For a smart man, you can be pretty darn stupid, Donovan. I'm talking about Patrick playing with his father's urn."

"Oh." Blue chuckled. "Patrick helped me put Bean in the first jar. We had a lot of fun doin' that. And he loved getting the urn."

Blue grew solemn. "I sure am glad Lan took the kids out back before I broke that jar. Seeing their daddy blowin' all over the hangar. Now that would have been unhealthy."

Swampy kissed her fingers and touched Billy's jar. Then she turned to Blue. "All right, you want Bill to see you work, let's get working. I need you to fill up my hopper so I can spread one more load today on Tyler's tomatoes."

# Chapter Thirty-Four

She flew back to the hangar near sundown, smiling for a change as she thought about Billy in his mason jar. Leave it to Blue to think up something crazy like that. She buzzed the hangar to let Blue know she'd need help pulling in the plane, and then circled around to hit the airstrip.

As she eased down into her landing, she saw the Camaro parked at the end of the runway. He was leaning against his car but pushed away from it to stand tall as her plane rolled to a stop.

She climbed out of the red-and-white Stearman the same way she had on that January afternoon that seemed so long ago. She removed her leather helmet and flight goggles, letting them hang around her neck. She tossed the helmet onto her seat, then slid onto the wing to jump to the ground.

Her ponytail swayed in the warm September wind. The sun haloed John as she slowly walked to him with tears flooding her eyes.

He took the final steps that brought them face to face.

"I'm John Reno. I was Jimmy's best friend in Vietnam." He wore an old army flight suit and a forest service badge, looking tired and rumpled and so damned good she laughed and cried at the same time.

"I like this introduction much better than before," she said as she stepped into his arms.

"I'm sorry about Billy. I was fighting a fire near Lake Tahoe and didn't get his letter until a few hours ago." John spoke into her hair, taking a deep, shuddering breath as he embraced her. "Is this the beginning or the end for us?" he asked hoarsely.

She was trembling in his arms, her whole body shaking as he held her. "What do you want?" She didn't have the strength to stop crying.

"Well, I just properly introduced myself, so I'm hoping this is a new beginning."

"Billy asked you to help me raise Patrick and Gracie, didn't he?"

"Yes, he did," John admitted.

"A life with us out in these dusty farmlands is a long way from a Virginia mansion. I read a newspaper article about you. Your family's looking for you. They're offering a large reward to find you."

"I'm no longer the son they're looking for. Luke Reno died in Vietnam. I never wanted the money or a mansion. You're my life. You, Patrick, and Gracie … if you'll have me."

He smelled like smoke and Juicy Fruit gum, and she leaned into him with everything she had.

"I love you," she whispered. It was the first time she'd said it before he did, and it felt so right.

"I love you too. Will you forgive me for Jimmy's death?" His words shook with emotion.

She held on to him tighter. "I forgive you." Something broke loose inside of her and flew away with the wind. She felt set free to really love him. Reaching up, she stroked John's scarred cheek, and then pulled his face down for a deep kiss.

A tractor hummed away in the distance. The breeze strengthened and pushed their bodies together as it gusted past.

Blue walked from the hangar carrying Patrick. Lan held Gracie in her arms. The warm wind that had rushed past John and Swampy hit their faces.

Patrick let out a squeal of delight when he recognized John. Blue set him down, and Patrick ran across the empty parking lot to them. John and Swampy stepped apart so John could scoop Patrick into his arms.

Gracie fidgeted around until Lan put her down to follow her brother. She toddled in Patrick's wake, the wind tumbling her wispy blond curls about.

Blue took Lan's hand, and they walked toward the others gathered in the shadow of the red-and-white Stearman. John picked up Gracie when she got to him and held both kids in his arms.

Everything was as it should be. The sun was warm and the wind soft. A meadowlark sang somewhere down the fence posts that rolled out of sight toward the Sutter Buttes.

Against the horizon, a flock of migrating swans wound their way home. They'd be settled into the rice fields by nightfall, having flown thousands of miles across an endless sky. Swans were created for this journey, and maybe John and Swampy had been created for it too. God had brought them out of the lonesome. Together, they were home.

*The End*

# A Note from Paula

It took me twenty-five years to write *Leaving Lonesome*, if I count from the beginning. I first wrote this story in 1995. It was my third attempt at a novel, and I started the book on New Year's Day. I had no idea what I was writing, but knew I had a story in me that needed to come out.

My husband, Scott, was an army helicopter pilot at the time. Both my fathers-in-law (I am blessed to have two because Scott has two dads) served in Vietnam. Scott also flew with a number of Vietnam vets when he first became an army pilot, and I loved listening to these older pilots' Vietnam stories. One of these veterans was Colonel Stephen Isle. Thank you, Steve for telling your Vietnam story to a young, wide-eyed journalist several decades ago as we walked the beach at midnight with your beautiful wife Bridget and my Scott, along with Mike and Gina in front of the Hotel Del Coronado.

My father-in-law Colonel Rick Fields most of all, lit the fire in me that became *Leaving Lonesome*. Colonel Fields received a battlefield commission in Vietnam as nineteen-year-old door gunner. I knew I wanted to tell Colonel Fields's story when I sat down to write *Leaving Lonesome*, so some of the battle scenes and the post-war toll on John, Blue and Billy in the story, came from Colonel Fields's heart. We call him Colonel Opa now and love him so dearly. After that battlefield commission in Vietnam, the Army sent Colonel Fields to college and when he came out, he returned to the military as an officer and an army helicopter pilot. Colonel Fields adopted Scott when he was a rebellious teenager, turning Scott's life around. Scott became an army helicopter pilot to follow in Colonel Fields's footsteps, and Colonel Fields pinned on Scott's army wings in 1991, the day after Scott and I had our first baby at Fort Rucker.

In 1995, when I started writing *Leaving Lonesome*, I also was up against my beloved Uncle Dan's suicide. Several years earlier, at twenty-three years old, I sat on freshly mowed grass beside my uncle's body. He was covered with a blanket awaiting the morgue's taxi. It was so like Uncle Dan to mow his lawn before killing himself.

Just hours earlier, probably after mowing the lawn, my uncle had come to visit me, bringing his record collection. We talked all afternoon, and the whole time, Uncle Dan held my one-year-old daughter Cami on his lap. Uncle Dan laughed. He cuddled Cami while sharing his favorite memories with me. He even talked about Jesus. I browsed through the records he'd brought along. I picked out my favorite one, "El Paso" by Marty Robbins, and told my uncle how much I loved this song.

I didn't notice as my uncle left, that he took the "El Paso" record from its album cover and carried it home with him. In his living room, he put the record on his stereo and turned up the volume so he could hear "El Paso" in his garage where he had work to do. Before doing that work, he wrote his family a note, telling us that he loved us but couldn't live any longer. The note was short, sweet, and to the point. *I've made my peace with Jesus,* was the last line before he signed it, *Love, Danny.*

My uncle then hung himself in his garage and devastated our family. The Marty Robbins's record played on in his living room, over and over repeating my favorite childhood song, "El Paso."

My Grandma Helen found my uncle in his garage thirty minutes after his death. Must have been her mother's intuition that took her there so quickly. She called me and her first words were, "He's done it."

Normally, I'm a crier, but not a tear fell over this shocking announcement. Not a single tear, until the next morning when I woke up sobbing, having slept the shock away. I sobbed for days. And then I buried my broken heart in work because that is my family's legacy. Work.

Years later, while writing about my uncle's suicide in a blog, my three-year-old son came to my office to tell me Mercy was in the house. My young son said this several times to help me understand about Mercy. All of a sudden it resonated with me. It felt like God was saying this about my uncle's suicide: Mercy is in the house.

The Mercy my son was referring to was actually our little rat terrier we called Mercy: the sweet little dog that had replaced Bell, the rat terrier puppy Scott had ran over in our driveway. And since that day, this is how I deal with suicide: *Mercy is in the house.*

But my uncle's suicide remains a scar on my soul. This is why I gave John Reno those scars on his cheek in this story. Wounds heal, but some scars never go away. The scar of my uncle's suicide remains. It has taken me nearly three decades to realize I am grateful for this scar. It has deepened me in a way nothing else could. The compassion I'm able to give others who are wounded is bone-deep because of my uncle's suicide.

But in the early days of writing *Leaving Lonesome*, I was still angry. I wanted to forgive my uncle for breaking my heart the way he did, but on an even deeper level, I wanted to forgive myself for not stopping it. The weight of being the last person my uncle talked to before he died was crushing. During that final summer afternoon he'd spent with me, what could I have said, what could I have done to stop his suicide? I can still see Uncle Dan sitting in my dad's living room recliner, holding Cami.

Uncle Dan is smiling. We are laughing. We are happy. We spoke of some hard things, too, like the Los Angeles riots and the school shooting that nearly took my teenage cousin's life, but overall, this last meeting with my uncle was sweet. I was the chosen one to receive the beautiful but brutal gift of my uncle's final hours. Just typing this sentence even now steals my breath away.

I wanted forgiveness for not stopping my uncle's suicide. I explore this in *Leaving Lonesome,* the need to forgive and be forgiven. At twenty-five years old, when I wrote the first draft of this story, I had no idea I was exploring the power of forgiveness. I thought I was just writing from my big imagination. *Leaving Lonesome* played out like a movie in my head and sitting at my kitchen table with my two small daughters playing around my feet, I just wrote what I saw.

I had no idea where the story was taking me. I was just following the muse, as they say, but I didn't know the muse was the broken girl in me being led through the valley of the shadow of death by a merciful God. Writing that first draft of *Leaving Lonesome* rescued me from a pain I was drowning in, though I didn't even know I was drowning and being rescued at the time.

In addition to forgiveness, I was also exploring a young wife's fear of losing her husband.

Each time Scott left in an army helicopter, I wondered if he would come home to me. This fear of becoming a widow at a young age was sharp and real and sometimes kept me awake at night. Writing *Leaving Lonesome* helped me process this fear. If I ended up an army widow, I would be okay because Swampy was okay.

When I first wrote *Leaving Lonesome*, I was a workaholic. Like Swampy, work was my refuge, the place that swallowed me whole. As long as I was working, I didn't have to face my brokenness. In my twenties, I fell into my first newspaper job and performed well. My bosses loved me. The people I wrote stories about loved me. I made them look good, and in making other people look good in stories, I looked good.

Work was the magic potion I drank that made everything better. I could hide my brokenness in work. I could succeed in writing. I acquired powerful friends because I wrote good stories for them. I worked really hard. *Leaving Lonesome* won me a New York literary agent and then a Hollywood movie option. I even went to Hollywood and met with a movie producer who showed me the town—but in the midst of reaching new levels of success and achievement, my marriage was crumbling. Just as my writing was taking off, my wounded soul began to wake up and howl for help. The howls inside grew so loud I could no longer work.

I quit my newspaper job and left my literary agent. The Hollywood movie option expired without a movie being made. I stopped writing for a number of years to tend to my soul and fight for my failing marriage. I write about these years in my memoir, *Farming Grace*. The ebook of *Farming Grace* is free on Amazon and all other digital outlets if you'd like to read my salvation story.

The truth is, just like the Lord was after my heart while I was writing *Leaving Lonesome,* he is after your heart as well. I'm praying you feel his cleansing love and bathe in his forgiveness if you haven't done that yet.

It feels so good to finally get *Leaving Lonesome* wrapped up. I want to thank my amazing author coach Alice Crider for too many things to mention. Above all Alice, you make me brave. Thanks for being a great coach! Thank you to my editors Jenny, Susanne, Abby, and Judy for making this story shine and to Janet McHenry for always encouraging me. And to my marvelous critique partners, Michelle Shocklee and Brooke French for making me a better writer and for your ever enduring friendship.

I hope you enjoyed the story. If you want to keep in touch, please visit my website *www.paulascott.com*. I love my readers and hope we can stay in touch. I'm on *Facebook* and *Instagram* under Paula Scott Bicknell and would love to connect with you there as well. If you enjoyed *Leaving Lonesome*, would you please consider a review on Amazon? Reviews help authors so much and I so appreciate them. They really encourage me. I'd also like to pray a little prayer over you before I go. *May the Lord bless and keep you. May he shine his face on you and give you peace.*

Love and peace,

*Paula*

Made in the USA
Middletown, DE
09 July 2020